Also by the author:

The Circle Leads Home, novel

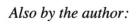

They Called Me Bunny

a novel

Mary Anderson Parks

Livingston Press

University of West Alabama

This book is lovingly dedicated to:

All adopted children, the blessed and not so blessed

Their parents and adoptive parents, flawed every one, as are we all

My writing groups, whose unflagging interest gives me hope

My husband, for his love, support and humor

My beautiful daughter, who devoted many hours to editing this book

The wonderful humanity of the people at Livingston Press

All of you I worked with in the Native community . . . you are with me always

All my relations

They Called Me Bunny

1

Somebody stole me from my real parents. Somebody bad. My parents looked and looked and yearned and yearned for me. They looked every damn place they could think of. But I was locked up in the orphanage. And before my parents could find me, Rose and Brad came and adopted me.

That's got to be what happened.

I hate thinking they just plain didn't want me.

Rose and Brad gave me the name Mary Martha. Then they called me Bunny. That's the only playful thing I've ever known them to do. They must have figured out real quick I could never live up to a name like Mary Martha.

"We call you Bunny," Rose's story went, "because you were born near Easter and to us you represent new life, which is what Easter is about, isn't it?" I'd nod and smile, trying to be bunny-like. "Scamper off and play," Rose would say. And I scampered off the way I imagined a small rabbit would. I even turned and grinned at her over my shoulder like Shirley Temple in the movies.

Other kids were comfortable with their parents. They didn't have to try the way I did. I never found it easy to call these tall, thin, flat people Mom and Dad. It got clearer and clearer how different from them I was, and what a disappointment. They blamed my faults on that year before they adopted me. I heard Rose tell the Bible Study ladies over tea in the living room, "I never believed character is formed so early. It says so in psychology books, but until seeing how Bunny is, I never really believed it, you know?"

"She had a whole passel of kids," Rose went on. I sat on the floor with my paper dolls, watching Rose's plucked eyebrows rise over her flowered teacup. "Dropped babies like kittens, can you imagine?" There had been seven of us, I decided. That number held magic, as if we were seven princesses and princes in a fairy tale.

Rose and Brad wouldn't tell me my real name, the name my mother gave me. I was sure she had given me a name. "That's all behind you now," Rose said, when I was old enough to ask. She said it like I was supposed to be glad it was all behind me. Like it was dirty and something to be ashamed of. I always felt dirty around Rose, even after she washed my ears, inside and behind, and every other part of me. "You scummy girl," she'd say, scrubbing hard on my skin. Maybe it was only one time she said that, but in my mind it happens over and over.

My skin is way darker than hers and Brad's. "Bunny tans easily," Rose says, as if that explains everything. My hair is about twenty-five shades darker than theirs, which I'd call blonde, though Rose says with a big sigh that it "used to be nice and blonde." They have light blue eyes and mine are a deep brown that's almost black. Sometimes when I tell people my name, Lundquist, they say, laughing, "You sure don't look Scandinavian." So I prefer to say, "Just call me Bunny." Often when I'm alone I stare into the mirror, wondering who I really am. Rose and Brad sure don't want to talk about it.

When I got old enough to wash myself, I tried to scrub the brown off my skin. I scrubbed until I bled.

When I was twelve, I used a whole lot of peroxide and bleached my hair so we'd look more like a family. That killed Rose and Brad when they came home and found me a blonde.

One way I'm not how Rose and Brad hoped I'd be is all the accidents I have. Like when our sixth grade class went ice skating, I fell and cracked my head and then I saw the blood and fainted. The worst accident was when I was thirteen and broke my leg roller-skating. Boy did I love all the attention.

Mary Anderson Parks

Every kid I knew wanted to autograph my cast. It got very dirty though, and that disgusted Rose, since Rose likes everything to be light and bright. After I got my dirty cast off, I sprained my ankle during a tour of a chocolate factory with the church teens.

We did some heavy television watching all those evenings I stayed home with my leg up. Television was new. Not many people had one. Rose and Brad liked *What's My Line, Hit Parade, The Perry Como Show*. Jackie Gleason was my favorite. I liked to watch him and Alice fighting and making up on *The Honeymooners*. Rose and Brad don't fight. They don't hug or kiss either. Ed Norton, the sewer man, was so funny. Even Rose and Brad laughed. Rose would make hot cocoa while Brad set up the TV trays. I tried to do my part to make us a happy family but it felt empty, like we were trying to be something we weren't.

I wanted to be out on the street "going wild" as Rose called it, playing kickball, moving aside and yelling "Car!" when someone drove through the sewer hole lids we used as bases, or hide-and-seek at dark, with a neighbor boy cornering me for kisses. I couldn't wait to see what form wildness would take next.

I started getting funny tinglings under my nipples. Then my breasts swelled up and got so big they needed to be covered and held in. Rose saw to that right away. We went bra-hunting and got me all fitted up. I didn't like the way Brad started looking at me when he thought Rose didn't notice. I tried to avoid being alone with him, which was hard because Rose took to her bed more and more with sick headaches. I wondered if she had them because I wasn't the way she wanted me to be.

I have the same birthday as Marlon Brando. I love that. There's nobody like him. No wonder Kim Hunter went to him when he yelled "STELLA!" I'd go in a flash. Margaret Schrader and I sneaked out of choir practice one evening and down to the Royal to see *Streetcar Named Desire*. Rose would take to her bed for sure if she knew.

When my fourteenth birthday rolled around on April third,

Rose baked a white cake with white icing. That's her favorite. It was just the three of us, as usual.

That night in my bed, I dreamed about my real mother, with brown skin and dark glowing eyes, black as coal, and in the dream there were seven of us children. We all looked alike and my mother was beautiful in spite of her dark skin. I held her soft hand in mine. It was my birthday in the dream and she looked straight into my eyes and drew me close with her love, and her smile included all of us children clustered around her. I knew she would never willingly have given us up, not one of us, and I wanted the dream to go on forever but then I heard heavy breathing close by me and my eyes opened, not wanting to, and there was Brad, his hot breath in my face. I sprang into a crouch, my dream mother a tigress roaring up inside me, giving me courage. I pointed to the door and spat the words at him: "Go away!" Like you'd tell a dog. I said it as a firm command, and Brad stumbled to his feet and backed out of my room. I swung my feet onto the cold floor, ran to the door and locked it. I locked my door every night from then on.

Mary Anderson Parks

2

Air raid drills. Earthquake drills. We kept having them even though nothing ever happened. It was San Francisco in the early fifties. Was I the only one wishing something would change? Men were in charge, wearing hats, suits, neckties. Women wore gloves, veils shaded their faces. Anything juicy was discussed in private, if at all. Everything was covered up.

Sex was never talked about. It lurked in shameful thoughts and dirty jokes. Back in sixth grade, our teacher showed the girls a movie put out by Kotex to teach us about menstruation. The boys had an extra long recess while all of us girls were in the auditorium. Somehow the boys got wind of what was going on. Most of them looked the other way when we trooped out after the movie except dumb old Michael Barnett yelled, "Here come the Kotex kids on the bloody trail!"

I told Rose about the movie. All she said was, "Well now you know about that." I should have known she wouldn't want to talk about it. Rose is always very private about things having to do with the body, almost like she doesn't want anybody to know she even has one.

I was becoming the opposite. Nothing was more real to me than my full-of-feeling body. On Sundays I'd go to church with Rose and Brad, run downstairs to Sunday school, peel off my white gloves to expose my bright red nail polish, then shrug out of my coat to show off my see-through nylon blouse. Girls got to wear these blouses for special occasions like church. Here we'd be with full slips on over brassieres and panties, seamed

They Called Me Bunny   5

nylons hooked onto the straps of our panty girdle or garter belt, and on top of all this we'd wear a see-through blouse buttoned to the neck. I saved up my allowance and bought a slip that was pure lace on top. None of the other girls had one. I wanted to make my see-through a double dose. I had my sights set on boys. And my techniques were beginning to work. Boys hung around talking to me. All I had to do was smile and say any dumb thing that came into my mind.

Church was where I tried out most of my stuff. Brad had decided our neighborhood minister carried on too much about sinners and hell, so he drove us downtown to Old First Presbyterian. The kids were a different bunch from the ones at school. I figured I had nothing to lose by being a little daring.

This one Sunday in March when I was in ninth grade, about to turn fifteen, I made my escape from Rose and Brad at the church door and ran downstairs to the bathroom. I applied two coats of black mascara and then gazed into the mirror, testing out new ways of holding my lipstick-coated mouth. My arm had just come out of a cast and I loved the freedom of my body being my own again, moving the way I wanted it to move.

Suddenly Mary Ellis, the minister's daughter, flung open the bathroom door. Mary Ellis is very intelligent but really shy. She stood there staring through my blouse at my lace slip, looking ready to back out the door and not come in at all.

"Come on in," I smiled. "How do you like this green eye shadow?" I held out the container for her to see. She let the door close behind her, but she didn't come closer.

"Your eyes are brown, not green," she blurted out. "I love blonde hair and brown eyes together. I think that is so pretty."

"Thanks," I said, surprised and touched that Mary Ellis would admire anything about me. "Actually, my hair's darker than yours. See?" I bent over and pulled my hair flat. "See the dark roots?"

Mary Ellis looked shocked. "That's not your real color?"

"No!" I laughed. "I bleach it. My parents just about had a cow. But I keep doing it, whenever it starts to show."

"Won't it ruin your hair when you get older? All that

bleach?"

Did she really worry about stuff like that? Her own brown hair was thick and long with a section on each side pulled up high on top of her head, held there by a tortoise shell barrette.

I grinned. "You mean I might end up bald? One o' those old ladies in a red wig?"

She looked at me wide-eyed. "I like how casual your hair is. Kind of uneven."

"I cut it myself," I told her. "It didn't come out right, so then I did a home perm. Which didn't take all that well."

"Bye," she said suddenly, disappearing into a toilet stall. I wished I could have made her feel more at ease. I fluffed my hair with my fingers to make it even wilder, put on another layer of red lipstick and went out to charm Robert Keller. He was an unlikely choice, but not many boys came to Sunday school. And I liked Robert. He was older than the rest of us and very much his own man. He never mentioned parents. Yet he was only sixteen. He must have had parents. All I really knew about Robert was that he went to the movies a lot. He saw at least four a week, usually at the Royal, down the block on Polk Street. While we'd wait for our teacher, Mrs. Pearson, who was always late, Robert would tell us about the latest movie he'd seen. It was like being there. He didn't leave anything out.

I was wearing my wide leather belt that made my waist look tiny and I must have cinched it too tight. I felt slightly faint as I entered the dark-paneled room with its purple velvet drapes.

"Hey, is that you, Bunny?" Robert called out. "Almost didn't recognize you without your cast!"

"Ha, ha, very funny. Wait till the next field trip, I'll probably break my neck!"

"Pull up a chair." That was Margaret Schrader, big and loud-voiced. I dragged one over next to hers and watched Mary Ellis come in. No one called out to her. She sat down at the other end of the semi-circle of chairs.

"So," Robert said, "that was how they met. When she rammed into his left tail light in a parking lot." He went on with his story. My gaze lighted on a boy I'd never seen before, taller

They Called Me Bunny   7

and leaner than Robert, with a superior, amused expression. Very handsome. His dark brown hair was slicked into a duck tail.

"Who's the new guy?" I whispered to Margaret.

"Celestine's cousin," she whispered back.

Celestine lived with her mother and grandmother. Something happened to her dad a long time ago. Just exactly what happened was never mentioned. When I first learned Celestine was missing a parent, I thought maybe we could be friends. It felt like we had something in common. But that turned out to be a big laugh, thinking Celestine and I could ever be friends. She acted like she was better than everybody else. So it didn't surprise me her cousin had that same superior look on his face.

Mrs. Pearson was later than usual and when Robert finished the movie, Margaret asked him to do the final scene from *Duel in the Sun*. We all loved that. As he neared the climax, a lock of sandy hair kept falling over his right eye and he kept brushing it away as he described the agony of Gregory Peck and Jennifer Jones dragging their bodies inch by inch across the dusty hillside, dying at last in each other's arms. Tears welled up in my eyes. I so much wanted to believe in love and romance. I wanted to believe they could happen to me.

Suddenly Margaret piped up, "You're all smudged under your eyes, Bunny!" Everyone turned to look. Celestine put her hand over her mouth and let out a giggle. Does everything I do have to turn into a mess? I headed back to the bathroom.

With a damp paper towel and soap, I finally got the black smudges off. My eyes were red and watery. I closed them, hoping they'd clear up. Pretty soon I looked sort of normal, even a bit interesting, like someone who has experienced deep emotion. I felt Jennifer Jones' and Gregory Peck's tragedy swirling around me as I left the bathroom.

He was there, waiting. Celestine's cousin. Leaning against the wall with a sly expression like the good-looking bad guy in the movies.

"Hi there," he said.

Mary Anderson Parks

"Hi yourself."

"You're pretty cute, you know?"

Maybe he wasn't such a jerk. "Where are you from anyhow?" I asked.

"I'm from Chicago."

"Wow! The big city, huh?"

"We live out in the suburbs, but yeah, it's a big city all right." At about five feet ten, he had five or six inches on me. He had one arm draped across the narrow hallway, the palm of his hand resting on the opposite wall. There wasn't room to get past him so I tried to come up with more conversation.

"How do you like it here? Is San Francisco at all exciting after Chicago?"

"It's great. I love it. Especially San Francisco women." Suddenly I was mashed against the wall and Celestine's cousin was pressing his mouth hard into mine and touching me everywhere at once. He used his strength and size to pin me into a helpless position. His hands were rough on my chest, squeezing and rubbing in fast circles. When he finally stopped, I slapped his face.

"I thought you'd like it," he said, with a half-embarrassed, half-sneering laugh. "You look like the type." He wiped his mouth with his hand and sauntered back toward the classroom, leaving me like a piece of garbage in the dim hallway.

I couldn't go back into that room with him in it. The worst part was I did sort of like it. His hands and mouth had excited me, deep down in the place I touch when I'm alone. Sickened by myself, I used my finger to remove my smudged lipstick. Then I walked up the stairs to the rear of the sanctuary and peered through the long glass windows until I spotted Rose, sitting straight and tall next to Brad. Thank God she was at the end of a pew and had a small space next to her big enough for me. When I squeezed in, she half turned, her face surprised and pleased. She even patted my wrist, giving me three light little taps with her white-gloved hand. That was a lot, coming from Rose.

They Called Me Bunny

3

My mind has chambers that frighten me. I'll be sitting in class and suddenly see myself naked. I stop the image, afraid it can be read on my face, unwilling to see the rest of it, to find out who is there with me. I go off into another chamber, but none of them are safe. It is only in books or plays that rooms can be safe. In real rooms, anybody can come in and bad things happen. It's why I lock my bedroom door. Sometimes I lock it even in daytime, when I'm lying on the bed daydreaming.

My bedroom is across from Rose and Brad's at the end of a short, uncarpeted hallway. We live in a white stucco house on Thirtieth Avenue in the Richmond district, halfway up the hill from Geary. It's a typical junior five, with a floor plan like most other houses in the neighborhood: a front room, a dining area off the kitchen, a hallway going to the back where the two bedrooms are, a bathroom halfway down the hall. And parquet floors. Rose makes a big deal out of the parquet floors. No need for a carpet in the hall with such a nice floor, is there? And I wonder, Am I supposed to answer? Half of what Rose says ends with a question. I usually grunt back in a friendly way, like a harmless bear. I often feel like a clumsy brown bear when I'm with Rose.

Across the street is George Washington High School, which takes up several blocks. It feels claustrophobic, the three of us cooped up in this airless house among long blocks of houses with no space between them, each built over a garage, so the families and the family cars are trapped inside together. There is one small outdoor space, open to the sky to let in light. Narrow French doors lead to it from the dining area. It is walled in on three sides by the house next door and portions of our kitchen and living room. Nobody uses it, but it's there as an escape hatch if I ever need to get out in a hurry. I'll scramble up on the roof and dash away over the rooftops.

Sometimes it bothers me that Mary Ellis thinks I'm stupid. Cute but dumb. That Sunday morning in the bathroom when I first knew she admired me, I was so happy. But after I thought about it I realized she just likes the way I look and that I dare to wear makeup and clothes she wouldn't wear, and she notices boys talk to me and not to her, but still, I'm stupid and she's smart. That's what she thinks and maybe she's right. Maybe I'm just this silly girl who lies on her bed staring at her bedroom ceiling with the door locked.

The thing is, Mary Ellis knows who she is, and I don't.

She's got these morals. She even talks about them in public and agonizes over whether, deep down, what she does is selfish, like when Mrs. Pearson had us do a project for the missionaries in China and Mary Ellis worked and worked on that stuff we were supposed to knit, and she was the only one who finished anything, and Mrs. Pearson told her she should be proud of herself. Mary Ellis looked stricken. I couldn't believe she'd let herself look like that with boys watching, her face all naked and tortured. She said, "No, the worst sin is pride. At least for me it is." And nobody knew what to say until Chris went over and patted her on the back and whispered so Mrs. Pearson couldn't quite catch the words. "Watch out or you'll turn into one of those goddamned saints, Mary. We can't have that." In his guttural tone that always goes right through me. I wished I'd done something to make him notice me like that. Mary Ellis looked at him, her face still naked, showing her insides, and I could see she was in love with him! Chris, the guy with alcoholic parents, in danger of flunking out, who hardly makes it to Sunday school. And she the minister's daughter. Then I remembered the way her father looked at her when Chris asked her to dance at one of the church socials and held her

They Called Me Bunny

close up against him. Her dad suddenly thought of something he needed her help with and made her stop dancing. So Chris cut in and danced with me and I asked him if he liked Mary Ellis and he said, "She's too good. Don't even talk about her. You're not in her league, Bunny."

Then he started doing something with his pelvis and I found myself sort of doing it back. And I didn't care whether Mary Ellis, or even Chris, thought I was stupid, because the only thing in the world he was thinking about right then was me. I felt shivers go up and down my spine, like I'd read about in romantic novels, but no, it was his fingers and the shivers both. I wanted more, but I knew I had to be the one to say stop. Rose told me so in that one talk we had when I first got my period and I couldn't figure out if it was me or Rose who didn't know what we were talking about. But at that instant, dancing with Chris, I knew. I knew from the feeling I was getting where his pelvis touched mine, and I guess Rose had taught me all I needed to know, but I didn't say stop. The dance ended and Chris walked away and I felt cheap and stupid.

Mary Anderson Parks

It's really true that people don't expect girls with bleached hair and too much makeup to be smart. It even kind of bothers them if we are. Not only boys, but girls too. You'd think us girls would stick up for each other.

I wish girls didn't have to give up so much of themselves. We're not supposed to win at games or be good at sports and nobody wants us to bring up ideas that show we've been thinking on our own. Rose and Brad have never known what to make of my ideas. One time when I was younger, Brad just about had Rose thinking I was crazy. I'd gotten up in the night thirsty and when I saw the kitchen light on and heard their voices, I stood in the hall listening.

Brad's voice was rough, and Rose's came back like the murmur of trees in the wind. It was rare to hear them have a conversation, I think that's why I stayed quiet.

"It's not normal," Brad said.

Rose murmured, "We've never been around children—"

"That's just it, she's not acting like a child! What business does a child have asking if I've ever wondered if there's any point in the things I do every day?"

I can still feel how my heart beat faster under my pajama top. Those were my exact words. He had, after all, been listening.

"She's only eleven," Rose said.

"What the hell does that have to do with anything?"

Why was he angry at Rose, I wondered, if I was the one bothering him?

They Called Me Bunny

"It could be a transition she's in, don't you think?"

"You read that in a book no doubt?"

I wasn't too young to recognize sarcasm, but Rose didn't seem to notice. She answered in her usual serious way. "Not about Bunny's ideas, the book didn't mention that. It said that eleven is a transition between childhood and adolescence."

"Well, that's obvious enough! You hardly need to read a book to learn something as obvious as that."

Rose was silent.

"Maybe she's going off her rocker. Could be the genes."

"Do you think so?" Rose sounded fearful.

"We don't know about the father, but the mother—"

"Brad, I don't want to talk about this." It suddenly felt as if Rose knew I was there, listening, because that's what she always does, cuts off any chance for me to learn who I am.

"You were the one who wanted to adopt."

"Don't, Brad, please."

"She's lucky to have us."

"Yes," Rose said. "Who knows what might have happened to her if we hadn't—"

Some impulse, I swear I don't know where it came from, maybe those crazy genes, pushed me into the kitchen.

"What might have happened to me?"

Rose's face stretched this way and that, trying to come up with its usual mask, a mask I hadn't known she wore until I caught her without it.

"Dear, we thought you were asleep."

"I know you did, but I'm not, and I want to know what you know about my—"

"Nothing for you to worry about," Rose interrupted. She got up and started moving canisters around on the counter. Her eyes lighted on the clock. "Brad, look how late it is! You have to be at work bright and early, don't you?"

Brad asked without looking at me, "What did you get up for, Bunny, a drink of water?"

"Yeah, I did."

Brad held a glass under the faucet, filled it and gave it to

Mary Anderson Parks

me, his hand trembling when it touched mine. Then he shuffled off down the hallway. He was wearing slippers, so I knew they hadn't gotten into their twin beds yet. If this were the middle of the night he would be barefoot, his steps making no noise. It was creepy to meet him in the night when I got up for a drink or to go to the bathroom. I began to shiver.

"You're freezing, aren't you?" Rose said. "Take a sip and run to bed now, Bunny. Quick like a rabbit!" After I drank the water, I did run back to bed, and I lay there wondering why I didn't feel safe. I was eleven then. It was three years later that I woke to find Brad breathing hard on my face. But something in me felt it coming. Somehow I knew.

5

Ilene Steele and I started eating lunch together the first day of high school. We latched onto each other so we wouldn't have to eat alone. I knew her from junior high. I guess what we have in common is we're both kind of boy crazy. We're the same height, too. Five four and a half inches. Ilene has a cute little figure and says the same about me. I hope she means it.

I'm now in the eleventh grade, sitting in U.S. history listening to Mr. Gershenberg explain the differences between capitalism and communism. I'm also watching Jeannie Erlickson, who is very pale and pretty and often absent for days, and I'm wondering why she gets sick so much. She has a steady boyfriend who must really care about her to be so patient and wait for the times she's well. I wish I had somebody who loved me that way. She doesn't even have to try. He's just nuts about her. He and I both watch Jeannie when she's here. I sit between him and Stan Miles near the back of the room.

I reach forward to take the note Ilene holds out, low, beneath desk level. When I see the words, "Stan Miles is watching you," my face heats up and I plunk my history book over the note. I don't look at Stan Miles, on my right across the aisle. Instead I keep my eyes on Ilene, who's on my left, two rows ahead. Her dark blonde hair drapes over her eye like Veronica Lake. She probably wears it that way on purpose to spy on people.

Mr. Gershenberg drones on but my mind keeps drifting. Sharon Jefferson eats with us too. While we munch through our sack lunches, Ilene gives us hints on how to attract boys.

Mary Anderson Parks

Always say "Why?" no matter what a boy asks you, Ilene taught us. I'm waiting for chances to try it out. Maybe Stan Miles will ask me something.

Sharon Jefferson is a foster kid, tall and skinny with frizzy shoulder-length red hair. Her sweaters look like hand-me-downs from someone a size smaller. I get the feeling a lot has happened to her she doesn't talk about. Sharon came at the middle of the year when everybody else already had friends. I noticed her eating alone and asked her to join Ilene and me. "Wouldn't I just be in the way?" she asked. I liked it that she'd come right out and say that. Every now and then she'll burst out with something as if she can't help herself. The first time she saw the Golden Gate Bridge from our bench where we eat lunch, she let out a whoop you could hear all over the stadium.

I feel light-headed, wondering if he is still watching me.

Ilene's eye that is not covered catches my eye and she winks. God, is Stan Miles watching this, too? The bell rings before it seems possible. In my rush to gather my books together I drop my pen. When I reach for it, Stan Miles' blond head is close to mine, near the floor. He hands me the pen, his face flushed. He's handsome in a sleek smooth way I don't quite trust. It is exciting to be so close to him. His eyes are blue and intense.

"Carry your books?" He asks it coolly, as I finally get everything collected. I hand my books over to him as casually as if we do this every day. We are the last ones in the room. Even Mr. Gershenberg has left. Fate, throwing us together! Stan doesn't make a move to go anywhere. He stands very still and the look in his eyes deepens. My heart pounds under my pink angora sweater.

"How about going to a movie Friday?" He narrows his eyes.

All too eagerly I say, "Sure, I could go to a movie Friday." Then I think, was I supposed to ask "Why?" A giggle bursts out.

"What's funny?"

"Nothing. I just giggle a lot." I bat my eyelashes, another

of Ilene's suggestions, but I feel like a bad imitation of a girl batting her eyelashes. Probably he thinks so too, because he laughs.

"Hey, give me your phone number!"

"You've got all my stuff," I point out. He sets my books and binder on the nearest desk. I rip off a corner edge of paper and write down my phone number and address. "I live right across from school. Here's the address, so you'll know where to pick me up."

He pockets the scrap of paper. "I gotta run. See ya."

What about carrying my books? What happened to that idea? I'm standing there staring when Mr. Gershenberg makes a sudden reappearance.

"Did you have a question, Bunny?" He looks hopeful, as if he wishes I did. History really fascinates Mr. G. I try to think of something. But what I come up with surprises even me.

"Communism didn't sound that bad. You know, when you compared it to capitalism?"

He eyes me questioningly, with a frown.

"What you said about regulators," I explain. "That the regulator of capitalism is competition and for communism it's cooperation." More comes back to me and I rush on recklessly. "The motivation of capitalism is self-interest and for communism it's the common good. That didn't sound so bad, you know?"

Mr. G sits on a corner of his desk, at eye level with me. Good. Now he's not as overpowering. "Bunny," he says, "I had no idea you were paying such close attention."

My face grows warm. I've always had a bit of a crush on Mr. G. He is earnest and kind, with a touch of shyness. And he doesn't just stick to the book. He brings up questions I wouldn't think of on my own.

"That was theory I was presenting," he says. "Practice is another matter."

"Anyway, folks in America like to be free to get rich. I guess that's why they'd never go for it."

He laughs. It is rare to see Mr. G laugh. I like the way it lights up his face. "Is that the aspect of freedom that first comes to

Mary Anderson Parks

your mind, Bunny?"

"Not really. What comes to my mind is the freedom to vote the way we want. I mean, we're free to choose any kind of government at all in this country. I like that."

"Except," Mr. G replies, "that congressmen like Martin Dies would make it illegal to belong to the Communist Party if they could."

"But that goes against freedom!"

"Yes, in that way people in France and Italy have more political freedom than we do. Bunny, this is my prep period, but aren't you due at your next class?"

I look at the wall clock. "Wow! I gotta get going."

"Thanks for giving me your thoughts, Bunny. You'll be interested in what I have planned for next week."

"What's that?" I pause on my way out the door.

"HUAC," he says. "We'll learn all about it and how it threatens our freedom."

I shrug and smile. I have no idea what he's talking about.

"What's wrong?" I ask Rose when I find her staring blankly into a kitchen cupboard.

"Your father won't be home for dinner," she says in a dull voice. "He *says* because of a meeting."

To cheer her up, I suggest, "Wanna have some Upper-Ten and Cheese-Its?

She brightens a bit. "Do we have any Upper-Ten?"

I open the refrigerator. "Half a bottle. Want me to walk to the store for another?"

"No, that's plenty."

I get out a tray of ice cubes, put three in each glass, then pour fizzling soda pop from the large green bottle. "I love Upper-Ten, don't you? It's zippier than 7-Up."

"What? Oh, I don't know."

She sounds awfully depressed. Sometimes the shock technique works. I blurt out, "Guess what? I finally got asked out on a real date."

Rose stiffens. Her eyes become focused. On me. And worried. Oh jeez! I've dragged her from the dumps into worry.

"What do you mean, Bunny, 'finally'? You're only sixteen!"

"Don't you remember that's when you said I should start dating?"

"I didn't say 'should.'" She pulls a handkerchief from the pocket of her housedress. Gosh, is she going to cry?

"You said something about sixteen being a good age to start dating. Aren't you glad I waited?"

"I said that's the earliest a nice girl would ever go on a date." She blows her nose into the handkerchief. "Who *is* the boy?"

Who is he? I wonder that myself. "He's just this guy. Kind of quiet and a good student."

"Well, that's nice."

I think about the strangeness in his eyes, the distance he keeps. Rose pours Cheese-Its into a flowered bowl, puts the box back in the cupboard and at last sits down with me at the kitchen table. I sip Upper-Ten, loving the way the bubbles feel as they go down my throat.

"Is he a nice boy?" Rose asks.

How the heck do I know? I guess I'll find out soon enough. "He's kind of deep," I say. "The silent type."

"Oh." Rose looks confused. "Maybe because he's so smart?"

"He's not *that* smart," I tell her truthfully.

"Where is he taking you? To a school dance?"

Aha! She's starting to accept it. I slump back in my chair. "No, a movie."

"But how will you get there?"

"He's got a car. I've seen him drive to school in it."

"Is he an *older* boy?"

"No, my age. I'm old enough to drive."

"But that's so young to have a car. I don't know if we want you out in some strange boy's car, Bunny."

"Just tell me when to be home and I'll tell him I have to be home by then." Sometimes I have to help Rose figure out the next step.

Her pale blue eyes cloud with worry. "I'll ask Brad to be sure to be here when he comes." It's the way things are supposed to be done, the father checking out the boyfriend. Brad won't like my going out with a guy. It wouldn't matter how nice Stan Miles was.

"You go do your homework, Bunny, why don't you. I'll figure out something for us to have later for supper."

I stand for a moment taking in the sharp, birdlike features that give Rose a slightly pinched look. Her short hair, set once

They Called Me Bunny   21

a week at the beauty parlor, never has a wave out of place. Maybe she doesn't roll around like I do when I sleep.

The phone rings and both of us jump. "I'll get it," I say, running to the hallway. "Hello?"

"Bunny?"

"Stan?"

"Yeah, it's me. I'll pick you up at seven on Friday, okay?"

"Sure, that's fine. I'll be ready."

There is a silence. Then he says, "How about if you just come outside? I'll be in the car waiting."

"Look Stan, my folks will expect you to at least come to the door. It's no big deal." I keep my voice low, hoping Rose won't hear. "Okay, Stan?"

"Okay. I'll come to the door."

Why does he sound so reluctant?

"Stan?"

"Yeah?"

"I just wondered if you were still there."

He laughs. "You're funny, Bunny."

"Yeah, that's me, funny Bunny. Well, I'll see you Friday night. And in class!"

He lets out another brief laugh. "Okay, Bunny." Silence again. "Does it matter what movie we go to?"

"No, you pick. I'll like whatever you pick."

"You will?"

"Sure, I like movies."

"Okay. Look, I gotta go."

"All right, bye."

The silences were weird. Will we be able to talk better in his car? He'll be driving, maybe that will make it easier. He'll be busy doing that and I can chatter away like I always do. Maybe later he'll kiss me at the front door at the end of the date, like in the movies, and my knees will feel weak.

After I finish my homework, Rose and I have lettuce salad with Thousand Island dressing and creamed chipped beef on toast.

"One little jar of chipped beef certainly goes a long way,

doesn't it?" she remarks.

"Yep, it sure does."

I wish we could talk about something that matters. Brad's not here, so I decide to give it a try.

"You know, sometimes kids at school ask if I'm Italian or what nationality I am, and I wonder is there anything you could tell me about—"

"Oh Bunny, don't spoil our nice dinner by bringing up unpleasant subjects!"

I spend the rest of the meal talking about nothing, hoping to make the line between her eyes go away, remembering the many times I've tried and failed to get her to tell me something, anything, about who I am.

For an hour on Friday night I try on clothes in front of my dresser mirror, standing on a chair, and still can't figure out what to wear. I want to wear the pink angora, so if Stan Miles puts his arm around me I'll feel all soft and feminine. But I had it on when he asked for the date. I can't wear it again. Finally I choose a pale yellow sweater set and straight dark gray skirt, then put on my favorite jewelry, a gold charm bracelet, for luck.

But wait a minute. I'm supposed to be a fun kid, daring. The raciest senior girls wear cardigans with nothing underneath except a bra and slip. I glance at my alarm clock. Five till seven. Already. I have to rush. I yank off the cardigan and the matching short-sleeve, then button myself back into the cardigan, leaving the top three buttons undone. I put on my gray coat. Quickly, I apply two coats of bright red lipstick, powder my nose, blot the lipstick and head out to the living room.

Brad is seated in his armchair, looking glum. Rose is perched on the edge of the middle cushion of the couch. "Oh, here's Bunny!" she says.

I forgot mascara. But it will be dark in the car and in the theater. Maybe it won't matter. The lobby, though, will have glaring lights. "I forgot something," I say, running from the room. I am adding a last touch of mascara when the doorbell rings. It sends shivers through me. My first real date! I wonder if he'll take me to Mel's afterward for a milkshake or a hamburger. Maybe we'll really hit it off and he'll end up asking me to go

Mary Anderson Parks

steady.

I come out to find the three of them standing awkwardly just inside the front door. Why is our entry so dark? I never noticed before how gloomy it is. Stan Miles is as tall as Brad, six feet. I can tell his neat appearance impresses Rose. His blond hair is carefully combed. He is wearing a tan wool sweater over a white shirt and tie. His face looks strained but relaxes a bit when he sees me.

"Nice meeting you," he mumbles, then hustles me out. I turn and wave to Rose from the bottom of the steps. Brad has disappeared.

Stan Miles holds open the door of his dark green Plymouth coupe and I slide in. He gets behind the wheel, starts up the car and drives off.

"What theater are we going to?" I ask.

"The Alexandria."

That's only about twelve blocks from my house. He doesn't say anything else and after a moment I ask, "So what shows are we seeing?"

"I don't know."

It seems odd that he didn't check out what's playing. Nervous, I start chattering about our history homework, about the Eagles, our football team, and finally, desperate to get a response, I babble about bleaching my hair last week when I spilled peroxide on my leg and got scared I'd have bleach spots on my skin so I ran a hot bath and soaked till I was wrinkled. He turns his head at the part about the bath and looks at me. Maybe I shouldn't have told him that. Something in his eyes scares me. This strong, silent act of his is beginning to feel creepy.

At least it's a short trip. He finds a parking spot near the theater and after he turns off the engine he just sits there, tense and straight. Staring through the front window, he asks, "You really want to go to the movies?"

"Of course!" I glance at the marquee. "One of them's got Gregory Peck in it!"

He looks at me then, and I am astonished how dark his blue

They Called Me Bunny

eyes are. I bite my lower lip and wrinkle my nose at him, to lighten the mood. "Hey, let's go in!"

He reaches over and gives my hand a quick squeeze before he gets out. I wait for him to walk around the back of the car and open my door, like fellows do in the movies. It takes so long I wonder if he started off by himself, expecting me to follow.

After a short wait in line, he buys the tickets and we go into the lobby with mirrored walls and thick red carpets. He doesn't offer to get us Cokes or popcorn or candy. And he doesn't ask me where I'd like to sit. He leads me to the middle of the very back row. The lights dim and a Bugs Bunny cartoon comes on. When it ends, Stan whispers in my ear, "Aren't you hot with your coat on?"

He helps me off with it. Maybe his manners aren't that bad after all.

But right away he drapes his arm around me and lets his hand rest on my breast. His hand starts to move up and down. I don't know what to do. My mouth goes dry. I sit there staring straight ahead, wondering stupid things like whether he can tell I am wearing a padded bra. Just lightly padded. Nothing like falsies. A few people come in late and the usher lights their way with his flashlight. As he comes back up the carpeted aisle, I pray he won't accidentally shine the flashlight on us. Maybe Stan Miles is thinking the same thing. He keeps his hand still. I have trouble concentrating on what is happening on the screen with his hand resting on my chest and me wondering should I have let him move his fingers like he did. But gradually I get caught up in the story. Somehow Gregory Peck looks different, not trustworthy like he usually does. It takes a long time for the movie to get to the first love scene. I can feel it building toward the moment he'll take the girl in his arms and kiss her. When he does, Stan Miles reaches his fingers inside the front of my sweater and then inside my bra, feeling and squeezing. He is hurting me.

There is no one else in our row or in the row in front of us. No one turns around when the cry "Stop!" comes out of me.

"Shh," he breathes into my hair. And with his right hand

Mary Anderson Parks

he reaches for mine and puts it on the crotch of his pants. I am horrified as he forces my hand up and down in a steady rhythmic motion. My jangling charm bracelet becomes part of it. Will someone hear his heavy breathing, turn and look at us and know what he is doing? He holds me tight with his left arm, unfastens his pants and presses my hand to his thing.

Why does he think he can treat me like this? This is a million times worse than Celestine's cousin. I yank my hand out from under his, grab my coat and stumble past empty seats to the aisle. I walk through the lobby and out the swinging doors as fast as I can without running.

I struggle into my coat and dash down the street. Parts of me begin to fall off. I know I'm imagining this, it only happens to me in dreams, but it frightens me. A middle-aged couple stare. I run and run and run until I'm panting so hard I have to slow to a walk. At last I'm on my block, sucking in deep breaths of air. I trudge up the front steps, take the key from my coat pocket, open the door and close it behind me. I hurry to the bathroom and wash my hands twice. Then, as I pass Rose and Brad's room, Rose's voice drifts out through their half-open door. "How was your evening, dear? Did you enjoy the movie?"

"It was great."

"You didn't stay for the second feature?"

"No. We liked the first one so much we didn't want to spoil it. Night!" I shut my door firmly. Slowly, soundlessly, I turn the key, shed my coat, pull the sweater over my head, let my skirt, garter belt and nylons drop to the floor. I remove the charm bracelet and lay it on the dresser.

"This should never have happened to you," I murmur to the crumpled heap of charms. "I'm sorry." Still wearing my slip and bra and panties, I get in bed, curl up under the covers and try to erase the memory of Stan Miles' thing in my hand. When I close my eyes, thoughts still more unwanted come. Why did Stan Miles choose me? Does he think I'm a slut? Not as good as he is? My skin is as dark as a light-skinned Negro girl in gym class. Why? Who am I? Does Stan Miles know I don't know

They Called Me Bunny

who I am? Is that why it's okay to treat me the way he did? I feel numb, ashamed. I wish I could disappear. And then tears come, tears of self-pity because I have no one to comfort me. Other than my occasional sobs, the house is deadly quiet, as if waiting for something. I open my eyes and roll over onto my back.

I don't have to wait, expecting disaster. That is Rose's way. I'm a fighter. I don't have to run my life by what other people think! I'll go to school Monday and I'll be gayer and brighter than I've ever been. I'll wear loud colors or any damn thing I please. I'll be a style setter.

I won't wear the charm bracelet. Not that. I get up and run to the dresser and stuff it far back in my underwear drawer. Then I hurry back to bed.

Stan Miles doesn't hang out with other guys. He won't tell. It is not something he'd want to tell anyone. I have to believe that. In the struggle to believe it, my mind exhausts itself and I drift into sleep comforted by a dream image of my real mother. I know she would understand. But the sound of the doorknob turning jolts me awake. My body goes rigid. Did I lock it? He turns it twice more. Then there is silence, and I breathe again.

Mary Anderson Parks

8

Stan Miles isn't in class on Monday. Mr. G tells us we are beginning a new current events unit. He explains what the initials HUAC stand for: House Un-American Activities Committee. Somebody in Congress started it back in the thirties. Richard Nixon has been involved and a man named Joe McCarthy, and Harold Velde is the chairman. Mr. G asks how many have heard of this committee. Two kids raise their arms halfway. "It's been going on for years," he tells us. "It's something you should know about." But I can't think about committees. I can only think how glad I am I made myself jump back in the water, or get back up on the horse, or whatever the saying is, and show up where I'm supposed to be. It never occurred to me that Stan Miles wouldn't be here, that he would be the cowardly one. I wouldn't for anything have missed seeing his empty desk.

Ilene passes me a note. I have told her nothing at all about the date. Do I have a guardian angel who kept me from talking about it? For an instant I almost believe in God. I unfold the piece of paper and read the first line: "What are you grinning about?" She's right. I am grinning. The grin spreads more widely across my face as I read the rest of the note: "Why are you dressed all in red?"

"I'm starting a new style," I write back.

The next day is harder. Stan Miles is in his seat when I enter the classroom. I feel connected to him in a way I hadn't expected. That comes as a shock. There seems to be a low buzzing noise around him that only I can hear. Mr. G starts writing words on the blackboard, and for me it is the movie screen far up there in front of me and I can't register the meaning of anything that is happening. The whole period goes by like that. The only part of reality I can sense is that Mr. G is asking questions and no one is responding, and Mr. G expects me to be interested and even to help him out, but I can't come through for him. I hate failing him. We should be there for people when they need us. I sure as hell could have used someone to be there for me. Finally, this guy with thick glasses, a real square, pipes up and gives an answer that disappoints Mr. G. I can sense feelings but not meanings. The bell rings and I spring from my seat, grab my books and move toward Ilene, feeling the need of a shield. But Ilene is talking to the boy in the seat in front of her, flirting, trying out her tricks.

"Bunny?" Mr. G speaks as I pass his desk. I turn to look at him. "I'd hoped you might have some opinions on today's topic."

Mr. G still looks trustworthy. That is immensely comforting. I rest my stack of books on his desk.

"Mr. Gershenberg, I need to ask you something. I mean, I'm sorry about today, I couldn't really follow what you were saying." What am I babbling? Where am I going with this? Then inspiration hits. "You know, I think my near-sightedness is getting worse. I couldn't read a thing you put on the blackboard. I wish I could sit up closer to the front. There aren't any empty seats up there, are there?"

He looks concerned. What a kind man! He pulls out his seating chart from a drawer. "I'll just switch you with someone. That's no problem." He studies the chart. "I'll move Albert Carrington back to your seat." That makes me smile. Albert is the square who gave the answer that made Mr. G wince. I wonder what he said. I am in a state where I see things I don't normally see. I see Mr. G's relief that there is a reason I was so unresponsive.

"What was the homework again, Mr. G?"

He rubs the side of his nose, something he does when a student is on the wrong track and he's trying to think of a tactful way to help them out. Suddenly I realize I just called him Mr. G to his face.

"Gee, I'm sorry. It's just that your name's kind of long—"

"It's all right, Bunny." He smiles. "The homework." He rubs his nose again. "I didn't assign any today, not that I remember."

He adds that part about not remembering just to be nice, so it won't be so obvious I wasn't listening.

I feel like crying. I have a weird impulse to tell him what happened Friday night and that what happened is the reason I want to change my seat. Who else could I tell? The thought hits me that there is no one I can tell. I'll just have to try to block it out of my mind. It can join all that other stuff that is in there somewhere, blocked out. It won't be lonely. But I will. I'll be—

"Bunny?" Mr. G is still there, the seating chart in front of him on his desk, with my name pencilled into a new space, in the front row.

"I was kind of distracted today," I tell him. "I've got some things on my mind."

He coughs. Is he wondering if he should ask what's on my mind? "Nothing serious," I say. "Well, I better get to my next class." I'm not late, though. There is still time for something to happen. I wait, knowing he wants to say more.

"Bunny, do your folks have a television?" This strikes me as an odd thing to ask. I have the feeling it isn't what he really wanted to say.

"Yes, they do." It feels safe talking like this to Mr. G in the empty classroom. It helps me feel real, like a person whose thoughts matter. Even though he hasn't said so, I feel that to him my thoughts do matter. It is the opposite of that night in the movie theater. Then I was . . . but I must listen. I must try to hear what he is saying.

"Watch the news tonight, Bunny. That can be your homework. Find out what HUAC is doing."

"I don't have to give a report or anything, do I?"

"No." He smiles. "Just give it some thought."

When I get home, the house is empty. I go through all the rooms to make sure. I stick my head in Rose and Brad's room. It smells like pine scent. Everything is put away so you'd never know anybody lived or slept there, but the spray can of pine air freshener sits right out in the open on the dresser, next to the vase of plastic lilies. I wander into the kitchen and open the cupboard where Rose keeps canned food. Why do I have this urge to cook, to mess things up? I take out a can of tomato sauce. I could make something with it if she has any vegetables. I don't feel I have a right to be holding the tomato sauce. Do all kids feel this way, or only adopted kids? Maybe it's all in my head. Maybe I'm crazy. I pull out a bunch of celery, a carrot and a big round cauliflower from the vegetable bin, then get out the can opener and open the tomato sauce. There! I've committed myself. I twist the sharp metal lid till it separates from the can, and I see blood gushing from my neck. What if Rose came in and found me dead in a puddle of blood? Would she cry? Or would she be wondering how to explain it to Brad and the people at church? She'd start by saying how happy and cheerful Bunny always was, then her hand would go to her throat and she'd turn her head . . . God, I wish somebody loved me enough to go crazy and not have any words to talk about it if I died.

"I hate what he did to me!" I cry the words aloud and realize it is Stan Miles' blood I want to see spurting. I chop the cauliflower into littler and littler pieces. I get carried away,

Mary Anderson Parks

chopping, and slice into the forefinger of my left hand. Blood drips onto the white cauliflower. I wish I had cut the other hand, the one Stan Miles held under his.

Rose appears at the kitchen door. "Oh my, Bunny, what have you done?"

Why can't we ever say to each other the things in our hearts? Why can't I say I was chopping vegetables and wishing I was chopping up the boy who took me on my first date and ruined . . . what? Maybe I don't have words for what he ruined. But aren't mothers supposed to understand even when you don't have words?

Blood drips onto the sleeve of my red blouse. I run cold water on my bleeding finger. "We could make Johnny Marzetti out of this," I say, wrapping my finger tightly in a paper napkin.

"But that's not how you make it."

"We could try something different. Experiment. Play a-round."

Rose frowns, disturbed by my suggestions.

"Everything can be salvaged," I say.

"Bunny, you need a Band-Aid for that finger, don't you? I'll go get one."

I squeeze my wrapped finger and pretty soon Rose comes back with Band-Aids. God, what a familiar smell! My whole life I've been stretching out a finger or a leg for somebody to stick a Band-Aid on. Mr. G once said that Band-Aid solutions are not good enough. I need better solutions. Ending up with a Band-Aid and a throbbing finger because I want to punish Stan Miles won't get me anywhere. I need fundamental change. And it is me I have to change. I sure can't change Stan Miles.

Have more dates right away, that's it! I'll use all Ilene's techniques and mine too, and throw myself in the path of somebody who isn't a creep.

"I could fry up some hamburger," Rose says.

"And stir all this in! Once I get it mixed together." Protected by my Band-Aid, that is starting to seep through with blood, I go back to chopping.

"Bunny, let me do that, why don't you? Don't you have

They Called Me Bunny   33

homework you should be doing?"

"Nope!"

"Well then, you might put on a pot of water for me to cook the macaroni. I'll finish those vegetables, all right?"

I catch on, finally, that Rose doesn't want blood seeping into her food.

"Great! That I can do. Oh, I do have homework, I forgot. I'm supposed to watch the news and learn about the House Un-American Activities Committee."

"Why would a teacher give an assignment like that?" Brad's voice comes from the doorway. His tone signals danger. How long has he been standing there?

"He just wants us to learn about current events," I say. "So we'll know what's going on."

"I can tell you what's going on. Those rich Jew commies in Hollywood are finding themselves out of a job." Why is his voice so mean? I know he resents rich people. I've heard him complain to Rose that he's worked at the post office all these years and where does it get him. But what does being Jewish have to do with anything? And why would there be Communists in Hollywood? I'm starting to get interested in the homework assignment.

"Our teacher likes us to look at all sides of things," I say.

"What is he, soft on communism? What's his name?" Brad's tone is so menacing I wish I had kept quiet. Wasn't this supposed to be just between Mr. G and me? I hate it when I do things that hurt other people. I'm used to messing up my own life, but it doesn't seem fair to mess up somebody else's.

"I can't pronounce it," I tell Brad. "It's too long."

"Some foreigner, is he?"

"Ooh," I squeal. "The blood's seeping through my Band-Aid. I need to get another one!" I run out of the kitchen holding my bandaged finger.

The Johnny Marzetti turns out to be the best we've ever had. It gives us something neutral to talk about. Me, I don't need much of a subject to get me going. I guess I'm opposite to Rose and Brad in that way, like in so many others. I wonder if

Rose and Brad ate in complete silence before I came into their lives. Maybe my chattiness is some sort of natural reaction to their silence.

Later, as we watch the news together, tension edges in again. Brad starts muttering about commies and why don't they go back to Russia, and Rose frowns at him and at the television and at me. I try to block all this out and listen, but it isn't easy. I don't understand the talk about the Fifth Amendment. What does the Fifth Amendment say, anyway? And then I figure it out because somebody declares, "I have the right not to incriminate myself." So it really is a crime in America to be a Communist! Maybe I'd better watch out what I say from now on.

"Only one person named names at today's session," the announcer tells us. "And the world is startled to hear of Kim Hunter's ties with the Communist Party." Certainly I am startled. Kim Hunter is one of my favorite actresses. She seems like she'd be a really good person, too. Someone with a conscience, like Gregory Peck. But I push away the thought of Gregory Peck, because now when I think of him I think of Stan Miles.

Movies are important. I learn about life from the movies. If I had to rely on Rose and Brad, my god, I'd be like one of the Puritans. I know what goes on in nightclubs, law courts, even prisons, because of movies. And this committee wants to put the people who've given me the best part of my education out of a job? That makes me fume.

"What ever happened to freedom?" I mutter.

"What?" Brad's voice is sharp-edged.

"I thought this was a free country."

"Bunny, those guys are *commies*! They'd take away our freedom."

"Kim Hunter? Somehow I find that hard to believe. Anyway, it hasn't been proved yet, has it? That she's even in the Communist Party?"

"Joe McCarthy'll get 'em," Brad hisses. "He's got a list. And it's getting longer every day." What weird satisfaction is Brad getting from this? He hasn't answered my question, but it doesn't seem like a good idea to point that out.

They Called Me Bunny

"Who is this teacher of yours anyway?"

"Just my U.S. history and civics teacher. The same one I had last semester."

"Is he some kind of pinko?"

"He just likes for us to see all sides of things. He's teaching us to be objective."

"There's only one side to this, Bunny. You're either a commie or you aren't."

I yawn, stretching my arms up over my head, and immediately, as if he can't help himself, Brad's eyes travel to my chest and hold there. I despise him, I really do.

"I've been thinking," I say, "if I take all solid subjects the first semester of my senior year, I could graduate early, in January."

"Why would you want to do that?" Rose chimes in.

"Why not?" I shrug.

"You'd miss the prom and all the senior activities."

"If it's dates you're worried about my missing, I can take care of that."

Rose doesn't know how to respond, and I smile. "Don't worry. I'm just thinking out loud. Anyway, it's not till next year."

10

As weeks go by, it becomes clearer and clearer why I want to graduate early. To get away from them. Especially Brad.

I bury myself in schoolwork. But part of my brain shuts down and the effort doesn't pay off. My eyes learn to stay open while my mind sleeps. Then one morning I awaken and my eyes and mind fly open as one. I stare at the ceiling and see up there in the whorls of plaster that I have let myself be knocked out of a creep. Me, the original bounce-back kid. The kid nothing fazes. Cheerful, resilient Bunny. What's happened to me? I've become this shell that walks around impersonating the real Bunny. Never mind that I don't know who the real me is. There is still this girl, this "Bunny," who's learned how to get by, how to crack a joke and grin, how to keep herself above water and not get dragged under by all the stuff she doesn't know about who she is. Stuff other kids take for granted, and even complain about. And what happened to my dating plan? I was going to cancel out Stan Miles with normalcy. Instead I've let myself drift along, afraid of getting hurt again.

I sit up in bed and fluff out my perm, deciding what to wear. I choose a knockout bright green cotton blouse and don't wear a coat even though the fog is so thick I can't see the school on the other side of the street. Ever since "the date," I have been rushing over at the last minute, sliding into my seat as the bell rings. This morning I get there in time to go to my locker first, like I used to. I watch Skip Henderson straighten up his lanky frame. He always jokes about being over six feet and having a locker next to the floor. He grins when he sees me.

"Hey, Bunny!"

"Hey, Skip!" I give him a friendly shove, leaning into him with my shoulder. Boys like it when you get physical with them. It breaks the ice. Leads to other stuff. But since the night with Stan Miles, I haven't felt like touching or being touched. Skip gives me a push back and lets his big hand rest on my upper arm.

"Where you been, Bunny?"

"Nowhere special."

"You look cold."

"Dumb me. I ran out without a coat. But all I have to do is cross the street. I didn't think I'd get cold."

Skip bends down and rummages in his locker. "I've got an extra sweater. Wanna wear it?"

"Sure!"

I love wearing boy's clothes. It's kind of a status symbol, too, when a guy lends you something to wear.

"This okay?" He pulls out a black vee-neck.

"Great. My green collar will still show. Good thing your sweater's not red, I'd look like a Christmas tree." The sweater comes below my knees. A few inches of skirt peek out.

"Don't get lost in there, Bunny!"

I'd forgotten how great it feels to start the day kidding around with Skip. I keep his sweater on until afternoon when the sun comes out, then drape it around my shoulders and tie the sleeves loosely in front. I feel protected by the sweater. It smells like Skip, healthy and clean.

At the end of the day, I'm walking down the hall with Ilene when Frank Gardner and Erwin Eliot saunter past. Ilene calls, "Hi Frank, Hi, Erwin," and they stop to chat. They're both really nice guys. Frank is in my English class and I ask him about the homework. During class, my mind had been wandering, as usual. Frank is honor roll, he's always on top of things. He gets out the assignment and goes over it with me.

"Gonna be a tough football game Friday," Ilene says. "Galileo's got a whiz of a team." I know she's hoping they'll ask us to go to the game and the dance afterward.

Suddenly I blurt out, "Let's all go together to the game. It'd be fun."

The surprise on their faces reminds me that girls don't do the asking. But when Frank grins, "You're right, Bunny. It'd be fun to go together," I am glad that for a moment I forgot. I plunge onward.

"We could go to the dance afterward and have a blast."

Ilene sends me a dagger-like look from her one visible eye.

"Why not?" Frank responds. Is it relief I see on his face? Maybe boys get tired of doing the asking, running the risk of getting turned down. Why should girls always wait to be asked? It's degrading.

"Ilene, you can come to my house," I go on recklessly. "And Frank, you and Erwin meet us at the gate on Thirtieth Avenue. I live just across the street from it."

Erwin studies me with interest. He is a straight A student who's known as a fun guy. I've wished I could get to know a boy like that and suddenly it seems easy. There's so much freedom we have that we don't use. The thought exhilarates me. No, it is the act of exercising freedom that exhilarates me. I feel an urge to tell Mr. G about the fascinating forms freedom can take!

"Is that the gate that has a quote engraved above it?" Erwin frowns, trying to remember.

"Yeah, it's from Plato. Something about first and greatest is for a man to conquer himself."

He stares at me in disbelief. "That's it exactly." There is more than a hint of admiration in his eyes. He must have thought I was really stupid if that's all it takes to impress him. I glance at Ilene to see if she is taking it in. Her confused expression tickles me. I give Erwin a playful punch on the shoulder.

"Ilene and I have to be somewhere," I say. "Goodbye, guys."

"See ya at the gate, four o'clock sharp," Frank calls, as Ilene and I walk away.

"Where do we have to be?" Ilene whispers.

I burst out laughing. "It's you who taught me that. You said it's a good way to end a conversation. And I do have to be somewhere. See you tomorrow." I run off quickly. I don't want to hear her rehash of what just happened. I want to keep on feeling free, like I could do anything.

11

We have fun at the game and then later at the dance, but no sparks fly except my own when I go crazy doing the bop, hopping all over the place. So I'm not surprised as weeks go by and Frank and Erwin don't ask Ilene or me out for a real date. And I guess I'm not all that surprised when Erwin and Jean Wallace start going steady. I'd never much noticed Jean Wallace. I don't think anybody had. She's this tall, plain-looking girl, not at all a sharp dresser or part of any clique like the Tawunas or the Echoes. But when Erwin asked her to go steady, everybody started realizing how nice she is. Smart, too. So it makes sense they'd end up together. Come to think about it, there's no way a boy like Erwin would go for one of the clique girls. Usually I don't think about cliques. I try to ignore them. The clique girls are not the best students, but they're popular and seem to have more fun than anybody else. They're the party girls, the ones who get chosen for "best figure" and "prettiest face" and "great smile" in the yearbook. Boys like them. Certain boys, anyway. But since nobody ever shows any sign of wanting to include me in their clique, I just try to have a good time on my own and be friendly to everybody.

Sometimes I worry, though, whether all of life is going to be like this, with certain people getting elected to office and certain people getting the best grades and certain people being the most popular and certain other people being left out, and once those reputations are established, there's no changing them. It's depressing to think the whole world might be like high school.

I hope I'm being honest in thinking it would actually bother me to be in a clique where the whole point is who's in and who's out. I know I don't like what it does to the people who are out.

12

One day, only Sharon shows up for lunch. Ilene is at a dance committee meeting. I guess she figures it's worth it to be at the dances any way she can get there. You won't catch me bustling around arranging decorations. But I suppose Ilene being on dance committee is an example of how she's the most normal of the three of us. Sometimes she tells us stories about her family, about the good times she and her mother and father and older brother have together. She and her mother borrow each other's clothes and makeup. I can't imagine Rose and me doing that. I laugh a lot to cover up that I have no family stories I want to tell, and so I won't have that far-off, sad expression Sharon gets.

"It's just you and me, kid," I say to Sharon. We sit down on our cold bench and she brings out this pathetic-looking peanut butter sandwich and starts munching away. I unwrap my corned beef on rye.

Sharon casts a gloomy, envious look at it. Did she even comb her hair this morning? It's all matted and dirty. Her too-small sweater is covered with fuzz balls.

"How're things?" I ask.

"Not so good."

"Hey, do you want to trade half a peanut butter for half a corned beef?"

"Sure." She trades hastily, as if afraid I'll change my mind.

"What's not going so good?"

"The family I've been living with is getting transferred to Los

They Called Me Bunny   43

Angeles."

I stop chewing. "You mean you'll move to Los Angeles?"

"No. I'll get put in a new home."

"Oh," I say, with peanut butter stuck to the roof of my mouth.

"They don't take you with them when they move." She lowers her voice. "Thank God."

"Why do you say it like that?"

"I wouldn't get to see my mom."

A pang of jealousy hits me hard in the chest. For a second I can't breathe.

"Do you see her often?"

"Only every month or so. If she's having her shock treatments, I don't get to see her. She has periods when she goes crazy."

"Do you have brothers or sisters?" I've never asked before. I can't believe I've never thought to ask, but when Ilene's with us we talk about lipstick, nail polish, our lack of boyfriends, and nothing real gets said.

"Yeah, a little brother." She says it so softly I barely hear the words.

"What'll happen to him?"

Sharon's jaw tightens. "We damn well better be sent to the same home."

"Have you always been together?"

"Yes." Fierceness flashes out of her eyes.

"How old is he?"

"Eleven."

"Gee."

"Yeah. He's got a long way to go."

"Sharon, when will this happen?"

"I think next week."

"You're kidding."

"I kid you not." She attempts a grin but it doesn't come off.

"Will you have to go to a different school?"

"Who knows? Sometimes they put kids out in Daly City. I don't care though. So long as they let my brother go to the same home."

Again I feel the pain in my chest, a surge of pure jealousy. She has a mother. And a brother. I'd give anything to be Sharon. Miserable as she looks, I'd give anything. She has what I don't have and never will. She knows who she is.

13

We are in the living room waiting for the clock to reach seven so Rose can turn on the television for the evening shows. Brad, as usual, sits tensely in the green easy chair. Rose is on one side of the couch and I'm on the other. A typical evening, except Rose has brought up something to talk about: a church banquet for fathers and daughters.

"You and your father will enjoy a night out together, won't you?"

The idea sounds so unlikely I hardly know what to say. All I come up with is, "I feel awfully old for a father-daughter banquet."

"The social director did have younger girls in mind," Rose admits. "There weren't many interested fathers, so he opened it up to all ages."

"Great." I roll my eyes.

"Now eighteen couples are signed up, but it's still small enough there'll be chances to get acquainted, won't there?"

We're attempting our happy family act. I have to figure out my lines.

"Yeah. Should be a barrel of fun." Brad looks at me closely to see if I am being sarcastic. I'm in for it if he decides I am, so I shift the subject.

"Will I need a new dress?"

"Oh no," Rose says. "Your brown wool should do fine, don't you think?"

I hate the brown wool. High-necked and long-sleeved,

Mary Anderson Parks

it makes me sweaty. Why'd she think of that one? Maybe because she chose it, back in the days when she picked out my clothes. She bought things big so I'd get more wear out of them. I wore that dress twice, then hung it in the very back of my closet.

"I'll ask Margaret. . . ." I pause. Does Margaret have a father? I've never seen her with one. Who the hell is going to be at this dinner?

"When is it?" Brad asks. He looks pathetically eager. Somehow that touches me. Maybe this is just what old Brad and I need, a banquet.

I peek over Rose's shoulder and read from the church bulletin. "Next Friday. We're supposed to come with stories to tell—well, *you* are—stories that will help your daughter know you better."

I can't imagine Brad doing that. He never talks about his past. It's like he doesn't have one. He's as bad as I am, and he's not even adopted.

I dream about the banquet the night before it happens. I dream Brad and I get lost. We wander around in a dark alley, bumping into trash cans, and I realize we are not going to get there in time, the church will be dark and the doors locked, and right on top of that comes fear . . . not of being lost, but of what? I am consciously thinking in my dream, wondering what I am afraid of. We pass a tramp, an old man crumpled in a heap against a brick wall. He opens one eye, takes us in, closes it. I tell myself there's nothing to be afraid of here. But I begin to shake. Then Brad turns, close to me in the darkness, and I know it is he who makes me shake with fear. We've never been this alone together, this far from help. I sit up in bed and stare at the door, then creep over to make sure I have turned the key. I have. I always do. I never forget to lock my door. Not since that night almost three years ago. The oddest and scariest thing is that neither of them ever says anything about my locked door. Does Rose even know? Doesn't she ever come to check on me? Someone came but didn't call or speak. In the first months of my locking the door, someone tested the knob, then went away, over and over, night after night. Now it happens only sometimes.

It takes me a long while to go back to sleep. I can't stop remembering how it feels to lie listening to the jiggle of the doorknob, immobilized by fear.

14

The night of the banquet, Brad and I are among the last to arrive. He had to change from his post office uniform into a suit and tie. Purple crepe paper streamers criss-cross the social hall, giving the place a festive look. Two long tables covered with white paper are set with silverware, cups and saucers, paper napkins and drinking glasses. Bouquets of daisies stand next to metal pitchers of ice water. Brad greets old Mr. Faber, who stands in a corner with his grown daughter. She must be forty. Is this some kind of joke? The younger girls appear subdued by the elegance of their party dresses. I wander over to talk to Lydia, the only girl my age. I barely know her.

"Oh good, you wore school clothes too," she says.

I look around the room. "I guess not many kids our age have parents who come to church."

"It's because we're a downtown church," Lydia responds. "You know Diane, who comes to Sunday school? Her father's a card sharp and her family lives in a crummy hotel. Did you know that?"

I shake my head, wondering how she found out and why she's spreading the story around. I doubt Diane would appreciate it.

Lydia lowers her voice. "He's a Jew."

"Oh. Yeah, well that might explain why they're not here, I guess."

"Does your father have a story?" she asks. I start to say I don't know, wondering if I'll add that we never talk to each other so how would I, but she goes right on without waiting for me to answer. "My father's going to tell about this flood he was in when he lived on the farm back in South Dakota." I am distracted by Brad, who keeps glancing at me from across the room.

"Let's go get a drink," I say abruptly.

"What?" An expression of shock comes over Lydia's chubby face.

"From the water fountain, silly."

"Gosh," Lydia giggles, "the way you said it . . ." I take her arm and lead her off to the hallway. When we return, people are starting to sit down. The place cards are arranged so that fathers and daughters are lined up in pairs, facing each other. Lydia and her father are at the other table. I watch him teasing her, saying things to make her laugh. They look a lot alike, Lydia and her father. All the fathers are in suits and ties and white shirts, like on Sundays.

The same women who help at all the church dinners bring in individual plates with food already on them. We make our way through the swiss steak and gravy, mashed potatoes and peas. We are spooning up our apple cobbler when Mr. Brown, the social director, gets the story telling started. He begins with one of his own about being trapped in the root cellar when he was "just a kid and still believed in the boogie man." All the stories turn out to be about some disaster the family lived through and came out all the closer for, or else they are funny. I am surprised what good story tellers a number of the men are. We aren't laughing to be polite but because they're funny. I begin to worry about Brad.

At last it is his turn. He gets up and clears his throat, then straightens his tie and makes the throat clearing noise again. Mr. Brown's eyes meet mine and he smiles, as if he feels sorry for me. That makes me mad, so I grin the way I do when I want to show I feel just fine and nothing's bothering me. I've gotten so good at that grin it makes me sick.

"My father used to take me and my brother hunting," Brad says, and then has to clear his throat again, as if his voice hasn't been used lately. "Rabbit hunting."

Mary Anderson Parks

Mr. Faber nods his head like maybe he and his dad did that together too.

"My brother was an excellent shot, even though he was younger," Brad goes on. "He and Father would bag all the rabbits and I'd come home with nothing." He pauses. For a moment it seems he is debating whether to go on with this tale or not. I stare at the daisies, wondering where this brother is now and why I've never met him or even heard of him before.

"My brother practiced a lot." Brad says it too low and has to repeat himself. "My brother practiced a lot. With an air rifle. Shooting tin cans off a fence. One day I got an idea. I thought, how about if I practiced on real rabbits. That way I'd have a moving target. If I could hit the real thing, well, I figured I'd be better than my brother. So I did. Every chance I got, I'd go off by myself and shoot at every rabbit that hopped in those fields out back of our house. I got so I could hit some of them. It took a lot of practice. Patience. The next time Father took us rabbit hunting, he and my brother were pretty impressed. We brought home three rabbits for Mother to cook, and two of them were mine."

A smile briefly crosses his face and disappears. He sits down. There are a few uneasy chuckles, then people politely clap hands. I don't think they know quite what to make of Brad's story. His face wears a satisfied expression, and I realize he thinks he has told a story that makes him look good. I am not at all sure that he has. I wonder if anyone else is thinking about all those bunnies he wounded, when he could have been shooting at tin cans like a sensible person.

Everyone here knows my name. I shiver and hope nobody sees the goose bumps on my arms.

They Called Me Bunny

15

Sometimes when I lie like this on the bed, staring at cracks and swirls on the ivory-painted ceiling, I think about how everything leaves signs of how it was and how it became what it is. The ceiling has lines and bulges that mean something, that show what has happened to it. The past is connected to the present. Maybe everything is connected. There is one crack over to my right and another I have to tip my head backwards to see. They're not big, split-open cracks. Someday they will be, and if the person who lives here then spends as much time as I do looking upward, maybe the cracks will get repaired. Or maybe that person will just let it happen. A live-and-let-live type. Is that what I am? I hardly get a chance to know, do I? I mean it's not like I could suddenly whip out cans of paint and start changing things. I'd paint these hospital green walls in alternating stripes of orange and yellow. That would be wild. But I'll be leaving this house soon. What a scary, exciting thought!

I've made it through the summer. I'm carrying out my plan to graduate early, in mid-year. I've found a way to take my life into my own hands and speed up the pace so I can get out of here faster. I don't know where I'm going, but I'm sure in a hurry to get there!

The swirls are a pattern the painter put in, an effort at being modern. Modern is dull. The most beautiful ceiling would be like the Sistine Chapel, with angels and marvelously complicated scenes you could gaze at forever and never be done seeing

Mary Anderson Parks

something new. Like the Dostoevski books I spent every spare moment of the summer reading. Thank God for libraries and art books. From pictures I've seen of gorgeous things, I transform my sad ceiling. In my mind, my reading and my imaginings connect to the beautiful music of Beethoven and Mozart I hear in church.

Does connectedness ever take the form of echoes? Did the fog bring that idea? All I can see from my window is a patch of furry gray sky. Where do thoughts go? Do they travel in the air until they bounce off something? Could be they float into the atmosphere, but they wouldn't be lost forever, even then. Just the opposite! That would give them immortality, to escape gravity and be out with the stars. Don't fly too close to the sun, thoughts of mine! You'll get burned.

Really, where do they go? Doesn't everything have to be somewhere? Thoughts aren't bound by gravity. Do mine reach my mother? Does she know I yearn for her?

I wish I could hear Rose's thoughts. She's right here in the same house. Why don't our thoughts meet and mingle? If they did, we might understand each other. I want to understand Rose. I don't want this awful, horrible distance between us that I don't know how to cross. When I try, I come up against the wall she keeps around herself. She'd have to venture out beyond the wall for us ever to meet, but she won't.

Because she's afraid! How do I know that? Has one of her thoughts reached me? Are her thoughts, and Brad's too, hanging in the air, really close to me, but I can't penetrate them?

Do I fear their thoughts, is that what keeps them away?

I'll empty my mind to make room, stay as open as I can, and try to be unafraid.

They Called Me Bunny

16

I had room for one elective and signed up for drama. I wish I'd known about drama sooner. It is a joy to leave my troubled self and disappear into the character of someone else. I hurry into class as the bell rings and head for my desk. Miss Pride is assigning new scenes today, from Shakespeare.

"Ouch! I stepped on a tack!" The whole class watches while I pull it out and then Miss Pride surprises me more than any tack.

"I want Lance Woodall and Bunny Lundquist to do the Romeo and Juliet scene." Miss Pride speaks in her usual measured tone. I can't believe she'd give me Juliet. I mean Lance *is* Romeo. He's tall, noble looking, idealistic, kind, handsome, but whatever possessed her to think I could be Juliet? I figured I'd be somebody's maid.

I steal a peek at Lance. He looks composed and serious, as always. I love how serious he is. I'll be serious too. I'll go against everything in my nature and become serious and committed like Lance. I'll learn my lines tonight. No, I don't want to learn my lines too quickly. I want to get in lots of rehearsal time with him. What did Miss Pride just say?

"Pardon?" I ask. "I didn't hear the question." Marcie Davis giggles. I'm sure the whole class knows I'm reeling from being chosen to be Juliet, with Lance as Romeo.

"I asked if you and Lance can have your scene ready by the middle of October. Would that give you enough time?" If we rehearse every day, I want to say. I look questioningly at

Lance.

"Sure," he says. "We can be ready in two weeks."

Two weeks? Is that how long we have, two weeks? How can he think so fast? This isn't a big deal to him. Of course. I have to remember that, or I'll make a fool of myself.

When the bell rings, I have no idea what's been going on or who else got assigned what scene. It's as if the world lurched to a stop and started up again.

"Bunny, I'm sorry about the tack," Miss Pride says. "I was putting up a play notice and it got away from me—"

"And I found it!" I laugh. Lance stands nearby. He's waiting for me! I gather my books and binder in a messy pile.

"Hey, take it easy. No need to hurry." Lance picks up the large history book about to fall off the top and balances it in one hand. "Want to rehearse tomorrow after school?" He says it so easily. Gosh, I'm in a scene, that's all. A scene we'll do for class and in two weeks it'll all be over. End of romance. How fitting! Maybe we'll kill each other off by mistake. I've got to get hold of myself. I plop everything down on the nearest desk and start rearranging.

"You'll make an interesting Juliet," Lance says.

"Really? You think so?"

"You'll make her more human. More real."

"Gee, thanks." What does he mean?

He hands me the book he's been holding. "The challenge for me will be to match your realness. You put your whole self into whatever you're doing, you know?"

I don't know but I throw my whole self into the smile I give him. "So where can we meet?"

"Don't you live right across from school?"

How does he know that? No way am I taking Lance Woodall to my house.

"Yeah, but Rose . . . I mean, my mother is usually there and, I don't know, it'd be strange to be Romeo and Juliet in our living room."

He laughs. Why? What did I say that's funny? What did I even say? I'm so rattled that as soon as words come out of my

They Called Me Bunny   55

mouth I forget them.

"Maybe an empty classroom," he suggests. "Or the auditorium, if it's free."

"Isn't it too big? All those rows and rows of empty space."

"I was just thinking it would be good if you could be up higher. You're supposed to be on a balcony. I could stand down below the stage."

"Yeah, you're right." Gosh, he's really thinking this through. "Maybe we could try it. See how it goes."

"Okay! We better run. We'll be late. Where're you headed?"

"History," I tell him. "Room 307."

"I'm going the other way. See ya tomorrow."

"Yeah, see ya!" I am halfway up the stairs when I remember it's gym I'm supposed to be going to.

By our third rehearsal, I am falling seriously in love with Lance Woodall. Not just with the way he looks but the way he thinks. This is new for me.

The day we're to do the scene I feel queasy. It's all going to be over, I keep thinking. And then the moment comes to begin. Lance was right to have us practice in the auditorium. It turns out that's where we have to perform. I peek out from behind the curtain and see the class sitting in the dim glow of stage lights or orchestra lights or whatever the hell lights they're sitting in.

"I can't do it," I tell Lance.

"Why? What's wrong?"

"My knees feel like jelly." I slide to the floor, my back against the wall.

"Bunny, it's just the class! People you know."

"That's why it's so awful." I can barely talk. "And I don't remember my lines."

"Listen Bunny, just go out there, take a deep breath and start. It'll come to you, I promise, the lines will come to you!" He takes hold of my hands and gently pulls me to my feet.

"I feel like we're really Romeo and Juliet, standing here like this." I say it softly, not wanting him to let go of my hands.

"Good. Keep feeling it." His voice trembles a bit.

Afterward, I don't know if we were good or not, but Lance

tells me I was wonderful, and Miss Pride looks pleased. In the class discussion, the only criticism is I need to project my voice more. Marcie Davis pipes up and says it's the first time she ever cried during Shakespeare. With watery eyes, she looks at me with new respect. That gives me an unaccustomed good feeling. But then I remember it's all over. Just as I'm thinking that, Lance touches my wrist.

"Bunny, could you go with me Friday night to Arthur Miller's *Death of a Salesman*?

I can't speak. He must think I'm hesitating whether to go out with him. He rushes on, "Miss Pride saw it already, remember? At Actor's Workshop. She urged us all to go if we can."

"I know. I'd love to go with you."

"Would you?" A beautiful smile lights his face. Lance laughs and smiles more now. I wasn't wrong about him being serious, but there is a part of him that wants to loosen up, and he doesn't know how to do it on his own.

The night of the performance, Lance and I sit side by side in the front row. It is theater-in-the-round and we are right there in Willy Loman's claustrophobic house with him and his wife and two sons, right there in the claustrophobic life he can't bear any longer. When it's over, we stumble out of the small downtown theater, hardly knowing where we are. Neither of us speaks.

"God, they were great," Lance says, after we get in his car. "I'd love to be able to act like that. They spilled their guts. Right on stage."

"Sometimes I was embarrassed," I admit, "to be that close when they were doing that."

"Yeah, theater-in-the-round takes so much honesty."

"I keep remembering what Miss Pride said, how Arthur Miller is one of the first playwrights to make a tragedy about an ordinary man. Willy Loman really was. He was so ordinary."

"That was Willy Loman's whole life we were seeing, Bunny, everything he had, all his hopes and dreams!"

"And illusions."

"Yeah, he held onto those as long as he could. That's what

kept him alive. You know, he couldn't help it, Bunny, that he wasn't rich or successful. That doesn't make his dreams and hopes any less important than any other man's."

"You're right. That's the point, isn't it?"

Lance looks troubled. "I could understand that awful trapped feeling he had."

"Me too," I say, wondering what it is that makes Lance feel trapped.

He starts the car. Lance's car is an Olds 98, the big luxury model. It looks and smells brand new. I was awed when I saw it. I asked if his parents gave it to him. He mumbled something about how he earned part of the money himself, then changed the subject.

"What does your father do, Lance?"

"He's a stock broker."

"What's that? I'm sure it doesn't mean he's broke, right?"

Lance laughs. "It means he spends all his time down in the financial district, helping rich people invest their money so they can get richer."

"Is that what you'll become?" I wink, to let him know I'm teasing.

"God, I hope not. He's hardly ever home. And my mom has to throw these big parties for people he wants to impress." I notice his jaw tighten.

"What does your mom do the rest of the time?"

"Oh, you know. Bridge parties mostly. She's a good player."

"Her whole life is parties?"

"She organizes something called The Cheery Ladies in Cherry Red. They do volunteer work in hospitals. She's clever and I guess those are the ways she's found to use her talents. What about your folks, Bunny?"

"I'm adopted," I tell him. "Rose and Brad aren't my parents."

"What's that like?"

"It's hard. The hardest part is . . . oh I don't know what the hardest part is."

Mary Anderson Parks

"For me it would be not knowing where I came from. Gosh, my mother can trace her family back to the Mayflower."

"I don't even know if I'm descended from the pilgrims or the Indians!"

"You're pretty dark. Your skin, I mean."

"I was joking, Lance. But would that make a difference to you, if I were part Indian?"

He looks at me in astonishment. "You're not Indian, Bunny! I just meant you might be Italian or something. There's an exotic look about the shape of your eyes."

"Is that a compliment?"

"Of course it is. But please don't be coy. One thing I like about being with you is how honest we are with each other."

He drives for a while in silence. "Would you ever adopt a child? I mean, after having had the experience yourself? If you couldn't have your own for some reason?"

"Why?" Finally I have an occasion to use Ilene's question and I'm asking it in all honesty.

"I just wondered," he answers.

I should report to her how ineffective it turned out to be.

"No, I never would." Part of me still reverberates from the way he said, "You're not Indian," as if it would be unthinkable. It's disturbing to think there are things I could be that Lance might not find acceptable.

"Why not?" he asks.

I pause to think and also to wonder why his asking will get an answer from me when I couldn't get one from him.

"I guess because I don't believe my mother gave me up willingly. I don't have proof, but it's one of the deepest beliefs of my life. And I wouldn't want to take somebody else's child if there was any chance that had happened."

He pulls up in front of my house and switches off the engine. "You're a good person, Bunny." He shifts sideways to face me. "You'll be a good mother." I'm wondering if now is when he's going to kiss me. "You know, Bunny, don't you, that I'm getting pretty serious about you?" When I stay silent, he goes on. "I want you to meet my mother. Can you come with me to my house Monday after school?"

I feel like I'm about to cry. "You know, Lance, you're the first boy who's ever shown an interest in who I am and in what I think."

He shifts his weight on the seat, edges closer. "You're really special, Bunny. I've never known anyone like you." I want him to go on thinking I'm special. I want to hang onto this precious moment and not let anything spoil it. I put my hand on the door handle.

"Thanks, Lance. Thanks very much. I need to go in now."

He gives me a long look that almost melts me. "Will you come to my house with me on Monday?"

"Sure I will."

He smiles, then gets out and comes around to open my door.

17

The weekend passes in a sustained glow. I feel beautiful and worthy because Lance Woodall told me I'm special. At Sunday school, Robert Keller appraises me closely and says, "Lookin' good, kid." I favor him with a Mona Lisa smile. At school on Monday afternoon I begin to get nervous. My eyes stay on the second hand as it lurches along its tortuous path. It amazes me how long it can take a minute to go by.

At last Lance is helping me into his Oldsmobile, true to his word, and off we go. He drives along Geary and then turns north toward the Golden Gate Bridge. It is the first time I've been more than a block north of Geary. We enter a neighborhood of large, imposing homes. A sign tells me it is Lake Street. Everything is so out of the ordinary, it wouldn't surprise me if we did come upon a lake. Unlike in most of the city, these houses are detached, with spacious, well-kept lawns. An Oriental man, clearly a hired gardener, is hoeing flowerbeds in one of the yards. My stomach clenches when Lance pulls up in front of a huge brick mansion and stops the car.

He drapes an arm around my shoulders as we walk up the cobbled path. The door is opened by a maid in a black dress and white apron. I just about faint. It is the first time I've ever seen a maid in real life. We step into a large, high-ceilinged entry hall, with gleaming mahogany woodwork and dark green wallpaper flecked with gold. The maid says something to Lance that I don't catch and then goes out. A dog barks sharply. Lance walks over to a basket in the corner and gives

They Called Me Bunny   61

the tiny dog a few quick pats. Lance seems different somehow, here in this house. He seems smaller.

"I'll run and get Mother. I'll just be a sec!" He gives me a close look. "Are you okay?"

I nod my head, not finding words, locking eyes with him, trying to find safety in his earnest gaze.

"I'll run interference," he says, and leaves me alone. Moments later, I hear his mother's shrill voice, penetrating like a high-pitched bell: "Who, exactly, is she?"

I can't make out Lance's well-bred murmurs and protests, only his conciliatory tone, lowered to protect me from distinguishing the words. I wasn't wrong in sensing kindness in him.

It is his mother's answers, cutting like a whip through the air, that tell me what he's telling her. "You mean she doesn't *know* who she is?"

No, lady, I ain't got no pedigree. The small dog regards me from its frilly satin basket with the name *Perky* embroidered on the side. The dog has its papers, I'm sure. It looks at ease, confident of its right to be here. I on the other hand feel ready to bolt out the door. If I alarm the mother to this degree, what will the father say? But the father is safely downtown, ensconced in the financial district, bringing in the money that makes all this possible. I hadn't known this neighborhood was here or that a street like Lake Street existed so close to where the rest of us, the ordinary folks, live. How clear it is Lance's mother wishes I hadn't found out.

"Well yes, of course I'll meet her, now that you've brought her here." They step soundlessly into the entry room where I stand. The thick rugs, inches deep, should have muffled her voice. But when I see her, I understand that nothing muffles this woman. In movement and attitude she resembles a highbred dog, an Airedale or a greyhound, not a small, soft-boned, fluffy dog like Perky. The nervous, high-strung temperament I heard in her voice blazes in her eyes. Her hair, like mine, is bleached. But no bathroom experiments with peroxide for this lady. Every strand shows the touch of a professional, blonde to the roots and stiffly in place. I feel sorry for Lance. As someone who has dreamed of a mother all my life, I know this lady is not the mother of anyone's dreams. She is all bones and angles, with skin drawn tight over sharp, handsome features.

"Mother, this is Bunny Lundquist. Bunny, my mother, Mrs. Woodall."

"How do you do." Mrs. Woodall's quick tight smile comes and goes in an instant.

I won't say, "It's a pleasure to meet you," I won't lie like that. It is so clear I don't have a chance. What the hell difference does it make what I say? I draw a quick breath. "Hi. You sure live a long way from school."

She regards me as though I've said something incomprehensible, which I suppose I have. I see her take in my home bleach job. My perm fluffs my hair out so the dark roots hardly show, but this lady can see them, I am sure. And I am wearing too much makeup. Under her glance, I suddenly know that.

Maybe because I am so determined not to say anything about the house, how big and impressive it is, I blurt out another inanity. "Lance looks a lot like you." She makes a tiny 'hmm' sound, in a way I've never heard anybody do it. I don't want to look behind that 'hmm' and see what's there.

"I hear from Lance you like to play bridge." I offer my most winning smile. But I win no points here. Not in this house. The disdain on Lance's mother's face alters into an expression suggesting she has noticed a piece of turd on her beautiful rug.

"I really must run," she says, glancing at her gold watch. "I'm late for . . . an appointment."

Bridge, I think, and the winning smile comes back of its own accord. It repels her, she turns away. "Lance, I need to have a word with you before I go. Excuse us, please." She bears him off. In her train, I can't help thinking, even though she is dressed in a Harris tweed suit.

On the drive home, I stay silent, waiting for Lance to speak. He doesn't live that far from school at all. It's a short drive. It's just that it's another world.

He pulls up in front of my house. "That didn't go too well, did it?" His eyes meet mine, his expression pained and unhappy. "You didn't like her, did you?"

I don't know how to answer. Doesn't Lance know I heard what his mother said in the other room? Didn't he see the disdain written on her face?

"I think the point is she didn't like me."

"Oh, well. . . ." He looks extremely uncomfortable, which gives me an unexpected urge to throw my arms around him, but we haven't been physical with each other and this doesn't seem the right moment to start.

"Don't worry about it," I say, and then want to bite my tongue out. I wish he'd worry about it for the rest of his life. Or do I? He no longer looks strong and wonderful, like the answer to all my problems. I look at him now and see the link between him and his mother, as if she has him on an invisible chain that Lance doesn't know is there.

Our goodbyes have a sad ring of finality. I go straight to my room, lock my door and stretch out face-down on the bed. Maybe I need to think less about boys and more about school. If nobody is going to want to marry me, and it sure feels that way right now, I better get an education and be prepared to support myself. Or should I be aiming lower, willing to give myself to some creep?

No, Bunny! Forget that.

It's hard, though, to keep from unraveling, hard to hold onto the pieces of myself.

18

I focus on studying and at the same time make a mighty effort to sustain the carefree, lighthearted manner that helps me survive. People take it for the real thing and then it becomes almost real. And so do I. The danger of vanishing into nothingness vanquished once again.

Sometimes school doesn't feel like part of the real world. It's a safe place where if you follow the rules nothing bad happens to you. Not all high schools are like that. I know Mission isn't. We hear about pachukos with knives and fights breaking out. Kids get hurt. But not at good old George Washington. It's got a lot to do with our principal, Mr. Hoffman. He's a huge, imposing man. Like God. He likes to boom out over the loudspeaker and talk to us during homeroom. He tells us stuff like how many George Washington grads went to Cal last year and what grade point averages they got and how he wants us to do even better next year and he's sure we will if we just study and apply ourselves. We did better than Lowell last year, he tells us. More of our graduates went to Cal. It makes me wish I were going to be one of them. But I'm not good enough to go to Cal. I've taken the courses though, the ones I'd need to get in. I'm not sure why I did that.

Why would Mr. Hoffman care that much about us? I wonder if he has kids of his own that he tells how much they can do if they try. Rose and Brad don't expect me to be capable of a whole lot. When I get an A, I can tell that surprises them.

The other big thing about Washington, besides academics,

is school spirit. We're famous for it. Mr. Hoffman praises us over the loudspeaker for that, too. We've got this football team that hardly ever wins, but we cheer them on until our voices are hoarse and we leave the stadium all wrung out and limp and virtuous. Some kids are more into it than others, but it's something anybody can be part of. I like that. It's not just for the smart or the talented or the popular. We're a school of twenty-two hundred, and most kids show up for the games.

We stay through the whole game without moving from our seats, so the flower design and whatever words we're spelling won't get ruined. The boys wear white shirts and the girls white or red blouses, and the cheerleaders arrange us into a design that can be seen from the playing field and the other side of the stadium. They plan in advance where the reds will sit and where the whites will sit. Then they mark the seats so we'll know which color goes where.

We've got the best cheerleading squad in the city when it comes to spirit but the girls' outfits aren't as cute as some of the other schools. I'd want to be at Mission or Galileo if I were a cheerleader. Their skirts are shorter. Our girls may not be the most coordinated but they're right up there when it comes to spirit. Between yells, they run up into the bleachers to take orders for pop and chips. We pass the money down the aisle and they get our stuff from the vendors and pass it to us, so we won't move around and mess up the pattern.

We sit there and laugh at other schools because their designs never look as good as ours in the first place, and by the second half all the kids are milling around and you can't tell anymore what their design was even supposed to be.

But our team almost always loses. Sometimes I wonder if there's a connection. I like sitting there with the others, being part of a design. I feel a sense of purpose that's kind of reassuring.

I'll miss that when high school's over. Not that the whole experience has been that great, but Mr. Hoffman puts his whole heart into our school and I appreciate that. It feels like he believes in us. It makes me want to be better than I am, and then I get embarrassed and think that's too corny. I wouldn't want anybody to know I'm touched by a principal's message coming out of a loudspeaker.

19

The only way I hear anything of importance around our house is by accident. Just when I've decided Rose and Brad will never discuss anything more exciting than whether he remembered to pay the P G & E bill, or if they'll go to the Wednesday night church dinner, I overhear something really weird. If I weren't so boisterous and didn't come in shouting, "Hello, is anybody home," I'd probably hear more. But maybe I wouldn't be able to handle more, maybe that's why I come in shouting. Or else it's like Rose says, that it's my nature to be boisterous.

On this particular Sunday, I'm in a quiet mood. I pad into the living room in my socks, in search of a place to study that's comfortable and has good light. I walk past the kitchen without making any noise, and Rose and Brad don't notice me. They are having a cup of tea. That's one of their big things they do together, sit down at the kitchen table for a cup of Lipton's tea, each of them reading a different section of the *Examiner*.

In the comfort of a big easy chair, I doze off, warmed by sun streaming through the picture window. The sound of Brad's voice jolts me awake.

"It's creepy, Rose, the way you are sometimes."

I've heard him do this before. He's baiting her.

"I mean, I hardly know if you're a sane person or not."

Rose keeps silent. That is her way. She has no defenses. I can imagine her sitting there, thin and stiff, her head bent slightly forward and to one side, as if waiting for more blows.

"The way your father died," Brad continues, "that's pretty

creepy, Rose. Were you there when it happened?"

I hear the clatter of dishes. Rose is using chores as a way not to answer. Maybe that's a defense of sorts. But then, in a voice shaking with anger, she blurts out: "You try to control me with that, Brad! You try to make me think I'm crazy!" Sometimes, rarely, angry words break out of Rose, and I know what will come next. Brad's voice will be tinged with satisfaction that he managed to bring her to this point.

"You don't think you're acting crazy right now?" He lets out a snort of laughter. "Your whole family is crazy, Rose. It's probably a good thing you couldn't have babies." He scrapes his chair back and with a suddenness I don't expect, strides into the room where I lie curled on my side in the big chair. I shut my eyes and wait.

"Bunny?" His tone is soft, testing, ominous. I sense his surprise at finding me here. "Bunny, you awake?" There is a long silence during which I wonder what he is doing and what he will do next.

Then I hear Rose whisper, "She couldn't have been there all along, could she?" That's Rose, all right, hoping to preserve Bunny at all costs from harsh reality. But it won't work. Reality is too strong. I let them think, though, that I am asleep, that I haven't heard.

I wait a few weeks, and then one afternoon as Rose and I sit in the subdued, drapery-filtered sunlight of the living room, I ask her. I am perched cross-legged on the couch with my geometry book. Rose sits in the matching chair, leafing idly through the new *Ladies Home Journal*.

I try to make my tone neutral. "I've just been wondering, were you still living at home when your father died?"

Her head comes up like a startled deer. I often think of Rose as deer-like, with her gently bent neck and her shyness that keeps her rooted to the spot after church service as she stands among people greeting one another, taller than most and seeming trapped in their midst.

"Why would you ask that, Bunny?"

I look down at the pink pedal pushers she bought me a long

time ago on sale. She's always liked to dress me in pink. "It's just that I wish sometimes I knew more about you. You've never talked about your father."

She stares into the half-drawn draperies. "I was home on vacation from nursing college." She pauses. "My brother was gone." I hear the catch in her voice.

"Where had he gone?" Again, I try to make my voice neutral. An image flashes past, of holding my hand out to a deer, not moving closer, standing still and patient to show the deer I am not an enemy.

"He never wrote. We never heard from him."

"A loner, huh?" How odd that both she and Brad have a brother who is gone from their life.

Rose's glance flits over my face and back to the beige draperies. "Yes, he always kept to himself. Like Daddy. We didn't know he'd leave like that, though. Turn twenty-one and be off and gone. And never let us hear from him again." Her eyes are sad, inward-looking, as if she has forgotten me and is talking to herself. "The farm wasn't making any money by then. Maybe he just didn't see the point in staying."

"Do you think your father was depressed about that?"

She turns her head sharply toward me. "About what? My brother leaving?"

"Yes. And about the farm, too. Not making any money."

Rose appears to be thinking it over. Maybe for the first time? A deep frown furrows the space between her carefully plucked eyebrows. "I don't think it was so much the farm. We could eke by. Mother tended the garden and I took care of the chickens."

"You fed them?"

"And gathered the eggs. If one of the hens disappeared, I'd go look to see if she was out setting on her eggs, hiding in the high grass somewhere." Rose's face softens. "I loved it when the little chicks were born. It seemed hopeful, you know? They were so cute and funny, the little fluffy yellow chicks. Running around." I watch her expression change as her thoughts shift.

"Mother slaughtered a chicken every Sunday. I tried to stay

out of the yard while it was happening, but she made me pluck the feathers. I hated watching her pull out the insides. I was glad she never expected me to do that part."

No. I can't imagine Rose pulling out the insides of anything. Especially a creature that was alive moments earlier, that she herself had been tending and feeding.

"The body jerks around the barnyard after the head's cut off. All bloody and awful." Rose looks directly into my eyes as she says this, but she seems to be in a kind of trance. I have the impression she is thinking and saying things she has never allowed herself to think or speak of. "My father hated it, too. He had a way of lurking around out behind the barn. Mother made fun of him. Accused him of napping in the potato field. She made it seem like he was lazy and she was the strong capable one. But he just liked to be alone, Daddy did. And to get away from her."

From my one meeting with the woman, I can understand that.

"We had an old piano in the parlor and the only time Daddy ever looked happy was when he was fooling around on the piano. He played by ear, and after supper he'd go in there and pick out tunes. I'd hurry to get done with the dishes so I could go listen. He'd smile at me sometimes."

I could see little skinny frightened obedient Rose, sitting small in a chair.

"You loved him," I say softly.

"Yes."

I feel reassured to know Rose is capable of loving someone. I wait, wondering if she will speak of how he died. She closes her eyes, then rises from her chair. "I feel so exhausted, Bunny. I think I'll lie down for a little nap."

After she goes, I try to focus on geometry theorems, but fluffy baby chicks hop around on the page, distracting me. I had wanted to draw Rose out and get her to tell me how her father died. I wish I could follow her to her room and lie with her on her bed, ask questions to help her open up and let loose the pain inside her. I'm worried for her. Brad won't let up. His next attack will be more brutal. How do I know that?

It's not something I have ever done, lie on a bed next to Rose. She keeps a space around her that no one intrudes into. Maybe she's trapped in there and wants to get out but doesn't know how. Was I brought into their lives to help her get out? I feel like such a failure.

20

His next attack comes two days later. We're in the kitchen after another strained meal during which I kept up a stream of babble. I'm almost done washing the dishes. Rose has been drying. I've run out of babble. It's too hard to keep up in the face of Brad's barely contained anger. What the hell is he mad at, anyway? Is he just an angry person and he'll be that way all his life? Maybe I should feel sorry for him, after that glimpse I got of his childhood from his rabbit hunting story at the banquet. He wasn't happy even then, as a child.

The last thing I talked about before I shut up was the essay topic we've been assigned in English. I told them we're to write about a scientist named Gregor Johann Mendel. We have to research his discoveries about heredity.

Brad broods at the table, picking his teeth with a toothpick.

"She could write about that crazy streak in your family, Rose."

And that mean streak in yours, I think, wishing I had never brought up Mendel and his theories.

"What do you mean?" Rose asks, setting herself up as usual. Does she do it on purpose? She should leave the room or keep on wiping dishes and ignore him. But no, she leaves herself wide open to be hurt.

Brad emits an unpleasant snort. "Your father hung himself in the barn and then your mother didn't tell anyone for two weeks. Left him hanging there." He looks at her sideways, not making eye contact, watching her. I feel her wanting to plead,

They Called Me Bunny 73

"not in front of Bunny," but his bluntness silences her. She is stunned, like a wounded animal trying to edge to safety but unable to pull its own weight.

I grab the other dishtowel from the rack. "Here, let me help, it'll go quicker." It's all I can think of to do. I would take the towel that dangles in Rose's hand, but she needs it there while she lives through this moment. She squeezes it hard in her fist, fighting for control of her face, then lays it on the counter and retreats to their bedroom. I give Brad a look of disgust, but he won't meet my eyes.

For weeks after that, whenever I glimpse Rose standing at the mirror applying powder, or mending Brad's socks, or shaking frozen vegetables into boiling water, I see a shadowy lean figure hanging from a rope tied to a rafter. Hanging by a broken neck. Her own father! And she loved him. Was it Rose who found him? How horrible that would be. She'd never get over it. Wouldn't it be better for her to talk about it? I wish I could help her try.

I feel us moving toward a new edge.

21

It's the first assembly of our senior year. Ilene and I are late. We stayed too long in the bathroom touching up our lipstick, combing our hair, re-tucking our crisp white blouses into our full pleated skirts. Two service society girls close the double doors just after we rush in. A second later we would have been reported. The girls look silly to me in their gray and scarlet berets. Or am I jealous because I know I'd never be voted in?

The rumor is that Jewish and Oriental girls have an advantage because so many of them are already in Girls' Service Society and they nominate their friends. I have to admit, though, that most of them are special, the ones who get in. I have a crush on the president, Judith Greenberg. She's in my homeroom, I see her for fifteen minutes every morning. She's small and slim with black hair and a face full of sweetness. Sometimes she makes announcements about events that are coming up. When other people talk, she gives them her full attention. She's respectful to everyone. She has been my heroine ever since the day I came into homeroom and tripped over an eraser that was lying on the floor. I landed on my butt. Judith helped me to my feet, then gathered up all my scattered papers and books and set them on my desk. She even put the eraser back in the blackboard tray. She did everything in a way that didn't attract attention, like it was the most natural thing in the world. Still, I suppose she barely knows I exist, even though I sit in homeroom every morning admiring her.

It's how it is, I guess.

Ilene and I pause at the back of the darkened auditorium, looking for two seats together. The section on our left is the Negro section. I stand near them and feel a low, rumbling energy that seems to come from the earth itself. It is nothing I can explain but it is there, seething below the surface. Is it the palpable presence of fear mixed with anger, strength, vitality? All of that together? A boy with skin so black it gleams glances at me, then looks away as smoothly as if our eyes never met, but I'm left with the feel of his eyes on my skin. Sometimes I wonder if I'm crazy, the thoughts I have. No, Bunny, just boy crazy, like you heard Rose tell the Bible Study ladies. There are worse kinds of crazy.

"Over there," Ilene whispers.

"Down in the middle?"

"Yeah, we'll have to climb over everybody."

The section she's pointing to, with two empty seats, is white kids, of course. It occurs to me that the Negro section seldom has empty seats. It must be wonderful to be close together like that and belong. No, it isn't! I'm stupid to think that even for an instant. It's just that I would so goddamn much like to belong, even to a group that suffers hate and prejudice. Do they stick together for protection? From fear of being rejected if they tried to sit anywhere else? I can't help wishing I had somebody to stick together with. Somebody like me.

Ilene is distracted by a boy as we make our way to the two empty seats in the middle of the row. We're never really there for each other, Ilene and I, just sort of half there. She turns to face him as she scoots past his knees, and murmurs something I can't hear.

Finally we settle into our seats. Where are the Oriental kids? They don't all sit in a solid block, I know that. There are scattered clusters of them. I see a bunch of Chinese girls across the aisle to our right. I know they're Chinese because I heard two of them talk one day about having to be at Chinese school by five o'clock. I asked if they went every day and they said, yes, and Saturday mornings. Wow. That impresses me. They too have a group they belong to. Stop it, Bunny. Quit feeling sorry for yourself.

My gaze travels around the auditorium. There's Pat Miyamoto with a group of white girls. It seems like the Japanese kids mix more. The girls anyway. I wonder why that is.

Ilene pokes me with her elbow. "Look at Mr. G," she whispers. I turn my eyes in the direction she is looking and see Mr. G at the far end of a row, next to the wall. He is not sitting with any of the other teachers like he usually does. I miss being in his class and seeing him every day. Why does he look so sad? Is that why Ilene pointed him out? But already her focus has shifted. Now she leans forward to glance from under her waving sweep of hair at the boy two seats down, the one she whispered to. The sideways peek he gives her makes me want to giggle. Ilene flashes her best smile and he looks away in embarrassment. Does Ilene have any idea how funny she is?

I only half listen to the speeches. It's the pre-election assembly and Dawny Preston stands at the podium. Dawny is so short you can see only her head and shoulders. She's cute and a good dresser and she smiles at everybody in the hallway. That's the type who runs for office. They must have some sense of civic duty the rest of us don't.

"If you elect me your school secretary, I promise to carry out the duties of the office to the best of my ability," she says, which is pretty much what all the candidates say. Campaigns have been going on for two weeks, with hand-lettered, hand-decorated signs hanging everywhere. Dawny leaves the podium and walks back to rejoin the other candidates, who are seated in a straight line across the stage. She reminds me of a bantam hen, with her little chest puffing out.

Now it is Freddie Stokes' turn. He is a Negro and he is in the Eagle Society, the boys' equivalent of GSS. When he's done with his speech, everybody claps for a long time. It's almost a sure thing he'll win. That is so ironic, that the school is about to elect a Negro as student body president. I guess we're trying to prove we're not prejudiced. I mean for real, to prove it to ourselves, because just about everybody wants to believe they aren't prejudiced. Freddie certainly has all the qualities

They Called Me Bunny   *77*

we expect leaders to have, and more. He won't be hard to vote for in that way. Freddie is as clean cut and nice a boy as you'd ever hope to find. He's truly interested in other people and a good student, not to mention being on committees and holding office in his homeroom every single semester. He's a good speaker, too. I've talked to Freddie. I asked him about himself, the old technique, right, when talking to a boy? I found out he's the oldest kid in his family and they all go to church every Sunday, and often he is asked to read the scripture, so he's used to getting up in front of people and talking.

Because he's an Eagle, he wears a beret and patrols the aisles during assemblies, but if he weren't an Eagle, or up on the stage running for president, he'd be there in the section with all the other Negro kids.

It's really great to see Freddie sitting up there, the only person with black skin. I look down at my own skin. My hands are so dark compared to Ilene's white ones. What am I? Will I ever know? There is one brown-skinned student on stage. Suzie Kobayashi is running for school secretary against Dawny. I'm planning to vote for Suzie.

I feel choked up after Freddie's speech. It's wonderful there are people like Freddie in the world and that his worth is being recognized. It seems like a kind of miracle.

I notice a movement off to my right and look over in time to see Mr. G go up the side aisle toward the back of the auditorium. Something is wrong. I can tell by the effort he puts into holding his shoulders up and back.

When assembly is over, we troop out, under orders, one section at a time. They must be afraid we'd stampede if we all left at once.

"I have to run to my locker," I tell Ilene. Instead, I head for Mr. G's classroom, guided by my instinct for trouble.

I find him emptying the contents of one of his desk drawers into a cardboard box. He has three empty boxes lined up at the side of his desk. I stand for a moment in the doorway, but he doesn't notice me.

"Mr. Gershenberg?"

He lifts his head. "Bunny. Come on in." He straightens up and sighs, then frowns. "I hadn't known I'd have a chance to say goodbye." He hesitates, as if he doesn't know what to say after that.

"Goodbye?"

He motions to the boxes. "I'm packing up. They've got a new history teacher coming in to take my place. Highly recommended, I'm told."

"But why, why would you leave so suddenly? I don't—"

"Yes. Well." He presses his lips together and stares at the box he has just filled with books, pencils, note tablets. "The administration thinks I'd be more comfortable someplace else, maybe at the college level. They think I'm too political for high school." He avoids looking at me.

"You're going to a college to teach?"

"Not that I know of. I'll be lucky to get a job anywhere as a teacher."

"But you're a great teacher. You're the best!"

"Thanks, Bunny." For an instant his eyes meet mine. "It's good to hear that. Teaching is my life, you know. It's all I know how to do."

"Then why are you leaving, Mr. Gershenberg? You were . . . comfortable here, weren't you?" Puzzled, groping to understand, I use the word he used a minute ago.

He glances at me sharply. "I wasn't given a choice."

I blurt out the thought that suddenly comes. "You can't have been blacklisted! Isn't that mainly for movie stars?"

"Oh, Bunny." He chuckles, shaking his head. I'm glad to have made him less miserable, even if it's because I sound stupid.

But now he's dead serious again. "These things take subtle and different forms, Bunny. The blacklist is just one form. There have been complaints about me from some of the parents."

"Was one of them Brad Lundquist?" The question pops out before I can stop myself.

"The administration didn't tell me who the complaints were from."

They Called Me Bunny   *79*

"But that's not fair!"

"No, it isn't. I'm glad you see that. I'd like to have a chance to question these people, have a dialogue with them." He stares out the window. "I don't seem to have enough fight left in me to make that happen." With a sigh, he turns to me. "I need to finish packing up here, Bunny. And you need to get to your next class." The bell rings, startling both of us.

I feel tears coming and am not sure why. Except that Mr. G is another one of those really good, decent people like Freddie Stokes, and the world isn't fair to him and I don't want him to leave.

"Thanks, Bunny, for stopping by. And don't give up on yourself. You have a good mind. Please use it." I feel tears welling up. And then I go.

I hate the way the world is.

Mary Anderson Parks

22

I'm on my way downtown to choir practice, standing with a crowd of colored kids in the back of the streetcar. I like being jostled up against them, our skin sometimes touching, cool and exciting, smooth and rough, all that at once, with heat underneath, and awareness. I stay quiet amid voices and laughter, absorbing smells, sounds, images. It is enough to smile if someone glances my way, to let that person know I am a friend and not one of those who looks down on or pretends not to see them.

The streetcar lurches and a girl laughs close to my face, warming me with the friendliness in her eyes. For this moment we can be unguarded. The noise intensifies, far in the back. Two boys push their way forward, the level of excitement rising. Are they getting off here? We're only at Stanyan. None of them get off till Fillmore. But no, he doesn't pull the cord, the one who comes forward, pushing and laughing. He and the boy behind him have shoved their way through to tease a friend. They feint punches at him, playing like young children. I can imagine them as small boys, though now they are tall and muscular. One of them catches my eye, holds it for the barest instant, then turns away, shutting me out.

Only one white girl hangs out with Negro boys. She is beautiful, dark-haired, secretive. I've never been in a class with her, I don't even know her name. I could be like her if I chose. And ruin my reputation as surely as hers is ruined. But isn't that Rose talking? To me these kids seem more alive and fun than anybody else, and I know it is a vitality, a resilience that grows out of pain. Because some of it is in me. It's how we survive.

I feel protectiveness coming from them, as if they wouldn't want me hurt for choosing to forsake my own and stand among them, even for this brief time. But who are my own?

Am I imagining the protectiveness? I see it in the way the tall, big-boned girl, grasping the shiny metal pole, her hand just above mine, keeps an eye on me as we jolt and sway; I saw it in the boy who turned away, so as not to let things get complicated. Or is it himself he's protecting?

These kids don't know me by name, nor I them. That is how separate the races are at school. I know a few Negro girls in my gym class by name, because when we square dance they call out to each other. They grow wilder and more riotous as the dancing goes on. There, too, I chose to be among them, because no one else did and that doesn't seem right. Soon I found out how much more fun it was to be with them. They jazz up Miss MacKenzie's instructions, call out their own do-se-does, and parody the hokey, hillbilly music. Eleanor Appleby is re-cast as Eleanor Applepie by a huge, jolly girl named Belle, who sings out the name in a broad southern accent, then makes eyes at Alice Valentine, an adorable girl with gleaming black skin. "Oooooh, looky there at that pretty little thing," she squeals, and it is all we can do not to collapse on the gym floor in a heap of laughter. Belle swings and twirls us around as if the idea of square dancing came straight from heaven to her. Miss MacKenzie doesn't know what she has unleashed. A natural force beyond her control.

The bubbling witches' cauldron we read of yesterday in *Macbeth*, why do I think of it? These kids are not in that class, not one of them. There is not one black face in my English class. Somehow they've set us on different tracks. Who are they, who control us without our noticing? Or do the colored kids notice? Of course they do! How could I think not, even for one deluded second? That is why they seethe, like the cauldron. Emotions bubbling, rising, uncontainable.

They troop out at Fillmore Street into the world of color

where no one else ventures. Or do some? Are there others like the beautiful dark-haired white girl who risk expulsion from their own kind? I take an empty seat and look out at buildings crowded against each other, no breathing space between them except an occasional dark crack. I feel elated and desolate, brimming with love I don't know what to do with, for people who suffer hate and give back life-sustaining energy. But how could hate not lie underneath? Doesn't hate beget hate? My head feels heavy. All the life, all the high spirits left when those kids got off at Fillmore.

Who would think Bunny has such thoughts? I chuckle, evidently out loud, because a woman a few seats in front of me turns, prim and straight in her veiled hat, her sharp nose lifted in the air, her ears alert to unexpected sounds. Was she here when all the wildness was going on, all the suppressed life that can't be suppressed? Did she turn then, too, with her disapproving frown?

I look down at my skin. Do I have Negro in me?

23

In the night I have a dream. I see a circle of brown-skinned people sitting on the ground, their faces lit by the flickering light of a fire in the center of the circle. Some of them are wrapped in blankets, or towels, I'm not sure which. But it doesn't matter. What matters is the intensity on the glowing fire-lit faces, the steady purposeful light in their eyes. I am there in the circle of people. I belong to them. There are men and women of all ages, a few quite old, and many children. I am one of the children.

A very old man moves slowly but with great dignity from a seated to a standing position. He holds something in his hands. I can't make out what it is. He looks around the circle at each of us in turn, with strong love in his eyes, but when he comes to me, as his gaze moves slowly from one to the next around the circle, his expression changes to sadness.

Now I am inside the old man, looking out, and I see that my place is empty. I am not there.

Mary Anderson Parks

24

Death on the Mountain. I saw that title in the library and now I lie on my bed wishing I were on a mountain. Not really. I'd be scared. More scared even than here at Rose and Brad's. I've only been out of the city twice, the time we took the train to visit Rose's mother and in seventh grade when our gym class went to a swimming pool in Marin County.

It felt heavenly by the pool, soaking up sun after coming out of the water. We'd play and swim, then sun ourselves like seals. But the teacher announced it was time to go at a moment when I was emerging from the water instead of warm and dry. I stripped off my wet suit in a cold cement locker room. I was shivering when we got back on the bus. We crossed over into the city on a bridge made invisible by fog.

Sometimes it feels to me this isn't the world I belong in. I want to feel grass and dirt under my feet and not have everything covered up by concrete. Nature in San Francisco is a well-groomed park or a vacant lot, and both can be depressing.

I'm having one of those scary moments when nothing feels real. Especially me. I keep my eyes on the ceiling and picture my body under my clothes. It's pulsing, waiting for something to happen. A tingling starts in my bare feet, travels up my legs and spreads upward. The feeling of wanting something to happen grows stronger. But nothing does, except Rose flushes the toilet and I listen to water fill the tank back up again.

Was my hair truly black before I bleached it? Is any part of me real? I raise my hand in front of my eyes. It is very tan. I am tan all over. Nothing changes that. When I'm out in the sun I don't burn, my arms and legs just get browner. I drop my hand onto my chest, where it rises and falls with my breath. If I think about the past hard enough, will I be able to figure out who I am? Don't torture yourself, Bunny. Damn! That isn't even my real name.

I want to honor pain. Stay with that thought. Why did it come? Because of the little girl on the streetcar. I sat across from her all the way from Van Ness to Thirtieth and Geary, coming back from choir practice, and watched the pain on her face. The woman with her leaned slightly away from her and had a pinched face, like Rose. I can't stand pinched faces. I watched the little girl's pain instead. I tried to gather it inside me and let it be part of my pain so she wouldn't have to carry it. She was about five, with brown eyes like mine. She could have been me, sitting there so separate from that woman who owned her but wasn't really her mother. I'm sure of that. They didn't have the same features or coloring. Like Rose and me. Anybody can tell she isn't my real mother. She just likes to pretend. Poor woman. Brad is going to leave us soon. Does she see the signs? My own foreknowledge must be rooted in my babyhood. I don't want to think about that.

I'll be stuck here, trying to help her through it. But I have to get out! I'll suffocate here.

"Bunny?"

I pretend I don't hear Rose's voice on the other side of the closed door. The selfish, rebellious part of me doesn't want to deal with her.

"Bunny, can I talk to you a minute?"

It's daytime. The door's unlocked. Why doesn't she just try it?

"Bunny?"

Her voice is fainter. She's about to give up. Gosh, Rose, you give up too easily.

"Come on in!" I yell.

I watch as the doorknob turns with excruciating slowness. God, a woman like Rose would drive me crazy, too, if I were her husband. Slowly the door opens and Rose peers in. I sit up against the headboard and pat the bedspread, inviting her to sit down, wanting to put her at ease, trying not to bust out laughing at this woman who can't say boo, who doesn't know who she is. Wow! Neither of us knows.

She reacts uncertainly to the big grin spreading over my face. "Bunny?"

"It's okay. Come sit down. I was just thinking of something funny."

She perches on the small, chintz-covered chair, with a flounce at the bottom, that sits beside my bed.

"So what's up?" I ask, when she doesn't come up with anything on her own. "You look kinda miserable." I scoot over to reach out and take her hand. I do that sometimes when she seems really bad off. Her hand is cool and dry and mine is warm and moist, and I wonder does that bother her, having old sweaty me touch her.

"Bunny, there's something I have to tell you, something I've been meaning to ask." Her words come out in a rush. But she doesn't know how to go on. She removes her hand to her lap and wipes the back and front of it against her cotton housedress. She probably isn't aware she is doing it. Wiping off the traces of Bunny. Don't dwell on stuff like that. Help the woman say whatever damn thing she's come here to say.

"Is it about Brad?"

She raises her eyes to mine and nods, like a mute. She looks about as pitiful as I've ever seen her. "If . . . if Brad and I were to live . . . apart, I mean if that were ever to happen, not that I have any reason to think it would, but if it were, would you want to stay here with me or—"

"Of course I'd stay with you." There. It's said. She was crazy to think there was any doubt on that score. But it means she doesn't know. I take a deep breath and am surprised to hear it turn into a sob. Hasn't she ever wondered why I lock my door at night? Is she really going to fall apart over losing a man like Brad? Why am I even worrying about her when what I want is to be free of this stupid house, free of people who never say what is real.

"Bunny, don't cry."

"For God's sake, why can't I? I'm crying for so many reasons I can't even begin to tell you. Part of it's relief."

Through my tears I see her eyes register shock.

I hope he goes, Rose, I want to say. But then I'd have to tell her why, and you don't just knock away illusions when it's all somebody has.

"I'm talkin' crazy. Don't worry. We'll make it. Together. Whatever happens." I reach for her hand again.

What I need is a Coke. I can imagine in my throat the sting of it. The strong, all-American corrupt taste. Why am I thinking that? I search back and come up with Miss Angstrom. "Beware of advertising," she taught us in English class. "They hire psychologists to exploit inner yearnings. We don't even know what's happening to us." I really appreciated her pointing that out. I'd maybe never have known, just gone out there buying stuff right and left. If I ever get any money to do that. Sometimes the corrupt stuff is what you want, though. The stuff that's bad for you. The problem is there is no Coke in Rose's refrigerator. And it has never felt in all the years I've lived with them that I could put something in there that was just for me. Well good then! Maybe that's about to change.

"I've gotta get a drink of water," I say, and pile off the bed.

(Rose)

I remember a day in spring, lush and lovely. How old was I? Five? Ten? A child. Innocent, awakening to my senses. Not ten. By then I had closed down. Maybe I was five that day I sat on the back steps of the farmhouse and put my finger in my pee pee place. It itched in a way that could be satisfied only by my moving finger, probing, pushing, turning. Oooh, it felt good! I pushed my finger farther into the secret place, possessing it, pulling joy out of my own center. The screen door squeaked and my finger flew out and Mother stood in front of me, blocking the sun, her hands on her hips, her face stern. I missed the sun's warmth. I missed the feel of my finger inside my secret place, probing the secret folds. I wanted Mother to move, to go away, to leave me to myself.

But Mother demanded, "Show me your finger!" I raised the finger that had been inside me. Mother grabbed my hand, held it under her nose and sniffed. Her face twisted; it became ugly. "You bad, bad, bad girl!" she said. More than her words, it was Mother's mouth twisted into ugliness by the smell of my finger that made me know the place my finger had been was bad. I never touched myself in that place again. When the impulse came, I would see Mother's face and stop. Did Mother say more? Did she say, "Don't ever touch yourself there again?" It felt to me that she had. The joy of those moments in the sun, of my finger finding the place that felt good when touched, shriveled into shame. It seemed to me that the hole itself shriveled and disappeared under the condemnation in Mother's eyes.

I was shocked, years later, when Brad pushed his long penis inside me, that there was room for him there. But the good feelings wouldn't come back.

Mary Anderson Parks

26

It is Rose's Bible Study afternoon. I can count on having the house to myself. The weather is unbelievable, a freakish day in the upper eighties. A blast of heat swamps me as I unlock the front door. Rose never opens windows. Most of them are painted shut. On another hot day, years ago, I couldn't stand it any longer. I pried open one of the two windows in my bedroom. So far no one has noticed. I keep stuff on the windowsill to hide where I wrecked the paint when I jimmied it open. I move all the stuff each time I open the window and put it back again when I close it. Rose would worry some man was going to climb up into my window and jump on me if she knew I leave it wide open at night. Little does she know how much closer the real danger lies. I think often about Rose saying, what if Brad were to leave, but the longer he stays, the harder it is to picture him actually leaving.

I love being in the house alone. Alone, I can do as I want. I stand in front of the picture of an old-fashioned girl on a park bench, painted in somber autumn tones. I turn it a couple of inches off center. There. The girl looks completely different. No longer demure. Her eyes gaze at me sideways now, with something sly in the glance that before radiated pure innocence. I kick off my oxfords in the middle of the living room. Later I'll fix everything, so nothing will appear changed. I have a plan, and no matter how hot the weather, I'm going ahead with it. Fog will surely roll back in tonight, or tomorrow, and I'll be ready with a skirt in the new, tighter style the popular girls are wearing.

Rose's sewing machine is in their bedroom. I pause at the door before entering. I hate the strong odor of pine scent that comes from this room. Rose sprays it around to cover up any real smells. Today it's even worse, because of the heat. Someday I'll plant a garden full of flowers and bring flowers into my house and have them in every room.

I sneeze suddenly, startling myself into action. I don't want Rose to suspect I used the sewing machine, because then she'll want to know why. I hate having to answer for every impulse, every act. I've got at least an hour.

What a relief to unzip my wool skirt and let it slide to the floor! I turn it inside out but am still too hot to work on it. First I need to free myself of the other clothes I wore this morning, not knowing the fog would lift early and we'd have blazing sun in the afternoon. My long-sleeved blouse is sticky and wet under the armpits. I unbutton it and fling it into the hallway, then pull my slip up over my head and toss it on the floor. There, that's better! I breathe deeply, thinking out my plan. I'll sew alongside the seams on either side of the straight skirt, making each side seam a good half an inch wider. That ought to do it. In the morning, I'll wiggle into the skirt, then put my coat on and pretend I'm in a rush to get to school, so Rose and Brad won't see my daring new look. I sit down on Rose's straight-backed sewing chair in my bra, panties and socks and spend a long time lining up the seam, to be sure to get it right. I stitch very slowly, just as Miss Cooke taught us in Home Ec. It makes me grin, thinking how domestic I'm becoming. I am so intent on the second seam that when I hear the front door close, at first I don't place the sound. Then I sit, unmoving, beads of sweat forming above my upper lip and in the creases behind my knees. All I can do is wait to be caught. Or maybe if Rose goes straight to the kitchen, I'll have time to yank the skirt out of the machine, grab my slip, get my blouse from the hallway and dash into my room.

But there isn't time to do any of this. I recognize the heavy step treading down the hall. It isn't Rose, clicking along in her two-inch heels. It is Brad. I freeze, my eyes on the doorway.

Mary Anderson Parks

He looks in at me and a slow, awful smile comes over his face. The sly look in his eyes is like the girl in the painting. He holds my blouse in his hand. His gaze drops lower. I feel like a person without a face, the way his eyes are glued to my breasts. It seems forever that he keeps on looking. Then he tosses the blouse so it lands a couple of feet in front of me.

I have to lean forward to pick it up, further exposing myself. Getting up angrily, I turn my back to him and thrust my arms into the damp sleeves. My fingers shake too much to do the buttons.

I hate you, I want to shout. Whatever you say about why you've come home in the middle of the day, I won't believe you. Then his horrible grasping hands come down on my shoulders, forcing me to turn toward him. His fingers dig into my flesh as he pins me against the wall.

He mumbles, "Be quiet, Bunny, just be quiet."

"Are you crazy?" I yell. His eyes are wide and staring, his mouth twists into a grimace as if he's in pain. His grip on my upper arms tightens.

"Let go of me!" I scream.

Suddenly, behind him, I see Rose's shocked face.

"Brad, what are you doing?"

I watch his face change as he struggles to get control of himself. He turns slowly to Rose. "Bunny shouldn't have been in here," he says. "I was telling her that."

Rose looks confused and afraid. She can't possibly believe him, can she? She moves aside as Brad strides out of the room. I want her to come and hold me, tell me I haven't done anything wrong, that I am normal, that it isn't my fault Brad would act like he did. But maybe she doesn't understand.

I start to explain, "Let me tell you—"

"No, just take your sewing, Bunny, and get dressed." Her face muscles are tight and she avoids looking at me. She turns and leaves the room. I am shaking as I rip the skirt from the machine, grab my slip, run to my room and lock the door. Harsh, deep breaths rattle my chest. I sweep knickknacks from the windowsill, push the window up as high as it will go and

They Called Me Bunny

stick my head outdoors. How stupid I was. Never again will I go outside this room without all my clothes on. I fill my lungs with air, over and over, and finally flop on the bed and lie there for what seems like hours, dreaming of escape.

Night has fallen and my room is completely dark when I hear Rose's pleading voice on the other side of my door. "Please come to the table with us, Bunny."

She wants to pretend everything is okay. She's going to act like nothing is wrong. I let out a deep sigh, thinking about how she stood there and that made him leave me alone. I am grateful for that. And now she needs my help. But I won't let Brad knock me out. I won't let him do that to me. I get up, switch on the light and hear Rose's footsteps take her back to the kitchen. I put on pedal pushers and a clean blouse, a loose one that hides my figure, then force myself to unlock my door and step into the hallway. I go straight to the living room to pick up my oxfords. They have been placed side by side near the couch. The picture on the wall has been straightened.

Rose serves warmed-up stew. I chew and chew on a chunk of beef, afraid I'll gag right there at the table. Brad keeps his eyes on his food. Rose darts fearful glances at each of us. I have to get out of here. I'll suffocate. But where will I go, what will I do? Will anybody want to marry me? Will they think, as Lance's mother did, that I am too much of an unknown? I hate it that if I ever have children they won't know who they are.

Mary Anderson Parks

I end up doing what Rose does. I try to pretend nothing has happened. I graduate early, mid-year like I planned, and a few weeks later the teen group at church has a Valentine's Day dress-up dance. I buy a powder blue satin dress with money saved up from my library job last summer. It's mid-calf length and has a low scoop neck Rose doesn't know about because I show it to her wearing the matching jacket that buttons to the neck. Maybe the dress will help me get a boyfriend. I hope it's somebody as different as can be from Brad.

Margaret Schrader and I get a ride from her older sister. The minute we step in the door, I take off the satin jacket. Margaret oohs and aahs at my neckline and the skirt that fits tight around the hips and then flares. She has on a modest dark green taffeta. Robert Keller asks me to dance and two-steps me around the crowded floor until Tim, the boy Margaret is dancing with, cuts in and we trade partners. We're supposed to be practicing steps we learned in the dance class we've all been taking, but two-step is what we end up doing, and way slower than Mrs. Pearson taught us. Forget waltz, tango and rumba. It was weird finding out our Sunday school teacher knew all those steps. I guess it's because she's as old as the hills. Can you do the bop, we asked her. She'd never heard of it. Dance class was fun though. It helped keep my mind off troubling things like not finding a job yet.

Margaret and I get returned to our places at the edge of the room. The social hall looks romantic with dim lights and pink and red balloons.

Margaret sniffs the air and grins. "We smell like a perfume factory. Mine's Lilies of the Valley. What's yours?"

"Evening in Paris."

"I bet your dress cost a bundle."

"Not really. It was on sale."

Suddenly she takes hold of my arm and points across the room at two boys I've never seen before. "See those two cute guys? They're Catholic. That's what Robert said. He doesn't know how they got invited."

"Don't point. They're looking right at us. God, one of them's adorable."

The two boys exchange glances, then walk slowly across the room.

The chubby, redheaded one asks Margaret to dance and they move off onto the dance floor.

The lean adorable one, with sandy hair, gives me a smile that makes my knees go weak. "Hi, my name's Joe Doolin. What's yours?"

"Bunny," I tell him as we walk out onto the floor. He takes hold of my waist and pulls me against him way more tightly than Robert or Tim did. He looks down at me and I can tell from his eyes how special he thinks I am. If he weren't holding me up, I might swoon. What we feel between us from the first instant is completely physical. We don't even talk after he asks me what school I go to and I tell him George Washington and he tells me he goes to St. Ignatius. He doesn't ask any follow-up questions. I'm glad. I don't want to tell him I've graduated early only to realize I have no idea in the world what I'm going to do next.

He snuggles his head against mine, his breath warm in my ear, and shivers pass between us. When the music stops, we stand waiting for it to start again so we can go back to the good feelings we give each other by the closeness of our bodies. We dance to "Only You" by The Platters, "Unchained Melody," and my favorite, "Earth Angel." Others, too. When we get to "Goodnight Sweetheart Goodnight," Joe Doolin puts his finger to my lips and passes it gently back and forth. My lips tremble. That makes him smile. It is a smile that shows he knows the power he exerts over me. His hand goes to the back of my waist and burns through my satin dress. He asks for my phone number and I give it to him.

When he telephones two days later to see if I want to go for a ride, I can hardly make my voice come out normal. It trembles like my lips did when he touched them.

"Why would he take you for a ride?" Rose asks later as she unwraps a package of lamb chops. "Where would you go?"

"I don't know. Just driving, I guess."

"How long would you be gone?"

"He said something about maybe a movie, too. I'm sure we'll be home by midnight."

Rose looks doubtful. "What do you know about him?"

"He's a Catholic," I say.

Brad suddenly walks into the kitchen. "They're the worst kind. They take advantage of Protestant girls and then go to confession."

I can't believe he'd have the nerve to say that after what he tried with me. But Rose just says, "Oh Brad, they're Christian too, you know, Catholics are."

He gives her a look.

"They're just so different, aren't they, in how they worship?" She turns to me. "I think you should try to be home by eleven thirty," she says.

"Okay. We'll try to be home by eleven thirty. But I don't know what the movie schedule is. And we might want to go out for a hamburger."

Brad turns from the faucet where he has filled himself a glass of water and sends me a look of cynical disbelief. I go on laying the silverware, not wanting to say anything to set either of them off. I try to hide the excitement tingling all through me at the thought of being alone with Joe Doolin. I can hardly remember how he looks. I remember the feel of him, the electric charge he sent through me with the touch of his hands and his breath in my ear, but it bothers me I don't remember his features.

We couldn't really see that well in the dim light and we were too close together most of the time to look at each other. I remember the clean flash of his white shirt in the darkness, and how lean and hard he was. I think he had freckles, but I'm not sure. I hope he finds me pretty when he sees me in full light. I worry that he won't.

28

Joe Doolin shows up in a hot-rod Cadillac, an hour late. We hear him screech to a stop at the curb. I rush out the door when he honks, calling goodbye as I go, ignoring Rose and Brad's disapproving frowns. Joe gets out of the car and saunters around to open the door for me.

When he gets back in the driver's seat and turns his key in the ignition, all that comes on is the radio, blaring out "Let Me Go, Lover" at top volume. I hear the words in capital letters, embarrassing, stinging, making my mind blank of anything it would be conceivable to say, given the state of excitement this guy puts me in. But he doesn't expect me to talk. We've had an unspoken understanding from the moment we met as to what we want from each other. Talking isn't part of it.

Joe seems lost in thought. When he speaks, I realize he is frowning at the gas pedal for a reason. "If I floor it, sometimes then it starts." With a roar it does. I edge closer to him. When we're halfway down the hill, out of sight of my house, he pulls over to the curb and reaches for me. I scoot toward him until our bodies are touching to the rhythm of "Let me go, let me go, let me go," and he kisses me, keeping his foot on the clutch so the engine won't die, but I don't know that until he says, "Wait! I've got to move my leg, I'm getting a cramp!" I want to go on kissing. I like the way he kisses, pressing his cool lips against mine with soft urgency.

"Sit tight," he says. "I'll drive us up to Twin Peaks. We'll look at the lights." He gives me a sideways grin. "Sorry it's too late

They Called Me Bunny 99

for the movies. I had to do some stuff for my mom. Couldn't get to a phone."

He does have freckles. And blue eyes. Why do I keep ending up with blue-eyed boys? Lance, too, has blue eyes. Joe's face is thin and long, like his body. His thinness attracts me. Is the mutual attraction that we find each other exotic? He's Catholic and I his princess of unknown origin. I can tell by his shallow breathing that he's as excited as I am.

At the top of Twin Peaks, Joe parks in a dark spot and then turns his full attention to me. I feel wanted, a feeling I don't often have.

He reaches inside my blouse for my breasts, cupping them, adoring them, and I can feel him adoring the whole rich essence of me that I hadn't even known was there until he touched me. Sighs and groans escape him as he unbuttons my blouse, kisses my throat and then below my throat. He can't help himself and I don't try to stop him. He is beyond stopping, out of control. I feel myself come alive for the first time as a woman. My body lifts toward him, my breasts rise up to meet him and his face presses into them, burrowing from side to side. Now my body is underneath his on the car seat, my head trapped so that I am afraid to raise it and bump against the steering wheel. My pelvis lifts with a will and life of its own. In swift, sure movements he pulls my panties down and I kick them off with one bare foot, feeling the abandon of a whore, a courtesan. This must be my true nature, to be welded body to body with this boy, yielding to his need and my own, giving him pleasure. I am hot and sticky when, all too quickly, he finishes with me. I'm not sure what to do. But he knows. He reaches for his jockey shorts, uses them first to wipe himself and then to cover me where I am warm and moist. It feels good and comforting and safe. Almost right. But not right. Something in me knows I have done what I was not supposed to do. This was what they meant by going too far. I have gone too far. But it feels good here in this place where I've gone too far. He extricates himself from me and gives me room to sit up. I don't want to. I don't want to face whatever comes next. It's way too

Mary Anderson Parks

soon to pull ourselves away from ecstasy. I don't want to sit up and be me again, awkward and unsure. I wiggle back into my panties, feeling like a bad girl. It feels good to be bad. I glance at him, conscious of a new light in my eyes and confidence that rises from knowing I have the power to bring him so much pleasure and to feel such pleasure myself. He grins, proud and embarrassed. His eyes are alight with the light I feel glowing in mine. I am back on my side of the car, and he is in the driver's seat. He reaches out an arm and draws me close, as if now I am something he owns. We kiss, a long, slow, deepening kiss that makes me think it is all going to start over again. And I want it to. But he pulls away and shakes his head. I don't know why he does that.

"We've got to get you home," he says.

"Why? I don't want to leave you."

"You have to, Bunny."

"Why? Why can't we just stay here forever?"

"You're crazy!"

"I'm in love." I dare to say it. And it works. He grabs me and kisses me long and hard, so that my lips are bruised and swollen when he's finished.

"Comb your hair. Fix yourself up," he tells me, with abrupt tenderness. I retrieve my purse from the floor and grope around for my comb and mirror. He switches on the overhead light and I see my shining eyes. I see myself as a woman, a happy woman. Have I ever looked this excited and glowing in my life? I turn to him, wanting it to be him and not the mirror seeing me.

He grins. "Ready?"

I shake my head no, wanting to hold his eyes on me.

"Come on," he says, and now there is impatience in his voice. "It's almost midnight. Your folks might be waiting up."

We make the drive back in silence. Every time he looks over at me, I'm looking at him, waiting for his smile and giving him mine. When we reach my house, he doesn't kiss me again, just leans over and opens the door for me to get out.

"Better not start up again," he grins.

They Called Me Bunny

I shut the front door quietly and tiptoe down the hall. The door of the room where Rose and Brad sleep in their twin beds stands open. No one calls out to me.

I lock my door, then shed my clothes in a pile on the floor and notice blood caked onto my panties. Maybe my period is starting early. I snuggle into bed, pull the covers up under my chin and relive the feel of Joe Doolin's mouth and face pressed into my breasts. Does Brad lie awake too, staring at the ceiling, imagining the hot, passionate fumblings that went on in that car? I fear the scent emanating from me will draw him. I try to still the stirrings of my pelvis as it rises and falls and quivers, but I can't stop remembering the thrust of Joe Doolin's body into mine, joining itself to me. Will he call tomorrow? Could I call him? No!

All my life I've heard you should never let them do it on the first date. Now at last I know what "it" is. But I don't know why we shouldn't have done it. And I didn't really let him, he just did it. It felt natural to do what we did. Maybe now he'll want to marry me! Is there a friend I could talk to about this?

No, there isn't.

Mary Anderson Parks

29

Joe Doolin hasn't called. I can't believe it. Does he have other girls he does this with, or what? It's been over a week and he hasn't called.

I feel overwhelmed by Marilyn Monroe. She's the last thing I needed this morning, but I go into the kitchen and there she is on the breakfast table, her bosoms hanging out and that stupid look on her face that seems to be making her famous. Did Brad leave the paper open to that page on purpose? If it makes me feel inadequate, think how it must make Rose feel. I've seen her face when Dagmar looms out at us on television.

I wonder sometimes if any women know who they are, if maybe it's not just me who's lost but the whole pack of us. Too bad we're not more like a pack. If we stuck together we might get somewhere, but no, it's like we're all competing, trying to get boys' attention, and I'm among the worst, I admit. But I don't want it to be that way.

I stand in front of the hallway mirror, hating my dark roots. I hate them more than ever now that he hasn't called. Or is it the stupid blonde frizz I've made of my hair that I hate? Was I trying to look like Marilyn?

I sure don't. I'm squatty-looking compared to her. And my breasts don't look like hers. Actually no one's do. Why? Trick photography? Falsies? In the locker room I see other girls' bodies and they range from flat beanpoles to lumpy cows, but nobody looks the least bit like Marilyn. Marilyn looks like somebody just took a lollypop out of her mouth and told her to reach for it with her face. There's no thought going on there. She's not a girl you feel you'd want to talk to or eat sandwiches with on a park bench. But I guess men feel differently.

I retreat to the bathroom and sink down onto the toilet with a sigh. "Forget about movie stars, Bunny. Everyday life is bad enough, without bringing movie stars into it." Somehow that makes me laugh. And slowly an idea forms. A way to get even with men?

30

What did she mean? "I'll be ready in a minute." And then, "Not that I really feel like going." It's always a guessing game with Rose.

Here she comes again. "This hat, don't you think?" She turns her head off to the left and waits expectantly.

"Sure, that looks real good on you."

Off she goes to her room again. She spends so long getting ready for anything. I read that Marilyn Monroe is like that, which makes me wonder if the two of them could possibly have anything else in common. Here I go again, thinking about movie stars. Rose always looks the same, once she finally does get ready. She has four hats, the small, sedate types the other Bible Study ladies wear. Except Violet Brill. I get a kick out of Violet Brill and her wide, floppy hats with flowers and fruit. Seems like she models herself after Blanche DuBois, and she's just as neurotic. All the Bible Study women seem neurotic. Couldn't say shit if their mouth was full of it. Now where did I hear that?

I can't stop wondering what goes on inside Rose. What thoughts does she have? What do she and Brad do alone in their bedroom at night? Do they ever join each other in one of the twin beds? Does Rose ever take her nightgown off? I am trying to picture that when she comes back in. "Bunny, my slip isn't showing, is it?"

I bend my neck to look downward. "Nope."

Her skirt is so long, how could her slip show? She is wearing

They Called Me Bunny

a cheerful red and white print. Nothing, though, ever makes Rose look cheerful. Her makeup is on. Soon she actually may get going.

"What about this pin?" she asks. "Does it go with the dress, do you think?"

"I'd wear one that stands out more." Now she looks worried and I wish I hadn't said anything. I get up and follow her to her room. She opens her jewelry drawer and doubtfully holds out a large silver dragon with fake rubies.

"That's perfect."

"Do you really think so?"

"Sure, the rubies go with those red squiggles on your dress."

No wonder Brad gets impatient waiting for the two of us. Right now I can hardly bear waiting for Rose to finish all her little questions and scoot herself out the door. Because suddenly I'm quite sure what it is I'm going to do when she leaves. I'm going to call Lance Woodall. I'm afraid to think too much about why. If I do, I won't have the nerve.

"Brad's working overtime the whole day today, right?"

"Yes. He is." Rose rubs her forehead as if it hurts. She wanders around until she finds her gloves on the small end table where she laid them a few minutes ago. "I've forgotten the text."

"The what?"

"The text for Bible Study today. Can you look it up, Bunny?" She points to where her Bible lies on the coffee table.

"Is it marked or something?"

"Yes, it's marked, dear, the Jesus Loves Me marker you got in second grade for perfect attendance."

She still has that? I can't believe it. Is this a trick to get me to read the Bible? I open to the page with the marker.

"Can you read it to me while I pin my hat on?"

I roll my eyes.

"It's underlined, the passage for today."

This must be the one book it's okay to write in.

I read, "For God so loved the world that he gave his only—"

"Begotten," Rose interrupts.

"Begotten son. That whosoever believeth in him shall not perish but have everlasting life." I snap the Bible shut and hand it to her.

Rose frowns.

Was it because my mother loved me so much that she gave me away? Does God love even me or just Rose and Violet Brill and the rest of the people who study the Bible? And if he does love me, will he stop loving me if I call Lance and tell him this is a good time to come over because we'll have the house to ourselves for two and a half hours, maybe three? Things were strained between us after that day I met his mother, but I've seen the way he looks at me. God, I hope he'll be home. I've been thinking it all out. I tested the drop from my window to the ground and Lance could do it easily if he had to, like if Rose were to get one of her sick headaches and come home. But that never happens to her at Bible Study. Somehow there she is charmed, protected. I feel like a responsible person, thinking ahead like this.

Rose is asking me something. "Would you?"

"Would I what?"

"Go along with me! You'd enjoy it, Bunny. You don't have anything planned for your Saturday and—"

"No, please, you wouldn't want me there. I wouldn't be right for it, you know? That one lady still has it in for me because of the time she caught me necking with Dickie—"

"Please, Bunny! Why would you bring that up? We've all forgotten about it."

"Well, you better go. I'll walk you to the bus stop, how's that?"

"Would you really?"

"Sure. I'll keep you company."

"I do seem to be ready. Wait! I forgot to get a clean handkerchief. I'll be right back."

Four minutes later she comes back, then fumbles through her purse, making sure she has bus fare and keys.

"But you'll be here when I get back, won't you?"

I feel guilty, thinking about what I hope will have happened by then.

"Probably!"

We are out the door at last, and Rose minces down the steps, clutching her Bible. Will she read it on the bus, or will her mind be off in that place it goes?

"Do you like Bible Study?" The question comes out without my having intended it.

"Yes, it's very meaningful." Rose's voice is distant. The words don't sound like her own. "It's better than when we went to that other church," she adds, with surprising energy.

"Why's that?"

"We get to ask questions. Last time one lady even questioned whether it's all true, everything the Bible says."

Rose has an odd, dreamy look on her face. "I guess I thought that's why you might like to go, Bunny."

I can tell she was impressed by that lady who dared to ask if it was all true. And I feel happy knowing Rose noticed something true about me, that I'd like being in a place where you could ask a question like that. Maybe if I could find the right questions to ask Rose, or listen to her better, or learn to hypnotize her, maybe she'd let go of the pain she holds inside.

I run back into the house. I left the door open and Rose didn't notice. It makes me feel wild and free to do things like that, to break the rules. I shed my clothes on the way to the phone, leaving them in a trail behind me. I take off everything and then stand there trembling, my hand on the telephone. Will Lance know I am naked? Something will be different, I feel sure. Maybe I'll even tell him. No, never! He's a nice boy. I take my hand off the phone . . . could Rose be right? A girl never calls a boy. She has said that more than once. Why? Does she know I am in danger of doing it? Ilene tells me the same, like it's one of the cardinal rules of dating. But I've gone beyond all that now. And Lance is never going to call me, so if I want anything to happen I have to do it myself. I pick up the receiver and dial. I know the number by heart. I've written it over and over, filled a whole page in my binder. The phone rings a long time. What if his mother answers?

When I hear Lance say "hello," I can't speak.

He says it again.

"This is Bunny." I clutch my right breast, massaging it. I feel like moaning. "I wondered if you'd like to come over. My mom went out and my dad had to work overtime today and I'm all by myself." I hear Lance breathing.

"Lance?"

"Okay, Bunny. I'll be there in fifteen minutes."

I hang up, shivering. What have I done? After I put my skirt and blouse back on, I sit watching the clock. I stay barefoot. It's a way to keep my nerve, to keep in touch with the part of me that was able to make that call. He rings the bell in exactly thirteen minutes.

I open the door with just my cotton skirt and blouse on and nothing underneath. He senses the wild craziness that's taken me over. That's why he got here so quickly.

I reach up, put my arms around his neck and press against him. The next thing I know we're down the hallway and on my bed. I must have led the way.

"I shouldn't be doing this," Lance keeps saying. He pulls up my skirt, opens his pants, gets his penis out, pushes it into me, all the time saying, "I'm sorry, I'm sorry, oh no, oh Bunny, oh no!" And then he explodes inside me, going up and down really fast and strong, as if there's no way in the world he could stop himself. I feel that power again that I felt with Joe.

Immediately though, he gets up off me. He turns his back to me, fastening his pants, and suddenly I know what a terrible mistake I've made. I pull my skirt down and lie very still.

"Do you want a glass of milk or anything?"

He'll say no. Or maybe he won't say anything.

He turns and looks at me with a horror-stricken face. "Bunny, I have to go. I'm so sorry."

I don't get up. I lie listening to his quick steps going down the hallway, then the sound of the front door closing. Why does it feel so empty? Why did I think I wanted this? To prove I could get Lance Woodall to come running to me? I hate the feeling I'm left with.

Tears run down into my ears and I squeeze my eyes shut, wishing I could disappear. Will this be the last time I ever do anything this stupid? Have I disgusted myself enough? "You scummy girl," I hear in my mind. Rose's words in Lance's mother's voice.

I suppose if Brad leaves, it is my fault.

I want to be a better girl. As I think that, God feels very real. As real as my shame and stronger. Maybe God actually is everywhere, even here on this bed.

Mary Anderson Parks

31

(Rose)

I fought it with every ounce of faith I could summon. I joined Bible Study because of it, hoping to find the strength to conquer my jealousy. I was jealous of Bunny even before there was any reason to be. Oh no, here I am trying to blame her. There was never a reason. How can one blame a child? And yet in every way, in every thing about her, she was calculated to seduce Brad into feeling the feelings he never had for me. Or maybe he had them once, but they died so long ago, right at the start. I can't even remember if they were ever really there. When I couldn't respond to him, it all went flat for us. And stayed that way. An awful emptiness that we tried to fill with a child.

When we brought her home, she walked across the living room and toddled into Brad's arms, not mine. The look of sensuous joy on his face when he caught her up in his arms and held her close to his body appalled me. It appalled me that a child could awaken responses I couldn't feel or awaken. But my jealousy appalled me even more. I fought to become a better person, I fought the jealousy. But the more I struggled not to feel it, the more confused I became. Christians don't have such feelings toward a child, a mere baby girl. She was so full of life and cunning ways. She was everything I didn't know how to be, and she had the best part of Brad, too. Now there was nothing left for me. Sometimes I wonder . . . if we had taken her sister, like the agency wanted us to, if maybe then I could have had

They Called Me Bunny

one child just for me.

Eventually, my efforts at self-control brought numbness, an absence of feeling. But I judged Bunny. I saw her mother in her. I saw the beautiful, brown-skinned woman they told us about, who was so young and yet had all those children. It was shameful, like a family of animals.

As Bunny grew into a robust child with that natural freedom of hers, that wildness of movement that couldn't be restrained and led her into accidents and trouble, I kept seeing her mother in her. I was jealous of them both and didn't understand why. I should have pitied them. I prayed on my knees, morning and night, until I managed at last to subdue the jealousy, but in doing so I subdued the part of me that might have taken risks and found joy. I became a walking caricature of the perfect mother, making balanced meals, saying the right things. There were no fights between Bunny and me, no squabbling, no back talk. But I was afraid to feel anything.

Then Bunny began to develop a figure. It happened so much earlier than seemed normal. I had to get her a bra so she wouldn't show. Her nipples were popping out, her little budding breasts bursting forth. The day after I saw Brad stare at her nipples, visible through her thin tee-shirt, I got her safely reined in and covered. But it didn't work. Soon she was bigger than I in the bosom and growing bigger by the day. That's when my headaches started. The headaches were so bad they drove all thought from my mind. Each time, as the pain eased, I prayed to be more Christian. Mostly, though, I just blanked out a lot of what I saw happening. Especially when Brad looked at Bunny that way he did. Bible Study helped. It taught me that even the greatest men fight temptation. And sometimes their better nature wins. At least with Jesus it did. But he was Christ, the son of God. We're just ordinary people.

Then Brad got so hateful to me. I started counting on Bunny for comfort. She's always kind, Bunny is. You can rely on her for that. I just wish I could feel real love for her, instead of trying to feel it.

Mary Anderson Parks

32

I get a job at our neighborhood bakery and am fired after one week for putting salt in a sheet cake instead of sugar. Six cups of it. The salt and sugar canisters were side by side and I reached for the wrong one, without thinking. Actually my mind was on sex. Joe Doolin finally called, three weeks after the first time, and wanted to go up to Twin Peaks again. I tried Ilene's question. "Why?" I asked. It was all I could think of to say. He just chuckled and said he'd pick me up at eight on Saturday night.

I don't let myself think about what it means that we're going to do it again. Except that I know it doesn't mean marriage. I'm not kidding myself about that anymore. I'm just glad he called. I'd been feeling utterly rejected and worthless. I mean, what kind of a screwball can't even hold down a job as a bakery assistant?

"God leads us in mysterious ways." That was our subject in Sunday school last week. Well damn yes! It's mysterious, all right. Here I am on my way downtown to get a job application at a department store Rose told me to try, when I go flying off the streetcar like a lunatic. "American Indian Service Center," the sign on the storefront window says, and under that, "Help Wanted." Why have I jumped off at a stop two miles from downtown? I walk toward the one story building's front door and stand there with my mouth going dry, arms hanging at my sides, the little black purse clutched in my right hand. Rose said I'd look more professional with a black purse. She added it as the last touch to an ensemble that makes me feel like a dressed-up pig. A professional pig! A girl with long, straight black hair pushes her way out the door and bumps into me.

"Oh, I'm sorry!" she says.

I back up, but she holds the door open for me with a warm smile that begins in her eyes. I mumble thanks and go in.

Suddenly I am in a room of black-haired people, with skin all shades of brown. I squeeze the purse with both hands and wait for something to happen.

"You here about the job?" A woman calls out from one of the desks scattered about the room. "Come on over here, honey." I walk toward her, watching the folds of flesh on her face crease into a smile. I feel good, like I'm swimming through air. "Sit down," she urges, pointing to an orange plastic chair. "Would you like a cuppa coffee?"

"Yes, please." 'A cuppa coffee' sounds so comforting the way she offers it.

"Do you take cream and sugar?"

"Just a little sugar, please." She pours coffee from a Thermos for both of us and produces two spoons and a sugar bowl from her desk drawer. I stir in a spoonful of sugar and take a sip of my very first cup of coffee.

"It's wonderful!"

"Hits the spot, doesn't it," she agrees. Her short-sleeved dress reveals soft rolls of fat along her neck and arms. Her brown eyes sparkle. "Do you have any work experience, dear?"

"I've worked at a bakery." I hope my answers will be the right ones because I want to stay in this place that feels warm and welcoming.

A tall, middle-aged man with black braids hanging down the front of his plaid shirt walks over to us. "Hey there, Noreen."

Noreen smiles.

"States must end racial segregation," he tells us. "Said that in the morning paper."

"Sure did, Art, that's right. I saw it, too. Every day it says some new thing in the paper, don't it? Don't mean it's gonna

Mary Anderson Parks

happen. Now honey, what did you do at the bakery job?"

"I mixed dough and put together custards and learned to use the ovens." I don't tell her about ruining the sheet cake or about dropping a pan of custard on the floor.

"I hope you get the job," Art says, and moves on.

Noreen chuckles, setting her chins wobbling. "I'd better start writin' stuff down." She pulls a form from a stack of papers. "What's your name, honey?"

I wish I could tell her I don't know. "Bunny," I say. "Bunny Lundquist." She doesn't respond that I sure don't look Scandinavian. Instead she asks, "What tribe are you from?" and waits, her pencil poised over the blank on the page where she is apparently supposed to write that.

I swallow. "I don't know." I start to correct myself, to say I mean I don't know anything at all about my ancestry but she speaks before I can.

"Well that's okay, honey. I'll just write down Indian for now."

I am so stunned that I don't hear her next question.

She reaches out her plump, smooth brown hand and lays it next to the purse I placed on her desk. It doesn't have identity in it, my papers are false, I want to tell her.

"Were you adopted?" she asks in a gentle voice and I realize that is the question I missed hearing. It is the link, isn't it, that explains why I don't know the answers she needs?

"Yes, I'm adopted by Rose and Brad Lundquist who are Scandinavians. They look really different from me and they won't talk to me about where I came from." Have I said that aloud, for Noreen to hear?

"Well, a lot of our Indian kids were adopted," she says, patting my hand. Am I dreaming? Are we both saying these things? She goes right on to the next question on her form. "Can you type, dear?"

"Yes," I tell her. "I'm a good typist."

I'll learn. I'll go home and get out that typewriter in the hall closet and practice all night.

"We need somebody right away," Noreen says cheerfully. "Right now Leanna's doing all the typing and the phones too.

She can sure use help on those phones."

"I like answering the phone, and I'm good at writing down messages."

"Can you start tomorrow?"

My smile feels like it stretches from one ear to the other. "Yes, I can!"

"And you just wear whatever's comfortable, honey. You don't have to be all dressed up."

First thing when I get back, Rose asks doubtfully, "Did you get the job application?" Why does she always expect me to be a fuckup? No, Rose, I didn't get the damn job application. I never wanted to work for stupid old Joseph Magnin anyway. And I am bursting with pride to be able to tell you what I am about to say.

"No, I got a job."

She looks amazed. To the point where it's kind of insulting.

"You mean they hired you on the spot?" Her eyes travel to the purse. She must be thinking, that's what did it, that last little touch.

"Not there. Not where you sent me." Because it was she who sent me. None of it was my idea. Certainly not the suit I've practically outgrown or the white frilly blouse.

"Not where?" Doubts rush back into her face.

"The job I got is at the American Indian Service Center. They want me there tomorrow morning at nine. Sharp."

Rose's face crumples. "You didn't have to go that far, Bunny."

Whatever the hell she means by that. Rose is a mystery. But for me everything is. I ask her if I can use the typewriter.

I love working at the Indian Center. Leanna turns out to be the girl I bumped into the first day. She is a patient teacher and we work together easily. She's twenty-two, and in my mind I pretend she's my older sister. A lot of joking goes on when the director, Clarice Rawlins, isn't around. I don't meet her until my third week, and then only briefly. She emerges from her office in a fur coat, ready to go to a luncheon.

Mary Anderson Parks

Noreen calls out, "Miss Rawlins, this is our new girl, Bunny, that I told you about." She acknowledges the introduction with a brief smile. Then she is out the door, banging it behind her.

"Stay out of her path," Leanna warns. "Try not to come to her notice at all, if you can help it. If she takes a dislike to somebody, she'll fire them in a minute."

"If nobody don't mistake her for a bear and shoot her dead first," Art says.

"She'll roast in that coat," Noreen comments, with a satisfied glance out the window. "Just look how strong that sun's getting."

"Mrs. Rawlins doesn't seem all that popular," I whisper to Leanna.

"Nobody can figure her out," she whispers back. "She's not like any other Indian I've ever known. She's always telling people she's part Spanish and French, like she wants to set herself apart from the rest of us."

Clarice Rawlins is the only one with an office of her own. The rest of us share the large room with a big kitchen at one end. Most of the time Clarice Rawlins stays in her office and doesn't come out except to hurry past on her way to luncheons and meetings. She is a tall woman, elegantly thin and extremely well dressed. She wears her black hair pulled up and back in a tight chignon that emphasizes her long face. Her aquiline nose and narrow features remind me of a hawk. I get a glimpse of the interior of her office only once, on a rare occasion when her door is left open. I am shocked how plush it is. Our part of the building has small, scarred desks and thin, mustard-colored carpeting splotched with stains. Clarice Rawlins has a large, highly-polished dark wood desk and matching chairs, a spotless cream-colored rug, and a huge black leather couch. She dresses to match her office, in clear creams and black.

"This place is getting to be like the BIA," Art says to Noreen. "Run by apples." I've learned that BIA stands for Bureau of Indian Affairs, and the U.S. government has been using the BIA to relocate Indian people from their reservations to the cities. Art sees it as a plot.

"If we all get assimilated like they hope we will, then they won't have to worry about those treaties they made, those promises they never intended to keep."

I try not to laugh at the heavy irony in Art's pronunciation of "assimilated," but he catches the grin before I can suppress it.

"Now what strikes you funny, Missy?" That's his name for me. He never calls me Bunny. He knows none of my names are my real names. He said a whole lot of Indian kids got stolen away from their families and put with white people. I had again the sense I should say something to set the record straight. But how can I? I have nothing to put in the place of not being Indian. If I speak up, I'll just go back to being nothing. I don't lie. I just keep quiet every time they say anything about it.

"Eh, Missy? What's that grin about?"

"What's an apple?" I ask, going back to the thing he said earlier that I didn't understand.

Noreen throws back her head and laughs. Then she answers for him. "Apples are Indians who are red on the outside and white on the inside."

I realize they mean Clarice Rawlins.

33

Clarice Rawlins is dangerous and unpredictable. Leanna didn't exaggerate. In my short time at the Indian Center she has fired two key people. From the scuttlebutt I hear, there was no good reason. She replaced the employment director with her nephew. At first we don't talk freely in front of him, but then it becomes clear he doesn't trust her either. Art and Noreen lie low and stay out of her line of fire. Art even gets a promotion. Clarice Rawlins appoints him to head up the elders program when she gives the ax to the director he had been assisting.

One day I'm a few minutes late because I twist my ankle getting off the streetcar. I come limping in and find Art and Noreen deep in conversation, looking worried.

"You'll be next, Art, if you cross her on that."

"A man's gotta do what he's gotta do, Noreen."

"She won't tolerate anybody crossing her."

"I can always go home."

"Are there jobs on your reservation?"

"Nope. But I've got family there."

"Why would you do this to yourself? This is the best job you've ever had." She glances at me and a smile warms her face. "Sit down, honey. What's wrong with your ankle?" She pats the seat of the empty chair next to her. Art is seated on the other side of her desk.

"It'll be okay. I just twisted it."

"Give it a good hard rubbing," she advises. I begin rubbing as she turns back to Art. "Why would you, Art, do this?"

"The elders have to have a sense of security," he says.

"So you're going to risk yours to give it to them." There is admiration in Noreen's eyes as she shakes her head at him.

"That hot lunch is the only meal of the day for some of those folks."

"I know, but Clarice thinks it looks bad having them line up out on the sidewalk every day at noon. She doesn't like the mess, all the clean-up."

"For god's sake, Noreen, so what? It's not like she does any of it herself. She's usually off having lunch at the Top o' the Mark or some damned place."

"Shhh."

"She's not here. I checked."

"But she may come in any second. And you know how good she is at sneaking up on folks. That must be the Indian in her." They both grin.

Art turns to me, his honest dark eyes probing mine. "Missy, how would you feel about helping with the lunch cooking for a while? Clarice fired the cook, thought she'd end the lunch program that way."

"She fired Manny?"

"Yep, maybe she thought he was eatin' too much while he cooked." Manny probably weighs three hundred pounds. He's kind and funny and all the old folks love him.

"I could never take Manny's place."

"Not askin' you to fill up all of it, just to help me turn out hot meals once a day."

"You're the one I'd be helping?"

Art nods.

"Sure then. I could do that."

Art is patient and easy-going. Working with him will be fun.

And it is. What I hadn't expected was how much I'd enjoy the elders themselves. Art and I put the cooked food into big rectangular pans and serve it up, and a couple of the old ladies are so tiny they can barely see over the pans. Art leans over and greets each of them by name and they ask him about his relatives and chat about old times. Maybe Clarice Rawlins thought firing the cook would end the lunch program, but she hadn't counted on a director who was willing to cook the meals himself.

One woman makes jokes about her drinking days. She's the one I like best. Everybody likes Pearl. She's the youngest of the elders, only fifty-five. She has a humorous, self-deprecating way about her and we're always glad when she's in a story-telling mood.

Today, Art forks a second piece of fried chicken onto her plate and I add a large spoonful of potato salad. She thanks me with a broad smile and goes to her place at the table. Having served all the elders, Art and I serve the staff, then fill our own plates and sit down with the others.

"Every so often," Pearl is saying, "I'd end up in jail, and I wouldn't be there long before somebody would call out from another cell, 'Is that you in there, Pearl?' And we'd all start callin' out to each other, havin' a good old time. It'd be kinda like a reunion!"

"Tell about when the headlights went off," one of the ladies says.

Pearl grins around the table. "Well, this one time we smashed up the car headlights, runnin' into a tree, but the car could still go, so two of the men sat on the front fenders and Rudy drove real slow and they were up there ready to tell him if he was about to run into somethin' else! It's real dark out there on the rez at night. They got to laughin' and carrying on so bad they both fell off by the side o' the road. When Rudy finally noticed they were gone, he got us all outta the car and we had to walk back quite a distance to find 'em. That sobered us up all right!"

Pearl shifts into a more serious mood and tells about going into the sweat lodge with her grandma when she was a little girl, and how safe and good that felt. Her grandma taught her to put a towel to her face, breathe into it and keep her head close to the ground to get used to the heat.

A much older lady says, "That puts me in mind of when I was little. My parents died of TB, and after that I lived with my

They Called Me Bunny   121

grandfather. He'd gone blind, so he needed me to do things for him. I'd chop wood, get the fire going and dig up potatoes and carrots my aunt had helped me plant. Then I'd make soup. We'd have meat in it when Auntie brought some. There were days I stayed home from school because Grandfather was sick and needed to be cared for. On those days, he'd have me read my lessons to him so I wouldn't fall behind. One day I came home from school and Grandfather was sleeping. He went on sleeping into the evening and I couldn't wake him up, so I went down the road and got Auntie. She felt for his pulse, but he didn't have one. He was cold all over. That frightened me, so I was glad I could go home with my aunt, but the authorities found out Grandfather was dead and made Auntie send me away to boarding school. She wasn't my real aunt, the white people said. She wasn't a sister to one of my parents." Her face closes down and all expression goes out of her eyes. "I don't talk about what happened at that boarding school."

34

"Can you rinse out your socks, Bunny, do you mind? I didn't have time today to do laundry."

Rose looks up from the bowl of white icing she is scraping with a spoon and table knife, wielding them so expertly there will be nothing left to lick.

"Oh, the birthday cake, that's why! Sure, I'll wash them."

"The cake looks nice!" I yell from the bathroom. I can imagine Rose wincing. She doesn't like yelling, even when I yell something she wants to hear.

I wash my socks and hang them over my towel. She keeps everything so tidy it would be a transgression to hang socks anywhere else. Before returning to the kitchen, I go to my room and change into the bunny slippers Rose gave me at Christmas.

"I'm sorry, Bunny, about the laundry. It's just that I wanted to get the cake done before Brad gets home." She sets it carefully in the cake saver.

I feel a sharp pain in my stomach. "Do you think Brad's been acting kind of different lately?" It's true, but I ask it to deflect my worry away from myself. I haven't had a period since that first night in Joe Doolin's car. And then there was Lance. What a horrible thought. If I have a baby I won't know who the father is. I wonder, did my mother know who my father was?

"Why no," Rose says, a little too slowly. "You don't think he is, do you?"

"I wouldn't have asked if I didn't," I mumble.

"What did you say, Bunny?"

"Nothing." Dirty socks are a smell I hate. Not mine. Brad's. Why am I thinking that? Why do I know how his socks smell? Why did I ever have to get close enough to him to know?

"It must be that your father's overworked. You've been noticing how quiet he is, isn't that it?"

"Yeah, I guess." Maybe Rose likes him better this way. At least when he's quiet he doesn't belittle her. "How do you know? That he's overworked. Has he said so?"

Rose looks startled. Caught in the headlights. "No, he hasn't. He doesn't really talk about work, does he?"

She may be asking something else, it's hard to know. The wall between me and Rose has no footholds, no way to climb over.

The phone rings and I run to get it, hoping it'll be a boy, any boy, asking me out. I would so love to escape. Most of all I want to escape from the scary thought I might be pregnant. I just wouldn't know what to do.

"Hello?"

I hear Brad's awkward throat clearing. "Tell Rose I'll be late."

"Do you want to talk to her?"

"No, I don't."

"Is there anything else you want me to say?"

"What do you mean?"

"She's expecting you. She's—" I look over at Rose, who has two fingers over her mouth, her eyes wide and frightened.

"Just tell her something came up." The phone clicks dead. This isn't like him. Something is seriously wrong.

"Something came up, he said. He said he'll be late."

"Why?" Rose asks. "What?"

"He didn't say. Whatever it is must be urgent. He had to get back to it right away, I guess."

Rose has a deep crease between her eyebrows. "Is something wrong?" she asks.

Yes, of course, everything's wrong. But I don't say that. "It's a good thing you have the cake saver. It'll keep the cake as

Mary Anderson Parks

fresh as it is now."

Rose blinks. "He didn't say when he'll be here?"

"No, he didn't." I can't stand the empty look on her face. "Geez, it's not like . . . well, he's not a kid. I mean, his birthday isn't that big a deal to him. Remember how last year he said he didn't want to celebrate. . . ." I trail off, remembering the grimness in his face when he asked, "What's there to celebrate?" Brad's birthdays have never been much fun.

My stomach twists in knots. "You know, I don't feel all that hungry."

Rose looks at me blankly.

"I'm going to go lie down."

"It's only six o'clock," she says.

I guess I can't leave her. Her eyes are too forlorn. How could anyone hurt a woman like Rose? Is this to be my eternal damned role in life, wondering how could anyone hurt this poor woman? Does she look so pathetic on purpose? I push the thought down and go to stand next to her. She lifts the lid off the cake saver with both hands, then holds it to one side so I can see the cake in all its glory. We gaze down at the glossy white swirls.

"I thought of sprinkling it with coconut but it looks perfect like this, doesn't it?"

"Yes, it sure does." My appetite makes a reappearance. Is it nausea or appetite that's a sign of pregnancy? "Can we eat a slice if he's not back by dark? Can we have cake and milk for supper?"

Rose looks shocked. Then she catches my grin and something loosens in her. "Maybe we just will. He can have cake when he gets here. If he's not too tired."

I take her by the arm. "Come on in the living room. I'll lie on the couch instead of in my room." I lead her to a chair.

"We might as well see what's on television," Rose says, so I turn it on and doze off. Later, we each eat two slices of Brad's birthday cake with big glasses of milk. Then we go to bed. I don't hear Brad come home but in the morning he is there, silent and grumpy-looking. He goes to work, comes home as

They Called Me Bunny

usual and right after dinner retreats to his workbench in the basement, where he's been spending more and more time. I went down there today to take a look. I couldn't see anything that he's made, or even anything in progress. But sometimes we hear him hammering.

(Brad)

I liked it that night I went to the movies and sat in the dark. For a while I even fell asleep. It was restful. Better than the basement.

Rose rarely goes out in the evening. She's afraid to. But tonight her prissy friends came by and took her to a stupid organ concert. Bunny isn't home either. Bunny goes out all the time. Bunny isn't afraid of anything.

I've already eaten all the food Rose left warming in the oven.

I wish Bunny were here. But she's making out with a boy. Getting into trouble.

I like thinking about how Bunny stands with her weight shifted to one side and her hip stuck out. It is a very suggestive way for a girl to stand.

I hardly have any hips. Rose doesn't have hips either. Bunny's are nice and round. Rose and I are too damn much alike, both of us tall and scrawny-looking. Why did I ever think I was in love with Rose?

She seemed kind. I thought I would feel happier close to Rose. I've never felt happy. But Rose didn't want me to get close to her. How did I not understand that until it was too late?

Too late for what?

"I'm all screwed up. I can't do anything right."

Why have those words come out of me?

It's because I looked at the clock just now. I tried to fix that clock one whole Saturday. Now it's running slow again. That's how my life is. It's slowing down and pretty soon it won't go anywhere at all. Except I'll still get up every morning and show up at the post office, weigh all those packages, listen to people fuss about what stamps they'll pick, and watch young students look at me in that arrogant way, like they think they own the world.

The young women excite me, even though most of them look right through me as if I don't exist. Maybe I don't. But I must, because I think about them when they're not there. During lunch hour I think about them, while other people talk and eat and joke, and I just eat. I think about the way they lean over the counter, especially that one girl who looks right in my eyes and startles me into believing I'm alive.

"I'm not such a bad guy."

Darn, I did it again. But so long as I don't talk out loud when anybody's around, what does it matter?

So what should I do with this rare evening alone?

Not watch television.

Not try to fix the clock.

I'll turn out all the lights! That's what I'll do. I'll sit in the dark.

Where? The closet! I'll take the alarm clock so I'll be sure to get out before Rose comes back. She'll be back first. Unless Bunny has an accident or something. Once she fainted at an ice skating rink. I wish I'd been there, been the one to carry her in my arms.

The bedroom clock ticks so loudly. Why do things look fuzzy? The room is sliding away. I must hurry into the closet and shut the door.

It's better in here, with the smell of clothes all around me. The darkness is close and comforting like when I hid among Mother's dresses. I feel steadier now, sitting on the floor, my back resting against the wall. The floor feels smooth under my hands. Rose keeps everything clean, even the corners of

Mary Anderson Parks

closets. When does she do all this cleaning? She's always going to Bible Study or making cakes and stuff.

Something is seeping away. Is it tension, easing out of me? Is this what it takes?

But living here in the closet would be impossible. What would the deacons think if they knew I was sitting here even for a few minutes, much less imagining Rose slipping in trays of food for me and letting Bunny come in and be with me in the darkness with the door shut.

"Bunny!"

Now I've shouted her name. This is worse than mumbling. None of this will be tolerated.

I'm better off alone. My mind can go where it wants when it is dark like this and I am alone. I see a small room with a little kitchen at one end. An apartment hardly bigger than a closet. At least it would feel like a closet if I were alone in it.

Damn the deacons to hell.

36

I hum to myself all the way home from my job at the Indian Center. Saturday night Joe and I went up to Twin Peaks for our third time. He doesn't like it anymore for me to tell him I love him. He told me so. I've decided that's okay. It's better even. Less complicated. Especially since I don't really love him. Only for those few moments when he makes the colored lights come on, like Stanley Kowalski does for Stella in *Streetcar*. Something that feels so good can't be bad, can it? I've been washing myself really carefully when I get home. Joe said I won't get pregnant if I make sure to wash right away. My period finally came, so I guess it's working. What a huge relief!

Being with Joe helps blot out the memory of the mess I made of things with Lance. Lance is the one who never called me.

It is weeks past Lincoln's birthday but Brad still has the American flag up over our doorway. I see it from way down at the corner. I feel loose and free, swinging along in my full summer skirt, my feet in sandals with double-wrap ankle straps. I'm glad to have skinny ankles. Rose is skinny everywhere else, but her ankles swell up. It feels so good, swinging along, not carrying anything. I pull the key from my pocket, open the door and call out, "Anybody home?" I know Rose will be here, probably not doing much of anything. She has a lot of free time. Not that Rose ever seems free. Even sitting in an easy chair, like I find her now, she is upright and stiff.

She smiles at me. It makes her feel safe when I come home

right after work. She likes it that I am working and that during those hours she knows where I am, even though she doesn't like the place where I work and won't even talk about it. I'm not going to knock myself out over that. Prejudice isn't something you can talk people out of.

"Do you mind if I open these doors?" I ask, on an impulse. "And take a chair outside? I'd like to soak up some of this sun!" Why, after all, can't we open the narrow French doors and use the little space as a patio? What's to prevent us?

"You want to take a chair out there?" Rose sits up even straighter, looking alarmed. "Which one would you take?"

"Just a kitchen chair, from the dinette set."

Rose frowns. "The vinyl might get too hot in the sun. Though I suppose you could lay a newspaper over it."

Already spontaneity is seeping away. I try to hang onto the joy I've been feeling but it's hard with Rose following close behind me, cautioning: "Now don't scrape the paint." I push the doors open and scrunch through with the kitchen chair hoisted up in front of my chest.

"I'll move this out of the way." Rose crowds into the small space with me and sets a dead potted cactus farther into its corner. "You'll need something to shade your face, won't you?"

"No! I want the sun on my face. That's the whole idea!"

She starts moving the chair around until I think I'll scream. Finally she goes to the doorway and watches me from there.

I sit down and close my eyes. "Do you want me to bring another chair out? I could scoot over and make room."

"Not out here!" she exclaims. "I don't want to get my face all black." I flick my eyes open and catch her look of embarrassment. "I mean, you don't burn, Bunny, but I'm so fair-skinned."

"Okay, just go back and rest, like you were doing."

"I wasn't resting, Bunny." Her voice is reproving, as if the very idea of rest is some sort of insult. "I was planning what to make for dinner."

After a moment of blissful sun on my face, I hear her voice

again. "Meatloaf, do you think? Does that sound good?"

"I'll be going out."

"Oh it's choir practice evening! You'll be having dinner there, won't you?"

"Yes." Thank God. At least I get one guaranteed night out a week. We sing for an hour, then have baked beans and hot dogs or whatever the church ladies cook up, and afterward a bunch of us go fool around at the corner soda fountain.

The sun's rays grow weaker, then go away altogether. I open my eyes to a huge gray cloud.

"All that fuss and now it clouds up!" Rose chortles.

"Isn't that the way?"

"Mom, I've been thinking—"

"What?" Rose is immediately wary. She knows the word *Mom* means trouble. I usually don't call her anything.

The cloud disperses and sun returns to bathe my face and tempt my thoughts away from this cage within a cage, this tiny enclosure into which I am sandwiched. The idea of being in a sandwich makes me laugh. Do I laugh like my mother? Were her feet and legs darker even than mine? Does this urge I have to throw off my clothes and sit in bra and panties in the sun, does that come from my mother? I think maybe she was a Negro woman and it's that blood in me that makes me like being with the Negro kids.

"Why should I go to college? I'd rather work fulltime at the Indian Center."

"Bunny, sometimes I think you just lie awake nights dreaming up ways to hurt me."

I undo my sandals and kick one into a corner, then send the other flying after it. This isn't about you, dammit!

"I'm not good at school. It's too hard." That isn't true. But I had whole days when I couldn't focus on what was happening. I felt like an impostor. I'd stare out the window wondering why I was there, why I had to go home to a home where I don't feel at home, to people who need a different-looking, different-acting girl from me. I don't make them happy, Rose and Brad. That is the message I get, loud and clear. They went to the adoption agency and were given this little bundle that was supposed to make them happy and instead she grew up to be me. A fuckup.

"You could always get into City College. Most of the women in Bible Study have children going to City, or else to State. One really smart girl's going to Cal."

I glance through the open doors at Rose's troubled face. She's worried what to tell the women in Bible Study. And clearly she doesn't think I'm smart enough to go anywhere but City.

How I would love to ride the wave of freedom cresting inside me right on out of Rose and Brad's house into the wide world. But escape is not easy. Twenty-five hours a week at my pay isn't enough to live on my own. Maybe I can get more hours.

Then something intervenes, to postpone my jailbreak.

Brad tells Rose he is leaving her. But she doesn't hear him.

I'm in the room the night he tells her. I could be a witness in court if needed. He comes up from the basement, where he's been since dinner, while Rose and I were doing dishes and cleaning up.

I am hanging up the dishtowel when he says, "Rose, I'm fed up. I've had all I can take. You'll have to go this alone." He gives me the strangest look. Almost like he wishes I could be going with him. His expression is one of weary yearning, of bewilderment, as if he cannot understand how his life could have come to this point. He walks dejectedly out of the kitchen and Rose draws her head out of the refrigerator to ask me, "Did he say he's fed up with meatloaf? I'll have to come up with something else, won't I?"

Why did he choose that moment, when she had her head in the refrigerator?

37

Too late! Why do I think that? I turn the key in the lock, push the door open and pause. Something feels wrong. There's a stillness in the air that makes my stomach queasy.

"Rose?" I call, for reassurance.

"Bunny, is that you?"

Did she hear what Brad said and not want to admit her humiliation? Maybe she thought she could take the power out of his words by misunderstanding them. But she didn't see the look on his face. I did.

"Your father won't be home for dinner," Rose comments as I enter the kitchen. "It's Thursday, his deacons' night, isn't it?"

Why does that ring a note of discord? A sneer passed over Brad's face when Rose mentioned the deacons last night. She wasn't looking at him and didn't see. She had her head bent over the stove watching the frozen block of corn thaw. Rose watches things like that more than she does people.

It won't go away, the feeling that something is wrong.

"You've scuffed your oxfords, Bunny." Rose gazes critically at my shoes.

What the hell difference. They get scuffed the minute I walk out the door. But Rose hands me the bottle of white Shinola.

"Don't want to look like a ragamuffin, now do you?"

I unscrew the lid and take out the polish-soaked brush.

"Not in here, Bunny!"

"Oh."

Mary Anderson Parks

"Just run to the bathroom and fix yourself up there."

I roll my eyes. She doesn't see that either. She sees so little.

As I start down the hallway, the feeling gets stronger. I pass the bathroom and go to Rose and Brad's room. Something is different. What? I feel like a detective, a scared one. The door stands open wider than usual. Brad's bedspread is rumpled, as if he's been sitting on it. No, that's not why. Like someone in a slow-moving scene from a horror film, I am drawn away from the bed with its imprint of a suitcase and toward the closet. When I open the closet door, my throat contracts. Rose has to be told.

I hurry to the kitchen, dripping Shinola, but for once it won't matter. I know how it feels to be the one left behind when the other disappears. I was a baby, Rose is a grown woman. Maybe she'll get through it better. I hope so. I try to take her hand, but she draws it back.

"Bunny, what?" She looks into my face, at last seeing something.

This is it, I think. It has finally happened. Thoughts rush in and crowd together. Where do they all come from? Yet there's nothing to be done. We'll go on, I know that. Maybe it will be easier even, once we get used to him being gone. I'm getting used to it already. For Rose, it will take time. I wish I'd stop feeling these feelings from before, when I was too small to do anything. My vision blurs.

"What's the matter?" Rose's voice sounds far off.

"Come with me."

Struck by my tone, she follows, after taking the Shinola bottle from my hand and screwing the lid back on. She is clutching it by the neck when I open the closet door and show her the emptiness on Brad's side. A black hanger lying on the floor. Nothing else.

Rose's eyes widen. I feel as if I shouldn't be watching. You aren't supposed to adopt a child and then have your husband walk out on you. I look away, embarrassed. But she needs me. She's all alone. We have that in common now. Will we be closer, because of it?

Her mouth has tightened and her face seems to be shrinking. Oh hell, I'd forgotten what will bother her most. She won't want anyone to know!

She gives me a lost look. I don't know what will help, so I try food.

"Come on, we've got to eat. No matter what."

"I'm sure there is some mistake," Rose mutters.

"What?" But I heard her right. I just hadn't expected that.

"Yeah. Could be," I manage to say.

We move away from the closet and out into the hallway.

"Yes, let's eat dinner. Maybe he'll phone while we're eating," Rose says, following me.

Why would he phone when he's run away?

"We'll just go on as usual," she says.

"Okay."

This time she lets me take her hand. "I'll put the Shinola away. You can polish your shoes tomorrow. That can wait, can't it?"

"Yeah, it can wait."

She looks at me with a little flicker of life in her eyes. "It can, can't it?"

"Yes. A lot of things can wait." Will I have to take care of her the rest of my life? "Uh oh, I smell the peas burning!"

"Oh my, they tell you to put only a quarter inch of water in and . . ."

"Sit down, Rose. I'll take care of it. And I'll flip the pork chops when they're ready."

"Turn off the rice, will you, Bunny?"

"Sure."

I can see we're not going to talk about this either. It'll be like everything else. Is that possible? I guess it is. I guess with Rose what's not possible is to talk about it.

We're halfway through our meal when she gives up. "I'll just go lie down a bit," she says. But then she remembers the room and its half-empty closet. I see her start of horror at the thought of it. She heads for the living room.

Mary Anderson Parks

I feel trapped. I was the one getting ready to leave and now everything's changed. But would my staying help Rose? Maybe I do more harm than good. In her dismal skirmishes with Brad, I was no help. Can I help now? I stare at my pork chop. I have cut the whole thing into tiny little bits. I feel small, as if I could be any age at all. Brad used to cut meat for me into bite-sized pieces. Now I've done it myself.

There is a door somewhere that leads out. Brad found it. He walked through it and left. The pork looks repulsive. I dump it in the garbage and leave open the cupboard door we always keep closed. So the smell of garbage won't stink up the kitchen, is that why we keep it closed? I won't have to lock my door at night. Not if Brad's gone. But is he gone? Or is there as Rose said maybe some sort of mistake? I don't think so. But I'll lock my door anyway.

I sigh, wondering how Rose will make it through the shame and get to somewhere else. I dump her food, too, in the garbage. But I still don't shut the cupboard door.

In the days that follow, I keep watch over Rose. She isn't doing so bad actually, even when she finds out Brad emptied their savings account of all but fifty dollars. She drags out some old nursing journals and spends hours reading them and gazing into space. I get an extra job addressing envelopes at home, to help pay the bills. It drives me crazy being around Rose so much. I'd go completely out of my gourd if it weren't for my work at the Indian Center.

Then she surprises the hell out of me. She calls up a hospital and gets herself a job. Turns out she'd been a nurse for eight years before she married Brad. We do more talking, now that it's just the two of us. Mostly it's Rose who talks. I listen. She goes to bed early. Her job wears her out. But it's a happier weariness than she used to have, and her headaches are pretty much gone. There's nobody around to hurt her feelings. At least I hope I don't. It's funny how Brad set himself free but it's really Rose he set free. He's probably still over there working at the post office. I don't think he intended any benefit to Rose or even thought about how his leaving would affect her. There was a lot he didn't think about.

I don't feel as sorry for her anymore. She loves being a nurse.

38

A day comes when I can't make myself get up. I can't think of a good enough reason. I lie in bed feeling sorry for myself until suddenly I remember it's registration week at City College. What the hell, I'll go! Noreen will fix it so I can adjust my hours. She'll be all in favor of my going to college. In fact she's been pushing me to do it. She says I learn so fast I'll be a wonderful student. I roll out of bed, dress quickly, then call Ilene at her secretary job.

"Lucky you, Bunny! It's so boring here I can hardly stand it. I wish I'd saved money for college." She knows I started a bank account when I got my first summer job. I've always thought of it as my escape ticket. Maybe Noreen's right: education is how to get where you want to be.

"The 43 Masonic bus takes you right out there," Ilene tells me. "Just catch the Geary streetcar and get off at Masonic. I wish I were going too!"

It is not until I get off the streetcar that I realize I don't know which way to go on Masonic. How dumb can I get? A small, dark-haired woman and her little boy come along, walking hand in hand, and like a dimwit I ask, "Excuse me, do you know which side of the street I should be on to catch a bus to City College?"

She smiles and points in the direction she and her boy are walking. "It's this way. You're on the right side of the street. It'll take about forty minutes on the bus. They run every twenty."

"Thanks a whole lot. I appreciate it."

They Called Me Bunny   *139*

"Good luck! You'll do fine, I'm sure."

But when the bus comes, I am afraid to get on. This has never happened to me before. I see how crowded it is, shrug and turn away. The bus takes off without me. Here I'll be for twenty minutes, waiting for the next one, while wind whips the last bit of curl out of my hair. And I've worn a skirt that will muss in the forty minutes I'll be sitting on the bus. If I get a seat.

So why am I starting to feel better? I think of the kindness of that lady and her little son with his serious brown eyes, both of them so interested and concerned. He glanced back at me a couple of times, holding tight to her hand as they walked off. Don't think about mothers who hold their children's hands, Bunny. That only leads to pain. Think positively.

So. Everyday I'll go through this. Except the part where I don't get on the bus! Forty minutes is a long ride, maybe that's when I'll do my studying. How hard can City College be anyway?

When I get there, I feel sure of it. We look like a bunch of losers. Addie Hillman is near the front of the registration line. I've never been able to stand Addie Hillman. I go quickly past, as she talks a mile a minute to the person behind her, and make my way toward the end of the long line. At least I won't have to listen to Addie babble about how she's going to major in home ec and minor in biz ed. I glimpse the lettering at the top of a bulletin board: "Prepare for your chosen career in two years." This whole place is a joke. How did I get so far off the track of the university-bound, as Mr. Hoffman called it?

I ended up loving the ride on the 43 Masonic. We passed USF, the Jesuit College, and by the time we reached the panhandle and its huge trees with solid thick trunks, the bus had partly emptied out and I had a whole seat to myself. I got that feeling that comes over me sometimes on the bus, of wanting to keep riding into eternity. Geez, Bunny, maybe you should go into a career in theology! At City you could wrap it up in two years!

It was great, though. We wound around all over the place, like the bus didn't know where it wanted to go. Maybe that's why I felt at home on it. It left Masonic and went up Haight, then

Mary Anderson Parks

got on a street called Parnassus and went up by the U.C. Med Center. That's where I wish I could be. Not the Med Center, but over at U.C. in Berkeley. I'd have a bridge and a bay between me and where I've lived my whole fucked-up life. But I'm not good enough to go to Cal, even if I could afford it.

Think positive, Bunny, remember? You were going to do that. Turn over a new page. We got onto some road that curved around and overlooked a lake, it was like being out in the country. We'd left the city behind and gone on to a place I hadn't known existed. I liked that. Then came a ritzy neighborhood and a hospital on a hill with green lawns, and after that a winding, pretty street called Miraloma, where the houses had yards. I moved to the front and asked the driver to let me know when we got to City College.

We came to an ordinary neighborhood, with the houses all stuck together, crossed Flood, went down onto Phelan and I could see City College on our left, set up on a hill.

"Here y'are, little lady," the driver announced.

I crossed the street, walked up tiers of stone steps to a long rectangular building with six tall square columns and stared at the words engraved over the entrance: THE TRUTH SHALL MAKE YOU FREE.

Yes, this could be a start, this place. Noreen said it's important to start my education and not put it off.

"Bunny!" I turn and there is the goofiest guy in high school, David Baum. He's also very smart. Smart-goofy.

"So what're you doing here?" He knows what I mean.

"My folks think I'm a nutcase." He flashes his wacky grin. "They don't want to invest a lotta dough in a nutcase."

I won't ask him what courses he's taking, it's too trite. He'd just ask me the same and I don't want to tell him I don't know. "Going out for football?" I say instead.

He snorts with laughter, through his nose, and everybody turns to look at us. Great. Already I'm attracting the wrong kind of attention. And then I have this weird feeling in my stomach and know my period's starting. It always happens at times like this.

They Called Me Bunny

"I gotta go somewhere," I mumble to David.

"Better get in line, if you want to register today. It goes way back there."

He's right. I can't even see the end of the line.

"I'll save you a spot!" he yells, as I walk off holding my thighs close together.

"Hey, Bunny!" On no, now it's Skip. "Are you okay?"

"Yeah, I'm great. Everything's great." I hobble off in the direction I hope is the girls' room. But when I get there, the Kotex machine has an "Out of Order" sign taped across it. I retreat to a toilet cubicle, trying to think what to do, wishing I'd never been born. Or is that too drastic?

I do the only thing I can do. I stuff my underpants with multiple folds of toilet paper. When I emerge, I feel like an elephant being scratched in unexpected places. At least I had the bright idea of tying my cardigan around my waist to cover the wet spot where I washed blood off the back of my skirt. David Baum is much nearer the front of the line now. People would get really mad if he let me in. Maybe I should go home.

But I'm not a quitter. I refuse to quit. Feeling heroic, like what's-her-name, Amelia Earhart—God, I wish I was flying away in a plane—I plod with my new gait toward the end of the line, which reaches outside the building. And then I know why all this has happened, because the cutest guy in the world is standing at the end of the line.

He looks the way I knew the man I'd fall in love with would look. Tallish, about five feet ten, with a shock of black hair and glowing dark eyes. Sensitive mouth that smiles easily. Large, well-shaped nose. Intelligent, intense gaze. His skin slightly tan. How has he managed to get suntanned? Maybe he lives in the Mission. Everybody says the Mission gets more sun. And he does look sort of Italian. Or something.

"We seem to be bringing up the rear," he says, when I take my place behind him. His voice shoots a thrill right through me. I notice his hair has a slight wave. I hadn't pictured my dream man with wavy hair, but I can adjust.

"I'm glad to have company," I say, grinning.

Mary Anderson Parks

"I can't believe I'm going through all this just to take two classes."

"Why only two?"

"I want to learn more about art and history before I go to Europe. That's always been my dream, to go to Europe. I don't want to seem like just another American moron when I get there."

Wonderful! He's easy to talk to and has something to say. By the time we reach the front of the line, he's helped me figure out what courses I'll take: English lit, zoology, P.E., French and world history. I told him I have a passion for history. So I'll be in one class with him without seeming too obvious.

39

A week later, he hasn't noticeably fallen for me yet. Let it go, I tell myself, and trip on the gym steps and think again what a fuck-up I am, and of course two guys from the track team are lounging in the doorway. One of them snickers, "Need a hand?" "Do I look like it?" I say, and realize how stupid I sound. So I grin. They both grin back and I say, "Here's lookin' at you," and they say, "Hey, that's not your line!" and I think how easy guys are to mess around with. It's making them fall in love with you that's hard. I use my weight to push open the heavy door to the girls' locker room.

And there she is. Cork. From zoology. The locker room is full of girls and all I see is Cork. The teacher called out names while he made a seating chart. When he said, "Cordelia Newberry." she told him, "My dad calls me Corker, but to everybody else I'm Cork." Then she smiled at me across the aisle. Her golden brown eyes had lights dancing behind them. I guess I fell in love then and there. It occurs to me I'm doing a lot of falling in love my first week of college.

I shift my armload of books. "Hi!"

She flashes that smile. "You must be here for tennis. I just finished."

I shrug. "I didn't think I could make an eight-thirty."

I plop down on an empty bench and start rooting around in my messy gym bag, but mainly I'm watching her. It's like she's used to being stared at and doesn't even notice. A girl stops by and tells her about her sick cat and I watch Cork talking and listening in that earnest way she has. When the girl leaves, she unwraps the white towel covering her and drops it, then leans forward into her bra, effortlessly hooking it shut in the graceful way she seems to do everything. Even her underwear is special, satin and lacy in a gorgeous shade of aqua. She pulls on a tan sweater I'm sure is cashmere.

She looks so expensive. It's not just her clothes. It's the sheen of her skin, the cut of her hair, the way she holds herself. Like a classy brunette you'd see in the movies in an evening gown. Deborah Kerr maybe, only Cork's energy and coloring are more vibrant. Ava Gardner, or Elizabeth Taylor. But Cork is taller, more healthy and wholesome looking. And so *modern*. She's the way I'll never be in a million years.

I kneel down to untie my saddle shoes. I'm sweating already and I haven't even started exercising. Probably Cork doesn't sweat. My fingernail polish is chipped, I'm wearing cheap perfume, and when she glances at me I remember my sock has a hole in the toe. I straighten up, not wanting to take my shoes off while she's looking, and somehow bang my head on the edge of an open locker. I reach up to rub the sore spot, which hurts like heck.

"Ooooh, that must've hurt," Cork says.

I stop rubbing. "No no, I'm fine."

"There's a little blood on your head," she says.

"Oh no!" I collapse onto the bench. "I'm scared to death of blood!"

"She is," Addie Hillman says. I hadn't noticed Addie standing there. "Bunny's scared of blood. These things happen to her all the time."

Did she have to say that? "Yeah," I respond. "I'd make a hell of a nurse."

"So what does that leave, if you can't be a nurse?" Addie lets out her inane giggle. "Not a teacher. You'd crack up the class."

Cork cuts into our senseless chatter. "Here, let me help."

The first time I saw her I thought of her as someone to admire from afar. Here she is, real and up close, putting a cool washcloth on my head. How did she even find a washcloth?

"That feels good," I tell her. I can picture Cork being anything in the world she wants to be. Ingrid Bergman, that's who she reminds me of! And maybe Jennifer Jones.

"She does this stuff to get attention." I distinctly hear Addie's words, muttered to someone I can't see. Did Cork hear? Will she believe her?

"I'm accident prone," I tell Cork.

She laughs. "Don't sound so resigned! It's not a genetic thing, is it?"

Why did she say that? Does she know I don't know where my genes come from? Has somebody told her?

"I'm adopted," I blurt out. "So I wouldn't know." I grin, to take the sting out of my words.

She doesn't respond. She just tells me the bleeding has stopped, that it was hardly anything.

"Good. Then I probably won't faint."

"Yeah," Addie puts in. "When we all went ice skating and Bunny cracked her head on the ice and bled all over the place, she took one look at the blood and passed out. It took two guys to carry her off the ice."

"Ice skates are heavy," is all I can think of to say.

Cork steps into her skirt, fastens it, then picks up her books. "I've got to run. I'm putting up a notice about apartment sharing. I need to get to the admin building before it closes."

Apartment sharing. It wouldn't occur to her to let fools like Addie and me in on it. She leaves in a flurry of organization, all her stuff falling into place in her arms like in a Disney movie.

"Be careful," she calls to me with a warm smile as she swings out the door. And then she's gone. I find myself vowing that I will be careful. I really will. My accident-proneness doesn't have to be a permanent condition. I want to be like Cork, with that same easy confidence. Her confidence is real, from deep inside. Not just a bag of tricks.

The next morning I'm at the administration building when it opens, looking for Cork's ad. It's easy to spot. It is the cleanest card on the bulletin board and the only one that is not overlapped by other cards. She must have rearranged the whole board.

"Looking for roommate," it says. "Neat, quiet. Student preferred."

I could be that, I tell myself. I could be that. If I really wanted to. And I'm already a student. I'm halfway there.

"What's up, Bunny?" Skip comes up behind me and lays his big hand on my head. "Looking for a pet?" He guffaws at his own joke. Sometimes I feel like I'm back in high school. So many of the same kids are here.

"See ya in class, Skip," I say, so he'll go away. He gives me a clap on the shoulder and moves on. I write down Cork's phone number.

At home, I wait until Rose is in the bathtub, then run to the phone and dial. Just like I blurted out I'm adopted. Is that the only way I can do things, blurt, act without thinking?

When she answers, her voice cool and collected, a second passes before I can speak.

"It's me, Bunny. Remember? You helped me when I busted my head yesterday?"

She laughs. "Of course I remember you."

"Why I'm calling is your ad." I lower my voice, afraid Rose will hear. "I could be neat and quiet. Most of the time. I mean, I could try."

She is silent for a beat. "I'm not really neat and quiet myself. I'm an artist and I make huge messes."

Is she trying to discourage me?

But then she laughs. "Let's give it a try!" Just like that.

"You mean I can move in with you?"

"Don't you want to see the apartment before you decide?"

"Not really. If it suits you, it'll suit me." Keeping my voice low, I add, "I'm anxious to get away from home."

"Well, we've got that in common!"

"Really? It's the same for you?"

"No kidding. I couldn't have stood it another minute."

"Yeah, well it gets to me, too."

"Do you have much furniture and stuff?"

They Called Me Bunny

I pause. I hadn't given any thought to the details. "I'm not sure I have any furniture at all." This will be the end of it. Why would Cork want somebody who doesn't even have her own furniture? But I can't picture that Rose would let me take anything with me. It's a maple bedroom set she got from her mother that's in my bedroom.

"Great! That's great!" Cork is saying. "My mom had all this antique stuff in the attic and I couldn't get her out of here the first few days. She was setting everything up and crowding furniture into the bedrooms. I thought I'd go crazy."

"Does she still come over a lot?"

"No, that's the funny thing. She's like that, though. Always throwing herself into some project, then going on to the next one. I guess I'm not it anymore. Thank God!"

"She sounds full of energy, like you."

"We're alike in some ways. After all, half my genes are from her!"

I make no response. Doesn't Cork remember my telling her I'm adopted? I should have learned by now. People don't stop to think how it feels when you have no idea where your genes came from.

"Do you want to start moving clothes and stuff in on the weekend?"

"That'll be great," I say, wondering how I'm going to break the news to Rose. As wonderful and unbelievable as it is to me, to her it will be Bunny acting headstrong and impulsive, giving her another headache. But she has the hospital job now. I don't have to worry about how she'll survive.

"Who was that I heard you talking to on the phone?" Rose asks, emerging from the bathroom.

"A girl I met at City. Her nickname is Cork. I like her a lot."

"Oh. I thought it might have been Brad. But you would have called me to the phone, wouldn't you?"

"Yeah, I would have."

I edge into the kitchen sniffing the air, looking in corners, habits I've had as long as I can remember. Why can't I remember way back? Whenever I ask Rose that, she changes the subject. What is she so hell bent on hiding from me?

She still has her nurse's cap on and a blue and yellow checkered apron tied around her to keep spaghetti spots off her white uniform. When Rose first started working, she came up with this neat spaghetti dinner in a box. We never got to have dinners from a box when Brad lived with us.

"Chef-Boy-ar-Dee?" I ask cheerfully. Here I am preparing to make my escape, yet still hoping to connect with her.

"You're not tired of it, are you?"

"No, I love it. Want me to open the Parmesan?"

"Why yes, Bunny. You can put it in that small blue bowl."

Rose cuts up half a head of iceberg lettuce, then shakes orangey junk all over it. I hate Thousand Island dressing. Briefly, I think of telling her. But all that would get me is Rose's standard message about how we don't hate things, not if we're nice, civilized people. We may dislike Thousand Island dressing, but we don't hate it.

Rose interrupts my profound thoughts with a story about the old lady in room twelve. She's becoming my favorite. She throws things at Rose when Rose comes in with her meal on a tray. She has a good aim, that old lady. Never hits the tray, just gets Rose, right in the head sometimes. So far not with anything sharp. The old lady has these two rag dolls, one white and one black, and she holds them up in front of herself and chatters away, being first one and then the other. But she gets more and more worked up and before you know it the dolls are in a fight, pushing and batting at each other, until suddenly she flings one of them across the room in a fury.

Will I miss hearing Rose's stories? She's already told the same ones more than once, but I don't mind. It's the first time I've ever heard Rose tell stories. I didn't know she knew how.

"Are you listening, Bunny?"

"Sure," I say, surprised. She's never asked that before. I've never thought of Rose as a woman of surprises. Lately though, it's different. Working at her old profession has changed her. She's more alive. At last she has something to say. She doesn't ask meaningless questions as often as she used to.

I set the bowl of Parmesan on the table. None of this bowl stuff for me when I'm on my own.

"Seems like your mind was somewhere else," she says. I am about to tell her right then that I am going to move into a place of my own. But she goes back into her monologue. "So I just couldn't believe it when she threw her new Raggedy Ann at me. She loves that doll. Her brother brought it to her. She's put the other two aside and just hugs it and cuddles it, but it talked back to her. 'Don't you dare talk sass to me,' she yelled at little Raggedy Ann. 'I'm your mother.'"

My mind goes off again. I've never sassed Rose. It's not allowed. So much isn't allowed. I can't be me here. Can't even be told who I am. Is that why Brad left? So much wasn't allowed? Me, for instance? I wasn't allowed to him? I should stay away from such thoughts. They drag me down like quicksand pulling me by the feet.

We sit, each in our usual place, and Rose says the same grace she always says, "Bless this food to our use," and then starts up again, talking about a diabetic woman who went into a coma right there in her hospital bed. There are twenty patients in Rose's section and I'm beginning to know each one of them personally.

Rose gains confidence every day as she gets more and more

Mary Anderson Parks

into the work she trained for as a young woman. It's all coming back to her, she says. I wonder what work I'll do. Sometimes I don't feel that I'm real to Rose. Suddenly I blurt out with my mouth full of Chef-Boy-ar-Dee, right in the middle of what she is saying, "I'm moving out Saturday."

At least I get her attention. "Why would you do that?" she asks, with a hurt look in her eyes.

"Why would I do that?" I say the words back to her, and she turns her face away. "Well, let's see. I'm grown up now. I got out of high school. Graduated, I mean. I'm ready to hit the big wide world."

"But no job you can get will pay for rent and all that."

"I've saved money and I have a friend I can move in with and share expenses. Remember I told you about meeting a girl I like?"

Rose looks blank, trying to remember. "Tootsie?"

"Cork."

"Her family must live out of the city, do they?"

"No they don't, they live right here in town."

"Well maybe that's good. I mean, she won't think it's odd then, that you live away from home when your home is so close."

"Is that what bothers you about my leaving, what somebody might think?"

"You must do what's best for you, Bunny." She says it like a martyr at the stake. I feel confused and guilty. I wish I wouldn't keep thinking about Brad, wondering if she used the same lines with him. If this keeps up, I'll begin to feel like his damned ally.

Rose brings her cloth napkin to her mouth and holds it there.

"It's the right time, Rose. I need to start my own life."

Her pale blue eyes widen, something frantic in them. "But this is your life, Bunny. What do you mean?" She lays the napkin in her spaghetti, not noticing. "What would I tell people?"

That's always the question with Rose. I try to answer it, to make that look go out of her eyes.

"You'll tell them Bunny's all grown up and on her own and

They Called Me Bunny   *151*

doing just fine."

"But—"

"No. I've decided, Rose. You'll be okay, I know you will. You've got your nursing." I am pleading. I hadn't wanted to.

"Yes, I'll work extra shifts." Her eyes dull and her gaze drifts off. She's shutting down, like she used to do with Brad.

"Maybe I'll have a baby," I say, to bring her back.

It works. She looks horrified.

"I was only kidding."

"Bunny! That you could kid about something like that—"

"Come on, Rose, take it easy. This is what's supposed to happen. Your baby bunny grows big and hops away from the nest! Right?"

"Not a nest," she mumbles. "I might as well just go back to work right now, this very minute, see if they need extra help."

"How 'bout a movie instead?"

"A movie?" She gets up from her chair, staring like a zombie. I knew escape wasn't going to be easy. I need to help her get prepared.

"There's a good one at the Alexandria. With Alan Ladd. You'll love it."

"We could take the streetcar down Geary, couldn't we?"

"Sure we can." I lead her to the coat closet, pull her coat from a hanger and hand it to her. Then I get mine. "Rose, I need to make my own life. It's a normal thing. It's not like I won't be close by and coming over to pester you every few days."

"I only wish I hadn't told my friends in Bible Study that you weren't going to college."

"Well now you can just tell them I *am* going."

"I don't go anymore," she admits. "I called and told the president about returning to nursing. How that doesn't leave me any free time."

I should have realized. We've stopped going to church, too, since Brad left. I know it's because she can't face those people. She doesn't seem to miss it, though. I wonder about that. I always thought it was church and Bible Study that held her together. Maybe it was, but now it's nursing.

Mary Anderson Parks

Things can change. I find that a hopeful thought.

Then Rose remembers we need to brush our teeth and put on lipstick before we go, so I know she's kind of back to normal.

41

The next day I feel my dreams coming true when Richard walks out of world history with me and says, "You got time for coffee?"

"Sure!"

"Today is the one day I don't have to rush off to work."

"Where do you work?"

"At my uncle's restaurant. I also live there. In the upstairs apartment with him and my aunt and their three kids."

I smile. "It sounds kind of crowded."

"It is. I sleep on a cot in the kitchen."

We step out of the building into the fresh smell of rain. Richard opens the big umbrella he's carrying. "Good thing one of us is prepared," he grins. I'm thinking how glad I am I don't have an umbrella because now I get to walk really close to Richard. Our steps fit perfectly together. It feels romantic, like we're in a little world of our own. I hope the coffee shop is far away so I can stay close to him longer. He is so near I feel he might hear my heart singing, "I've finally found my guy!" Keep your feet on the ground, Bunny. Don't scare him off.

"Do you mind?" I ask. "Sleeping in the kitchen?"

"It's fine. I'm with my family and that's great. Also, I get to save almost all I earn because I don't have to pay for rent or food."

"What kind of restaurant is it?"

"Armenian. I'm Armenian, you know. Did I tell you my last name's Hagopian? A lot of people know right away from that.

I have this huge family in Fresno. Eight brothers and sisters and a whole bunch of cousins, aunts and uncles. I go there whenever I get a chance and we all have a big time together. We eat up a storm! And have lots of laughs."

"Gee, that sounds wonderful." I'm thinking how I'd love to meet them. Bunny Hagopian. I like the sound of it. I'm also thinking I won't be such a fool as I've been with Joe Doolin. If I'm going to go through life making stupid mistakes, I might as well learn from them. I want to put Joe Doolin out of my life and be the kind of girl a guy like Richard can respect. Can I do that? If I had Richard for a boyfriend I'm pretty sure I could.

We come to a coffee shop and Richard holds the door open for me, the umbrella dripping from his other hand. We sit down in a booth and Richard orders two coffees. He gives the waitress a quarter and a dime and tells her to keep the change.

"Thanks," she says, giving him a big smile. "You can have all the refills you want."

"Have you ever heard of the writer William Saroyan?" he asks me.

"Didn't he write that play *The Time of Your Life*?"

"One and the same! He's an Armenian, like me. He's a great guy." I see the flash of pride in Richard's eyes.

"I bet you're saving up for traveling, aren't you?"

He gives me a grateful look. "You remember me telling you how much I want that. Say, what do you think of our world history teacher?"

"So far it's been a history of war and intrigue."

He nods. "You're right. And class struggle. That's what it's really about, that and greed for land. I hope the teacher will talk about the connections."

"Don't forget the church," I say. "I've been surprised to find out how much power the church used to have, especially the Roman Catholic church."

"Hah!" Richard says. "You'd be surprised to find out how much power it still has."

We talk on and on and finish off two refills. We don't leave until the waitress starts setting the tables with paper place mats, getting ready for dinner.

We go out to find the rain over and late afternoon sun breaking through the clouds. We stroll along, talking about life and what we hope to get out of it and what the meaning of it might be. I tell Richard I haven't thought much about the future. I've just been trying to make it through the present. He throws back his head and laughs when I say that. I do wonder about the meaning of it all, I tell him, though sometimes it seems dangerous thinking too much about it, because what if there isn't any meaning. He takes that seriously.

"I think life has meaning if we take a bigger view," he says. "This country is just a small part of the world, yet we think we're the center of everything. We forget other countries were here centuries before us. Maybe it's because my parents and aunts and uncles are immigrants that I've learned a different way of thinking."

"It's really neat," I say, "the way you think. I love hearing your ideas."

He grins. "Hey, I better rush off. My aunt doesn't like it if I'm late for dinner." He gives my arm a quick squeeze. I feel his grasp strongly through my coat sleeve. All the way home it tingles where he touched me.

Mary Anderson Parks

42

Things are going pretty great with Richard. We talk for a few minutes after every world history class and then he heads off for work. And I love my life here with Cork in this bright, sunny apartment. I've been here two weeks now. I know it's going to change my life. It's at the corner of Granada and Ocean. We're at the top, on the third floor. Cork chose the place because the corner window and south-facing windows get really good light. She says running up and down two flights of stairs will put us in tiptop athletic form. She played volleyball in high school and had private figure skating lessons. But she's given all that up for art.

The apartment's not as crowded as she made it out to be. The big front room has a daybed, covered in a dramatic red and black sailcloth print, a pile of red pillows next to the hope chest we use as a phone table, an antique bureau, and Cork's art supplies and easel. Her paintings are everywhere, even in the bathroom. They're abstract. I've never seen anything like them. The colors are as vibrant as she is. I love how bohemian our place looks, how free it feels. There's a fire escape we can climb out the window and sit on, facing Granada. It takes only ten minutes to walk to classes.

Today Cork's doing my fingernails. She goes about it like a professional. Gosh, even in something like this she manages to impress me.

"Maybe it's because you're a painter," I murmur.

"Maybe what's because I'm a painter?"

"You do it like a pro."

"I am a pro. Susan made me paint her nails every weekend. As soon as she learned I could."

"You mean Susan bossed you around?" I can't picture anyone telling Cork what to do, not even a big sister.

"You bet."

She finishes my right hand, as absorbed as if she were in front of her easel. We are in the kitchen, at the cherry wood table, my hands spread flat on the smooth, glossy surface. Cork lifts my right hand with gentle fingers underneath my wrist, to inspect her work.

"Every damned thing you do, you do with style, do you know that?"

She doesn't answer, just meets my eyes with a steady gaze. Maybe I shouldn't have said that. I've begun to feel comfortable around Cork, but it may be a mistake to feel too comfortable too soon. I can't help it, though. I want our friendship to be real. I want someone I can talk to without having to be careful.

"Sometimes I think you don't see me as a real person, Bunny." She looks at me with an expression I can't fathom. It isn't unkind. I can't imagine Cork being unkind.

"What do you mean?"

"You think I'm this perfect person, don't you?"

"In a way I do," I admit.

"Well cut it out. You'll be disappointed."

"That's a laugh." I smile into the impossibility of Cork ever disappointing me.

"What the heck's funny?"

"Just that all my life I've been the one who's the fuck-up, disappointing people right and left."

Her face softens. "Is that how they made you feel?"

"It's how I am, Cork. I'm not what anybody wants me to be. I never have been. Maybe for a while in my bunny rabbit stage, when I was little."

"How do 'they' want you to be? And who are 'they,' anyway?"

"Whoa! You ask hard questions, Cork." I thought I wanted

Mary Anderson Parks

directness, but the conversation is moving too fast.

"What are the answers? That's what matters. Are we talking about your adoptive parents?"

"Of course." But maybe I wasn't what my birth parents wanted either. Is that why they gave me up? "I wish I could remember back to before I was adopted," I tell her. I don't mention that lately I've been having memories of being with my real family.

"But you said the other day you were only twelve months old."

"I know I said that."

"Is it true?"

"How do I know, Cork? I've never seen any papers. They can tell me anything they want."

She puts the bottle of polish back in her manicure tray. "You're right. I never thought about it that way. How weird."

"What? What's weird?"

"To have papers, like a dog or a horse. I mean, all I've got is a birth certificate, and who knows where that is."

"It's different though, Cork, for me. Don't you see? To me it would mean everything to see the birth certificate I was born with. For you it doesn't even matter."

"They might have got me mixed up in the hospital with some other baby." She crosses her eyes and sticks her fingers in her ears.

"You can kid about it because you know who your parents are. You can look at them and see the ways you resemble them."

"I look like my ding-dong mom."

"See? That's what I mean. You take it for granted!"

"It's no big deal."

She doesn't understand. I talk about what hurts me more than anything in the world and she doesn't even get it. Maybe she's disappointing me already. Maybe she'll keep on disappointing me. Maybe that's what it means to be a real person.

"Let's go to the drugstore for Cokes," I say.

"Yeah, let's! That's what I like about you, Bunny. You're

always ready to go!"

"I like that about you, too." I'm pulling back from her and she doesn't even know it.

"We're quite a pair, huh?" she says, throwing an arm around me, giving me a quick hug. A few minutes ago, I would have thought that was all I wanted or needed. But I should have known the loneliness in me doesn't have a cure. I've never found one yet, have I?

In the drugstore, I go nuts. I play "Shake Rattle and Roll" on the juke box for starters. I yell out to the girl at the soda fountain to turn up the volume. If nobody wants to hear me when I finally open up and say something that matters, well then, I'll just clam up. I'll make sure nothing but fluff comes out of my mouth. I raise my straw and blow Coke on the neck of the boy in the next booth. It surprises me how angry I feel. I want to smash my glass against the wall, smash all the glasses lined up behind the counter. The boy and his friend stand up. They want to join us, for god sakes. It works every time, Bunny. Just go nuts, get crazy. A sure way to attract boys. Cork sends them away, and I am impressed all over again.

"Isn't this where you met that guy you went out with last week?" she asks, taking me by surprise. "Here at this drugstore?"

"Yeah, he wasn't much." I drape my jacket around my shoulders. "Gee, this Coke is freezing my insides. Maybe we should take a walk, huh? How far do you think it is to the ocean?" I don't want her to ask me about him. I don't want to tell her I had sex with a guy who picked me up while I was buying toothpaste. And that he hasn't called since.

What was I thinking? The trouble is I wasn't thinking! He took me for a ride in the middle of the afternoon, out to the Presidio or some place with a lot of trees and grass, and he brought out this army blanket and spread it on the ground. He said nice things about my figure and hair.

Had I hoped Richard would see us out for a drive together and get jealous, be afraid of losing me? Yes, I hoped that. And I lied to Cork. I told her I met this good-looking guy and he took

Mary Anderson Parks

me out for a hamburger at Zim's. Was I trying to impress her? I had to tell her something, because I got home really late. I'd forgotten we were going to go to the library together. I'm a first-class fuck-up.

But I don't want to be. I think about how Cork sent those guys away just now. That was classy. That's how I'd like to be. And when Richard asks me to be his girlfriend, I'll never do anything stupid again. I really won't.

It is cold at the Shakespeare Garden, but we're prepared. We took the bus and Cork brought a blanket, folded up under her arm. We sit on it and gaze around at the statues. I try not to think about the last time I was on a blanket in the grass.

I tug my knitted hat down over my ears. Cork produces the thermos she packed into her tote bag. She pours hot sugared tea into two large plastic cups and opens a package of Oreo cookies.

"I love the way you think of everything."

"Bunny, you've got to quit this. I'm getting a big head."

"Not you. That would never happen with you."

"There you go again!"

"I can't help it," I mutter. "You're perfect. Face it. Everybody thinks you're the neatest person in the world."

"Look, Bunny. I'm not the smart one in my family, okay? So I try to make up for it with personality."

"Jeepers." I stare at her for a long moment. "We've got something in common."

"Yeah." She stretches her face in pretend surprise. "I'm glad you finally see it. You're the one who's Miss Personality, Bunny. You bubble like a fountain!"

I grin. "I have to do *something*. To distract people from noticing I don't know who or what I am."

"So we end up together. That's pretty funny."

"It is, you know?" I look at her and we burst out giggling.

"Geez! I spilled tea all over myself!"

Mary Anderson Parks

"Good, it'll warm you up. Bunny, I've got something to tell you. You're my best friend, right?"

I try to suppress the joy her words bring. It scares me to feel this good. I nod my head and lean closer.

"I've met a boy, Bunny. Handsome and intelligent and—oh, I don't know what! He makes me dream."

"That's wonderful, Cork."

"I think he's crazy about me!"

"I don't see how he could be anything else. Whoever he is. Is he in one of your classes?"

"Art history! Isn't that perfect? He adores art."

"Yes, it's perfect! Tell me more about him."

"His name's Richard. Richard Hagopian." She beams, savoring the syllables of his name. I feel a wave of nausea. How could this be happening? No wonder all he and I do is talk. He's crazy about Cork.

"Did you hear me? He's *Armenian*. My parents will *die*!"

I find I'm unable to say even a single word, but Cork doesn't seem to notice.

"So far all we've done is go out for coffee and ice cream. But the last time we did, he tried to kiss me! And now he wants to take me to his uncle's restaurant. He says he can't wait to show me off! Oh Bunny, I'm so thrilled, but I try not to let him see it. He's so much the right one for me."

I look down into my cup, blinking quickly, hoping she won't see my eyes filled with tears.

Because of school, I had cut my work at the Indian Center to twenty hours a week, enough to pay my share of rent and food, but after what Cork told me at the Shakespeare Garden, I decide to ask for extra hours. It would help to be busier. Work takes me out of myself and my own troubles and at the same time makes me feel more myself than I've ever been. Is that how it is for Rose, I wonder.

I arrive early the morning I plan to ask for extra hours. The room with all our desks crowded together looks small when empty of people. Soon all the desks will have someone sitting at them. Whole families will be gathered around, mothers, fathers and children fresh off reservations. Noreen will call all over the city and the East Bay, helping fathers find jobs. We'll go with mothers to enroll their kids in school, because some of them speak only Indian. But before jobs and school come food and housing. It keeps us all running, that's for sure. I've never felt so needed in my whole life, though I wonder about the over-all effect of what we're doing. Most of them want to go home. They're used to having aunts and uncles, cousins and grandparents to help with the kids. They feel lonely and out of place here in the city.

They look so lost when they first arrive, and it doesn't get better. The families who've been here awhile aren't happy at all. Nothing is how they thought it would be. The BIA promised a good life would be waiting for them. I've already seen some give up and go home.

Mary Anderson Parks

Just as I'm thinking someone must be here because the place was unlocked, the door to Clarice Rawlins' office opens and I hear her voice, loud and strident. She's on a rampage.

"I want you to get rid of that girl," I hear her say.

Then Noreen's voice, placating, trying to soothe, "Well now, she's been doing a fine job helping out here. Folks like her and she's getting to be—"

"I don't want to hear another word. I just want her out. The BIA people are coming tomorrow and if they decide to cut off our funding, we're up shit creek without a paddle. I don't want any dizzy blondes running around, do you hear? Get her out today!"

Noreen is silent. She's probably thinking about her kids and how much she needs her job.

"Donations haven't been what I expected," Clarice Rawlins goes on. "When we opened a year ago, I thought we'd get half our funding from private sources, but it's a wrestling match to dig even a dime out of people's pockets."

"I guess they don't understand how desperate the need is," Noreen says.

"I certainly tell them! I have to go to all those boring luncheons and teas with people in furs and expensive suits. That's why I have to dress well myself. I don't know if anyone here understands that. Part of the budget has to go for my car upkeep, too."

"I wasn't questioning any of that," Noreen says cautiously.

I start backing toward the front door, hoping to get out before I'm thrown out, but I trip over a wastebasket. I am sprawled on the floor when Clarice rushes out, Noreen close behind.

"Were you spying on us?" Clarice Rawlins' face is contorted with fury. She looks like the wicked witch of the west.

"No, I just got to work early is all. And somehow I fell over." I get back up on my feet, cradling a sore elbow.

Noreen is at my side, examining my arm, clucking over me like a mother hen. "Poor thing, you've got a bruise coming on."

"Well!" Clarice draws herself up to tower over both of us.

"You take care of telling her, Noreen." She retreats into her office, slamming the door.

"Oh honey, she's all pushed out of shape." Noreen keeps her voice low. "The auditors that were here last month are questioning some of her expenses, and now she's afraid we'll lose our funding. She's in such a state, I'm afraid we're going to have to let you go. I feel so bad."

"Don't feel bad, Noreen. I'll find a job. All I need is part-time. Maybe the bakery will take me back." I say it to make her grin and it works. I've told her about the lady who returned the cake I put salt in instead of sugar, and how she demanded the baker and I eat a slice while she watched.

"Really, Noreen, I'm sure I can find another job. It's just that I'll miss all of you." I hold back my tears.

"You be sure to come and see us, honey. Anytime." Her eyes dart toward Clarice's office. "I could maybe slip out with you down to the corner for a cuppa coffee." But we both know that won't happen. Clarice doesn't let anybody go slipping out anywhere. And Noreen knows I heard what Clarice said about me and that I won't feel comfortable coming back.

"Say goodbye to Art for me? And the others?"

She nods, puts her arms around me and pulls me to her bosom for a long hug. Rose has never hugged me like this. Not in all these years. I wish I could stay forever in Noreen's hug.

"I hope we'll still be here when you come by next time!"

I wave from the doorway. We both know we'll never see each other again.

Back on the sidewalk, I feel cold. I stare at the closed door remembering that last week I heard Noreen make a call to an adoption agency for an adopted woman who wanted to find out what tribe she was.

Would somebody at an adoption agency talk to me if I called? Would they tell me who my mother is? I walk slower, thrilled and frightened by the thought. Maybe someday I'll find the nerve to try. Right now I feel pretty crushed. First I lose Richard and now I have to give up these people I've loved so much being with.

Mary Anderson Parks

I've been trying to act like my usual self, which is sort of all I have, and I've thrown myself into studying. I want to go deeper, figure out the mystery of why I'm the way I am. I've been trying to find the answers by reading. That seems safest and easiest.

A couple of teachers at City have surprised me by how good they are. They've helped me understand the depth involved in learning and that so far I've been skimming the surface. We're reading Virginia Woolf in English lit. "We'll start with something that appears simple," the teacher said, "but it isn't."

Virginia Woolf's writing stimulates the part of me that grows in silence, deep inside, apart from other people and their power to crush and diminish what I think before it is half thought. Reading *Mrs. Dalloway*, I yearn to immerse myself in the ocean of love and life, lower myself into its depths and swim there with no words necessary. Her writing goes beyond words, to a place inside. So why do I scribble word after word in this little blank book Richard gave me? Yes, I see a lot of Richard now, thanks to Cork. He thinks my ideas are interesting and I ought to write them down.

Cork is just about perfect, so it shouldn't surprise me to find out the boy I'm in love with is like an adoring puppy around her. I guess it is Cork who'll get to meet that big wonderful family of his. I console myself that I'll see Richard often with him hanging around Cork so much and us being in world history together. I just hope I can take it.

He came by yesterday when I was reading zoology. Cork was out. Somebody had left the door to the apartment building unlocked. I recognized his knock and yelled for him to come in, madly fluffing my newly permed and peroxided hair. Last week Cork and I gave each other home perms. Hers is light and mine is tight. I was sitting on the daybed by the window in the sun, propped against pillows, my bare feet planted on the warm coverlet. Over my bra and panties, I had on one of Cork's father's discarded shirts. I had just taken a bath. I've picked up the habit from Cork of wearing an old white shirt around the house. For her it's a painting smock. For me it's freedom.

Cork teases me about how much time I spend in the bathtub. We both think it's great to do exactly what we want. We never make our beds and hardly ever put clothes away. We laugh about her ad. "I was still thinking like Mother," she explained. "When things are drilled into you for nineteen years . . ." A socialite: that's how she describes her mother. A woman who spends thirty minutes at her dressing table putting on her face and has two huge, very organized closets of clothes. Some things she wears only once and then gives to charity. Cork says her mother spends her days shopping, lunching, telling the cook-housekeeper what to do, and going to the beauty parlor. She swears her mother doesn't read the magazines she gets, but only looks at the pictures, and the only book she reads is her appointment book. Cork's mother sometimes stays in her bedroom with a sick headache, like Rose used to do before her job at the hospital. We will be spared that fate, Cork and I promise ourselves.

I told Richard all these things when he came by to visit Cork and she wasn't here. I stayed on my end of the daybed, my knees drawn up to my chin, the tails of Cork's father's shirt tucked under my bare feet. Richard sat on the other end. He had a thoughtful, worried look when I told him about Cork's mother. Maybe he's intimidated like I am by how rich they are. He tried to change the subject. He wanted to hear about my family, but I didn't want to talk about Rose and Brad. "They're not my real family," I announced, to get it out of the way. "I'm adopted,"

"Wow," he said. "Whew!" He got up and paced around the room the way he does when he's stirred up and thinking something through. "You should write about that, you know? How that makes you feel." Then he surprised me. "Some day I want you to meet my aunt and uncle and their kids. They'd love you."

Will he take me and Cork both? At the same time? Maybe he's just saying what he wishes could happen. From what he's told me, I know that most of the time they're all busy working in the restaurant. It would be fun to visit them there. I could pitch in and help, like one of the family.

By the time Cork got home I was dressed and ready to go to my new job at the school bookstore. I didn't tell her about receiving her boyfriend in my underwear and her dad's shirt. I don't think she'd understand. Other than that, I was good. I kept my mind on what we were talking about, like he was doing. I'm proud of that.

All I told Cork was that Richard dropped by, hoping to find her in.

"How did you get your mom and dad to let you do this?" I sit in the middle of the daybed, gazing at a room dominated by Cork's paintings, a wild swirl of motion and color. Cork is doing push-ups on her exercise mat, in white shorts and a red polo shirt.

She flips over to her back and starts her sit-ups. "Do what?"

"Move into your own place."

She finishes a set of thirty with knee-lifts, then rises to a sitting position and presses the soles of her feet together.

"What I did is I started painting in my bedroom. I'd been using my allowances to buy oils, brushes, canvases, an easel." She lowers her upper body flat on the floor between her outspread legs.

"God, I wish I could do that."

"You could. You need to do it every day until you can get all the way down."

I wiggle my bare toes, which feels like enough exercise.

"The ultimate betrayal," Cork mutters to the floor.

"What?" I lean forward, trying to see her face.

"I got red oil paint on her pink rug. The one she dragged me to ten stores to pick out."

"I knew your room would be pink."

Cork sits up straight, shoots me a look of disbelief. "Do I look like a pink type of girl?"

"No," I laugh. "I just knew your mom would surround you with pink."

"Mauve." Cork lengthens her mouth to say the word. "That's what she calls it. Shades of mauve and rose."

"So you spilled paint on her mauve and rose rug?"

"I did it on purpose." Her eyes gleam. "I got paint on the wall, too, and on the lampshade. Even on the canopy over my bed."

"You have a canopy bed?"

"She saw a picture of one and decided that's what I'd always wanted."

"Did she do that to Susan, too?"

"No, Susan she couldn't touch."

"Is Susan really different from you?"

"She's a straight A student. Hell, she's better than straight A. She got extra credit in all her math and science classes."

"How much older is she?"

"Four and a half years."

"Was that hard on you? Did anybody at Lowell remember her by the time you got there?"

"Are you kidding? I was known as Susan Newberry's little sister. The athletic one. Only I'm not littler, I'm bigger." Cork drops her head and rolls it slowly from side to side.

"And more beautiful. I bet she's not nearly as beautiful."

Cork scrunches up her face like a pig, making me laugh.

"Susan's got Daddy's brains and coloring, but not his size. She's a little blonde mouse with thick glasses."

"And you're brunette!"

"Mom has some Greek in her, that's where it comes from. She's mostly Swedish, though, and Daddy's pure English." Cork stretches her arms out behind her and clasps her hands, looking at me searchingly. "What are you, Bunny? You've got the darkest eyes! I love your eyes. They're almost black."

"I don't know what I am. Remember?"

"Sorry! I was caught up in thinking how it would be to paint you."

I reach for the bottle of nail polish and change the subject.

"Tell me more about Susan. Is she a teacher or what?"

"She's in medical school."

"You mean she's going to be a nurse."

"No, I mean she's going to be a doctor. Like Daddy."

"But she's a girl!"

"I know. Unbelievable, isn't it? I think it helped her to get admitted because of Daddy. She's the only girl in her class."

"I didn't know girls could be doctors."

"Nothing stops Susan!"

"You admire her, don't you?"

"Well, yeah! I mean, who wouldn't?" Cork stares off into a corner, resting her hands on her thighs. "Susan lives in a world of her own. She has this love, this actual love, for science. Nothing else matters. She never even knows what she's wearing."

"Does it bother you? Her being such a good student?"

"Not exactly. We're so different. She and I have always known that. I just wish Daddy could . . . I don't know. Appreciate me the way I am, I guess."

"What happened after you got paint on everything?"

"Mom backed me up when I told him I needed to be on my own and have a place where I could do art." Cork smiles gleefully. "I even dribbled paint on the hallway carpet. I told her it's a necessary hazard when you don't have a sink in your room to clean brushes. It worked!"

Cork is devious. It's not something I would have suspected. A little troubled, I file this new trait into a corner of my mind.

"You shouldn't patch up your nail polish like that, Bunny. It's better to remove it and put on a new coat."

"It's a habit." I'm still thinking about her doing all that paint-spilling to get her way. "Couldn't you just have explained? What you needed?"

"What do you mean?"

"Did you ever just ask your parents if you could move out on your own?"

"Directness doesn't work with them. I've tried it. I tried to get them to let me go to art school, but all they care about is for me to bring up my grades so I can go to a 'real' college." She makes a disgusted face. "Anyway, it's hard to get their attention.

Daddy's never home. And when Mom is, she's usually on the phone."

Our phone rings and Cork sighs. "That's probably her now." She picks up the receiver and says "Hi." I watch her face change. "It's Richard." She mouths the words. For one second I wait. Do I think he might be calling for me? As I watch her settle back against the red pillows, looking gorgeous with her gleaming brown hair curling perfectly around her face, I realize how dumb I am. I flee to the bathroom and am plucking my eyebrows when Cork's voice intrudes, calling me. Why? I stick my head out the door.

"Bunny, Richard wants to know if you and I will go with him to a poetry reading." She says it like she's never heard of such a thing.

"Sure, why not?"

"I don't get it," she tells him. "Are you coming over here to go with us or what?" I hear the deep tones of Richard's voice. "You're over there right now? Well, what's it called? Where is it? Write this down, Bunny. City Lights? Near Broadway? Wait, Richard, for Bunny to find a pencil."

"I know where City Lights is."

"How do you know a thing like that?" She looks adorable in her puzzlement. I'm in love with both of them, so the three of us being together may not be that bad. Didn't the poet Shelley have two women? Is that where Richard got the idea? Maybe I'll ask him. What the hell.

"I don't know, Richard," Cork says, "this sounds so weird. My mom would drop dead if she knew I went to a place on Fillmore." She pauses to listen. "He wants to talk to you."

"Why?"

"I don't know."

She hands me the phone as I sit down next to her.

"Richard?"

"Listen, Bunny, can you explain to Cork what City Lights Bookstore is? Tell her a guy named Lawrence Ferlinghetti started it. He came out here from New York because this is where things are happening."

They Called Me Bunny   173

"Yeah, I know who Ferlinghetti is."

Richard breathes out a sigh. "Well, that's good. Cork didn't have a clue what I was talking about. She'll love it though, once she gets here."

"You want us to go right this minute? To a bookstore?"

"Geez, Bunny. This isn't just 'a bookstore.' Everybody's down here, all fired up about the reading on Fillmore. It's at a place called Six Gallery that used to be a garage. Allen Ginsberg and some other beat poets are reading there tonight."

"Beat poets! Is that what you call them?"

"It's the Beat Generation, Bunny. We're part of it. It's the cultural revolution of the century. God, Cork's an artist and doesn't even—never mind, just meet me down here, okay? You can't go over to Fillmore by yourselves."

"Ferlinghetti wrote 'Pictures of the Gone World,' right?" The title stuck in my mind because it made me think of the part of my life that's gone. Only I don't have pictures. I wish I could tell Richard how that feels. I know I said the title to impress him. It's not like I'm hiding that from myself. Maybe this is one guy who the way to reach him is through his mind. The thought excites me. But Cork grabs the receiver.

"This is me again. Remember me? Cork? What should I wear?" She listens with widening eyes. "What in god's name is a granny dress? You're kidding, aren't you? You're so cute, Richard. You really are." She hangs up. "What should I wear, Bunny?"

"What's wrong with what you have on?" My mind has taken off on a path of its own.

"I'm wearing shorts."

"Cork, are you a virgin?"

The question brings a quick frown to her face. "That's not something we talk about." She looks at me sideways. "What are you laughing at?"

"You! I bet you sounded just like your mother when you said that."

"I probably did. But I was brought up that way, you know? Not to talk about certain things? So I feel uncomfortable when they come up." She pulls on a pair of white socks. I know she wants to ask me if I'm a virgin and can't bring herself to do it. I've already gotten my answer. She is. There's an innocence about Cork. For all her beauty and the confidence it gives her, she's still an awkward athlete, uncalculating about her body's effect on others. There's purity in her. Nobody has scarred her. Suddenly the last thing in the world I want is for her to ask me if I'm a virgin. I pull out a bureau drawer and start flinging sweaters at her.

"What on earth are you doing?"

"I want you to pick one for me to wear. No, I've got an idea! Let's trade, okay? You wear mine and I'll wear yours."

"Yours won't fit me, Bunny. I'm four inches taller."

"Hmm. I didn't think about that."

Cork ends up wearing her white twin sweater set and I wear my brown one. I've never had a white sweater. That seems fitting, somehow, maybe even symbolic.

"So what's the big deal about this City Light Bookstore? How do you know about it?"

"From a terrific English teacher I had in high school, Miss Angstrom. She took us there and we met Lawrence Ferlinghetti."

"Who's Lawrence Ferlinspaghetti?"

I laugh, though I'm not sure she mispronounced his name on purpose. "He's this beatnik guy who writes poetry. He owns the place."

At City Lights, we're the youngest ones there. And the most ordinary looking. Everybody else is wearing black or dressed like a gypsy with drooping clothes and heavy jewelry. I hadn't noticed such a large number of odd people when we came here with Miss Angstrom. Our class took over the whole place. The rest of the scene became a backdrop for our kidding around and noise. Richard leads us through aisles of books, pointing out titles. I guess one old guy sizes up the situation and figures out I'm the fifth wheel. He sidles up and offers to buy me a cup of coffee.

"Uh, no thanks. I'm actually headed out of here pretty soon for a poetry reading."

"Yeah, me too. I wouldn't miss it." He looks gentle and harmless, though over-eager. He's probably about thirty. It's hard to tell with the beard.

"Do you come here often?" I ask.

"Yeah, I live here in North Beach. My name's Dave."

"Who's Bunny talking to?" I hear Richard ask Cork.

Dave pulls a roll of Lifesavers from a pocket in his baggy trousers. "Want one?"

"Sure." I take a red one from the top.

"Is that the color you want?"

"Yeah, red's my favorite. Next to grape."

He grins, like we're old friends already. I'm starting to feel I could get into this beatnik life.

"Is Allen Ginsberg around?" I ask.

"No, Al's probably already over there."

Gee, he knows him, calls him by a nickname even. Suddenly Richard leans close and whispers in my ear, "Watch out for that guy, he's after you." I go hot with excitement from Richard's breath in my ear.

"He's old," I whisper back. Richard chuckles and shakes his head.

Cork draws Richard away and Dave asks, "What's your name?"

"Bunny."

"Hi, Bunny!" We both laugh for no reason.

"Want to go over to the reading with me? My car—"

"Bunny's coming with us." Richard takes hold of my arm and pulls me with him. "We better get going. It'll be crowded."

"Bye Dave. See you there!" I call over my shoulder.

From my seat on the bus, behind Cork and Richard, I look out the window and see more and more Negro people. Why is the poetry reading in the Fillmore? Is that part of the cultural revolution?

Once we're inside Six Gallery, I can't see anything because I'm too short and everyone is crushed together and the air is thick with smoke. A crazy-looking guy comes by with a jug of wine and offers us a swig. We don't take him up on it, but Richard whispers close to my ear, "That was Kerouac!" His excitement floods into me. I wish he'd whisper in my ear forever.

"Who is Kerouac?" I ask, but Richard doesn't hear.

"My mother would die," Cork keeps repeating and Richard keeps answering, "Isn't it great, though?"

"What's that funny smell?" Cork asks.

Richard inhales a deep breath. "I think it's marijuana."

How handsome Richard is, with his glowing dark eyes. Of the three of us, he is the only one tall enough to see what's going on.

"Hey," he tells us, "Philip Lamantia's going to read first." He puts his arm around Cork as quiet gradually comes over the room. The black painted walls, lined with people, seem to be pressing everybody close together. The words of Philip Lamantia and then Philip Whalen pass over my head as I stand uncomprehending and unseeing in the crowd. The next one is someone called Michael McClure. Richard gets even more keyed up when he is introduced. He helps Cork and me wedge ourselves forward so we can see. I have never before heard the word "fuck" said in public to an audience. This guy belts out a whole poem in which "fuck" is the most frequent word. Cork rolls her eyes and we both get the giggles. The funny thing is, he's wearing a suit and he's the most proper looking of them all.

There's a short intermission, and then Richard tells us, "Here comes Allen Ginsberg." Allen Ginsberg has a mop of black hair and horn-rimmed glasses. He says he's going to read from his poem "Howl." The guy named Kerouac has gone up to sit on the side of the low stage and is drinking from his jug of wine. The words of "Howl" roll out and over us like a torrent, disturbing and shocking. I feel swept along inside the rhythm and the images. This guy Kerouac yells out "Go, go, go!" at the end of some lines. He's a real character. Other people join in with shouts and I know I'm not the only one getting all stirred up. I feel the words and thoughts beating into me, my mind racing along with the flow of them.

"Whadda ya think?" Richard whispers.

"I've never heard anything like it," I whisper back. "He questions *everything*."

"I know. Isn't it great?"

"I also think he may be drunk," I add. Richard laughs out loud and Cork turns to him in surprise. "They're all drunk," I whisper to her. "Or else it's the marijuana."

"Yeah, it's crazy, huh?" She looks as beautiful as I've ever seen her, her face flushed, her eyes shining.

When Allen Ginsberg finishes reading, everyone explodes in applause and he leaves the stage in tears. I've never seen a man cry before. It makes me think his poem really is a howl that comes from deep inside him. What a mind the man has. He's got this whole roomful of people filled with emotion.

Another man reads poetry he's written, but I'm still thinking about "Howl."

When we start making our way out, everybody's moving slowly in a communal, dreamlike surge. We're caught up in the energy of what's been happening and don't want it to end. On the sidewalk, Richard takes a deep breath of cold night air. With a tender smile on his face, he says to Cork, "I'll always remember being here with you tonight, October 7, 1955." He looks deep into her eyes. My glance drops to the pavement.

48

A few days later I twist my ankle coming up our stairs and the next day I tell Cork it hurts too much for me to go with them on the picnic we had planned. I limp around making it seem a lot worse than it is. The real reason is I don't want to have to watch Richard look into her eyes the way he did on Fillmore Street. I help her make ham and cheese sandwiches.

She is gone five hours and comes back with a new and different sparkle in her eyes. She moves differently, too. I notice right away but of course I don't say anything.

"We went to Muni Pier. It was marvelous, Bunny." I notice she doesn't say she wishes I had been there. "The pier curves out into the bay and you can see so much all at once just by turning around. Alcatraz is so close! Richard calls it 'The Rock.'" Even the way she says his name is different. "He made me see it through the eyes of the prisoners, how it must be for them looking out the windows, thinking about escaping by swimming to shore."

"Did you do any sketches, like you wanted to?"

"I started one, but I didn't get very far." She blushes and tries to hide her face by busying herself with unpacking the bag she took with her.

"I'm going to go lie down. My ankle is killing me."

Stretched out flat and hopeless on my bed, I try to shut out thoughts of Cork and Richard holding each other, Cork and Richard making love. I hear her humming in the kitchen, contented, fulfilled. Where did they do it, I torture myself by wondering. Neither of them has a car.

Weeks go by without Cork and me having a real conversation. I tell myself it's not Cork's fault I am so miserable. It's just the way things are. I act like everything's fine. I'm good at that, I've had a lot of practice. I keep busy with school and my job at the bookstore but I'm so lonesome I can't bear it. I need Cork back in my life. I feel myself slipping away. I decide to confide in her about Rose and Brad, about what's wrong with us.

"They don't know how to love each other, so how could they love me?"

"People do, though."

"Do what?"

"Love their kids better than each other."

I file my thumbnail to a perfect oval, then flick my wrist to admire it and knock over an open bottle of nail polish. Cork shakes her head. She's getting used to my clumsiness. I grab her paint cloth to mop up the spill, then screw the lid shut. "Maybe it's that Rose and Brad don't know how to love themselves." I wonder how I know that, and if it is true.

"Maybe nobody's ever really loved them." Cork speaks in her innocent, wise way. We sit cross-legged on the floor, she directly in front of her easel, waiting for inspiration.

"We visited Rose's mother just once." I shudder, remembering the clean, bare kitchen and the tall, stern woman who said, *So this is the little girl,* and then whispered to Rose, *She's awfully dark, I thought you said she wasn't that dark.* "Rose seemed afraid of her mother," I tell Cork, and I move a little closer to her. "I felt sorry for Rose."

"Don't you think Rose felt love when they first adopted you?"

"For Rose, it was 'discharging a loving duty.' I've heard her use those exact words. That's how she and the ladies in Bible Study talk."

"But there was love in it, she used the word *love!*" Cork's eyes grow very round.

"I know you want me to feel loved, Cork. And I do, that's the funny part. I must have been loved a lot in that first year when

I was with my real family."

"Enough to last a lifetime by the look of you."

"You mean you can see it in me?"

"Love sticks out all over you, Bunny."

"Maybe it's just my need for it that sticks out! I'll tell you one thing, and I'm dead serious."

"You? Serious?" She wrinkles her nose.

"Yeah, me serious. I'm never doing *nothing* out of duty. Everything I ever do will be from love."

"Wow. You sound like you mean it."

"It's my manifesto."

"What are you, some kind of Communist?" Cork grins and gives me a push, toppling me over into the pile of pillows.

"Yeah, I'm some kind of Communist." My voice comes out muffled.

"I liked what you said once about the way communism is supposed to be. What was it? From each according to his ability, and to each . . ."

"According to his need."

"Yeah, I like that!" A hint of worry creeps into her eyes.

"What?"

"Would I be able to paint in a Communist society? Would that count as an ability?"

"It should. I know I need your paintings. They make me feel things I didn't know I could feel."

"So. I'd be meeting your need." She looks satisfied. Then she leans forward, peering at me intently.

"Why are you looking at me like that?"

"You have the most amazing cheekbones."

"I do not. My face is too wide. I look like the Cheshire Cat in Alice in Wonderland."

"Stop grinning like an idiot, Bunny. Can I draw you? Will you hold still?"

"Really? You want to draw me?"

"Think about something serious and look up at that painting over there." Cork reaches for her sketchbook.

"But you never do people."

"I want to get the way your bones are, Bunny. There's something different about you. The way your eyes are, too. Just a sketch, okay? It won't take more than a few minutes. I'll either get it or I won't."

Cork glances up frequently, working steadily. After several minutes, she drops her hands to her sides.

"Can I look at it?"

She turns the pad and lets me see the sketch.

"You've made me look wistful and sad."

"I see that in you, Bunny. You cover it up, but it's always there."

Tears spring to my eyes. It is the first time anyone has recognized that part of me.

"Someday I'll do a painting from it." She looks thoughtfully from the sketch to me and back. "Something about the way your eyes are set above your cheekbones. So lovely."

I get up, find my history book and go to the daybed, where I sit gazing out at the sky, my book unopened.

"You don't seem like an only child," Cork stands at her easel, contemplating its white blankness.

"I'm not. What do you mean by that?"

"What do you mean, you're not?"

"I'm not, Cork. I've got a family somewhere. I know it. I used to be with them. Somewhere in my head all those memories are there."

"Memories of what?"

"I can't tell you, it's nothing clear. They come and go. Someday when one is happening, I'll tell you." I watch her stir paint, then pace around the room like she does before she starts a picture. "What did you mean, that I don't seem like an only child?"

"You're social. You get along with people easily. And you're not spoiled rotten."

I grin. "It's hard to imagine Rose and Brad spoiling anybody rotten."

"What are they like? I still can't see them."

"I don't know, that's the problem. I've never felt I know them.

They Called Me Bunny   183

For some reason they decided to adopt a kid. I guess 'cause they couldn't have one and everybody else had kids. They're not very original. Then, once they got me, oh I don't know, let's talk about something else."

"No." Cork frowns at the blank canvas. "I want to talk about this. How old did you say you were when they got you?"

"They said I was one year. But why do I remember things from before, if I was just a year old?"

"Maybe you were older?"

"I don't know. After Brad left, I thought maybe I could get Rose to tell me more, but it didn't happen. I never talked to them much. I always played outside with other kids. It felt lonely in our house."

Cork makes two bold red strokes across her canvas. "That's why," she says.

"Why what?"

"Why you're not like an only child. 'Cause you played a lot with other kids."

"Why I played with other kids is because I was used to being with other kids." I say it stubbornly, wanting it to be true, the big family of my dreams.

"Why would you have ended up being adopted? I don't get it."

"Maybe my mother was crazy. Or people thought she was. Maybe she was a drunk and they took us from her. Maybe something bad was happening and she thought we'd have a better life with white people." I listen to my own words in astonishment.

"You are dark, aren't you?"

"Of course I am."

"You could be Italian."

"Why do people always say that? I could be a lot of things."

"Sorry. I didn't mean it as an insult."

"I know. It just drives me crazy, not knowing anything about who I am. And wondering how much Rose and Brad know or don't know."

"You could do something about it."

"What?"

"Go to the agency where you were adopted and ask. I know a girl who did. She really loved her parents, the people who raised her, and she didn't want them to find out she was doing it and be hurt. But when she was twenty-one, she went secretly to the adoption agency and—"

"Did they tell her who her parents were?"

"All I know is they told her that her father was Irish and her mother German and French."

"How did she know which agency to go to?"

"She found some papers in an old box of souvenirs."

"And that's all they told her, that she was Irish and German and French?"

"They told her stuff like how tall her mother was and how much she weighed and what color—"

"What if her mother were still alive, she might have wanted to meet her daughter if she knew she was asking about her."

Cork looks shocked. "You've got to think about her right to privacy, Bunny! Maybe she married somebody who didn't know and—"

"What about my rights and every adopted person's right to know who the hell we are, doesn't that count?"

"You're getting awfully emotional about this, Bunny."

I stuff a pillow over my face so Cork won't see me cry.

"Bunny, are you okay?"

"Of course I'm okay."

When I uncover one eye, Cork is at work on the lower righthand corner of her canvas, painting in something brown that might be an animal. "You could even be . . ." Her voice trails off.

"What? I could be what?"

"Oh, I don't know."

"No, what were you thinking?"

"Nothing. Really nothing, Bunny."

That's me, I think. Good old nothing.

I don't tell Cork about the thousands of times I've wondered why they didn't want me, why they didn't come and get me. I don't tell her how hard it is to hang onto the memory of being loved, how it takes every ounce of strength I have, and how sometimes it all seems like a sham, a trick I've played on myself.

The only time I feel wanted is when I'm with a boy. The act of making love, of fitting into each other's bodies, that's the most fulfillment I get. Work and study are satisfying, but the yearning for someone to be with doesn't go away. Sex makes my world fall into place. While it's happening and for a while afterward, it's the be-all and end-all. That's why every now and then I still call up Joe Doolin. He knows why, I know why. Someday he'll get married and that will be the end of it. I wouldn't go with a married man, even if he wanted me to.

We do it during my safe period. Joe taught me about safe periods. The five days right before my period starts and right after it's over. I'm pretty regular so that makes it easy to know when we can do it. I still wash afterward, too.

We are side by side on Cork's bed, our backs against the headboard. It is very dark outside.

"Cork, I remembered something last night."

She lays down her textbook and looks at me. That's one of the things I like about her, that way she has of giving herself to you. I waited half an hour to say those words, not wanting to interrupt her studying, or maybe I was afraid to say them.

"What? What did you remember?"

"A big sister. Kind of like you."

"Like me how?"

"Like I could trust her."

"Good, that's good." She lengthens herself out on the bed, her head on the pillow. "What else do you remember?"

"Yawning darkness." I say the words into the lighted room and fear courses through my veins. Cork senses it.

She reaches up and takes hold of my hand. "Something happened to you in the dark. Stretch out. Like me. You'll feel better this way."

"No, I can't tell you what I remembered unless I stay right here." I lay down the book I'd been pretending to read.

"Go on then."

"It was a darkness that yawned because something hid in it."

I feel her waiting, but I can't go on.

"Something really bad happened, to hurt you."

"No. It didn't, Cork. It didn't because of my big sister."

They Called Me Bunny

A smile touches her face, a relaxing of tension around her mouth and eyes.

I remember more as I tell it. "She used to bring mattresses from all the beds and put them side by side in the corner. With hers in front, nearest the door."

I fall silent and Cork asks, "Did you all help? Were the rest of you big enough to help?"

"The bigger ones did." Suddenly I see a baby's wobbling head. "I think there was a baby."

"Were you all girls?"

I chew on my lower lip, counting shadows. "I think there was a brother. And six of us girls. Or five. I was a little one."

I squeeze my eyes tightly shut. It works. More memories come to flow out of my mouth and into Cork's listening body. "My big sisters put themselves in front of us little ones. Like frontline soldiers. When the grownups—" Something snaps as I say that word and tears run down my face. "They weren't, were they? Grownups. They hadn't grown up at all. They just drank until they didn't know shit."

Cork frowns and tightens her hold on my hand. "No. They weren't grownups, Bunny, or your sisters wouldn't have had to protect you from them."

With my eyes squeezed shut, full of tears, I see the room with us children huddled on mattresses. "My big sister had a knife," I whisper. "That's how she protected us when the drunk men came to the door. She was like you, Cork, confident and strong and sure she was right. They sensed that in her, drunk as they were. They backed out with their hands in the air, laughing."

"How many times did they come?" Cork breathes.

"I don't know. I think that was the last time. I don't think my sister got the knife until after . . ." I lose clarity as I see her carried away by a drunken man. "We slept like that all together with the big ones in front, us little ones piled like kittens in back of them. Except cats wouldn't do that to their kittens."

"Yeah, they do." Cork scoots herself up to sit against the headboard with me. "Cats don't get drunk. But they fuck their children and brothers and sisters."

Mary Anderson Parks

"We're all animals."

"Humans have brains," Cork says. "We're not supposed to use them to mess each other up." I feel her struggling to help me, unsure how to do it.

"It's okay, Cork, I'm glad I remembered more." But it isn't okay. Where was Mother?

"Could I sleep here with you?"

"Of course," she says. I slide under the covers and Cork goes on sitting there, her hand resting on my shoulder. With her other hand she reaches out and turns the bedside lamp to its lowest setting, so it is dark enough to sleep but not scary dark.

When I awaken in the morning, she is asleep beside me with her mouth open, her breath as gentle as the fall of rose petals, and I think for the thousandth time how beautiful she is. Then I remember something else. Something happening now, in the present. The last time Richard phoned, it was to talk to me. He called at a time he knew Cork wouldn't be home. We talked for an hour.

How could I let myself hurt Cork? But why am I thinking that? How could he be interested in me, the fucked-up one? An image comes of Richard's body pressed against mine. I push it down with other images buried in the pit of my stomach and ease out of bed. Cork turns to the other side and closes her mouth, goes on sleeping. I am surprised how light I feel. Have I lost weight from all the memories that came out? I go to the bathroom and study my face in the mirror. One of us ought to do some cleaning, it's getting hard to see my reflection. But I look okay. I even see why Richard might call to talk to me and then I feel guilty, thinking that. But Cork has so much. She's always had everything, how could she mind one guy lost? She could. I need to get out of this place, not be here when he calls.

I splash cold water on my face, get dressed, put on lipstick and mascara and hurry off to my job at the bookstore. I get there half an hour early and the place isn't open. In my rush to run away from my thoughts I forgot to eat, so I buy milk and doughnuts at the student union. After three hours of work I go to English lit, then head straight for the library and get in some studying. Cork isn't home when I return to the apartment. Probably she's with Richard. On an impulse, I pick up the phone and call Rose.

"Hi, how're you doing?"

"Your father called two nights ago." There is a pause. "To find out if you were still living here. When I told him no, he wanted your address."

"I hope you didn't give it to him."

"I had misplaced it."

I breathe a sigh of relief. "What else did he have to say?"

"That was all. He seemed anxious to hang up. Like he hadn't even wanted to talk to me in the first place." I notice the odd, dry tone of her voice. There is an awkward silence.

"Is work okay?"

"Yes, it's fine. I'll be quite busy for the next two months. I'm taking a refresher course. To bring my skills up to date."

"That's wonderful, Rose. What a good idea."

"It's important to stay up to date. There've been big changes in medicine."

"And you'll be right on top of them!"

"Well, I'll try."

It never occurs to her to ask how I'm doing, so I tell her.

"School's going along pretty good."

"Oh, that's nice. Bunny, *What's My Line* is coming on. I better go."

"Sure, don't miss the beginning. Well, 'bye then."

Rose has never come to see the apartment, never asked me to bring Cork over to meet her. She's been hurt badly. I need to remember that. It's selfish to wish she cared how I'm doing. It must be hard for her that when Brad finally called, all he did was ask about me. I should go see her, make sure she's all right. My visits have become less frequent, maybe because neither of us seems to get much out of them.

On Saturday I jump on a bus and pop in unexpected. I find Rose standing in the hallway, an envelope in one hand, an official-looking letter in the other. She looks startled to see me, even a little scared.

"Hi, what's up?"

Rose just stands there, holding the letter out to one side, as if it might be a time bomb.

I try humor. "Did Brad get drafted or what?"

"Bunny, could we go in the kitchen and sit down?"

Am I imagining the quiver in her voice? I am surprised to see a fire going in the fireplace. I can't remember ever seeing the fireplace used before.

"Sure! It'll be good to take a load off my feet."

We sit in our usual places. Rose has the table all cleared off and wiped clean as usual, but I notice dirty dishes in the sink. She stares at the white-flecked yellow formica. "Bunny, there's something we should have told you, your father and I."

She is covering the name on the letterhead with a trembling hand.

"Something about the letter? Something about that?"

There is a film over her eyes. I can't read her expression.

"Bunny, we never thought you'd need to know. I mean, it didn't seem to matter, we didn't want it to matter . . ."

"What?" I ask. "What didn't you want to matter? Is this about me?" A strange feeling creeps into my stomach.

"What I mean is, we always hoped you'd feel like our very

own daughter, and the past just wouldn't matter. It was the adoption worker who said we should tell you that you were adopted. I thought we could keep that a secret, but she told us it wouldn't be a good idea."

I take a deep breath that comes out all shaky. "Is that a letter from the adoption agency?" I am dying to read it, to hold it in my hand. It's something about my mother, I feel sure.

Rose frowns at the letter. "Yes, but it isn't they who did this. They're not the ones who enrolled you."

"Enrolled me? Enrolled me for what?"

"Bunny, you're always so direct." She heaves a heavy sigh.

Yes, I think, and you drive me over the wall the way you can't face anything. I bite my lip to keep from screaming. I can barely resist the urge to rip the letter from under her hand.

"We hoped you'd never have to know, Bunny, that you're . . . that you're Indian."

"Indian? I'm an Indian?"

"Of course you're not all Indian. Just enough to be enrolled in your tribe. I mean most of you is white. We thought it best for you not to know about that other part so you'd fit in better and not feel inferior . . ." Her voice trails off.

My heart flips into ecstasy. I am Indian! Noreen had it right!

"What tribe, Rose? What tribe am I enrolled in?"

She seems surprised I would ask that.

"It says in here somewhere. Oh yes, here it is. Some name I can't pronounce."

She turns the letter toward me for a brief second, points to an unfamiliar word, then stuffs the letter in her lap. I can't pronounce it either, not in the time Rose gave me to look at it. But there it is. My tribe. I feel a surge of pride so strong it could sweep me right out of San Francisco and off to wherever this tribe, this tribe I belong to, is waiting for me. When will she let me read the letter? It's the first thing I've ever seen about who I really am. I want to hold it!

Rose sees my eyes full of tears. "Now, Bunny, don't be upset. I knew you'd be upset."

"I'm not upset!" I shout. I want her to share my joy. I want the whole world to share it. "Do you know what this means to me, Rose? Can you imagine what it means?"

"I know it must be an awful shock—"

"No, no! It's not a shock. It's an answer!" I lay my arm next to hers. "It's why I'm brown, Rose. We've never talked about that. I wasn't supposed to notice my skin is tan and yours is white, and my hair is dark and . . . we all just pretended and pretended till I had no notion who I was, Rose. Can you try for a minute to imagine how that feels?"

She stares at me, her eyes full of doubt and confusion.

"Try to imagine how wonderful it is, Rose, to find out I belong to a whole tribe! Not just a family, a tribe! And they found me! I wonder how they knew which agency to write to?"

"Maybe they knew somehow you were adopted in San Francisco. Then there wouldn't be that many agencies to write to."

"Why didn't they write sooner?" It comes out a cry of anguish as I think of all the years that have passed.

"They've been holding money in trust for you."

"For me?"

"Apparently one of your birth relatives enrolled you. We never knew about it." She looks dejectedly at the letter in her lap. "Something they call per capita payments have been held in trust for you all these years, and after you turn nineteen next April the tribe is going to send you a check for the money. They said it may take several months."

"They're giving me money?"

"There's also a possibility the Bureau of Indian Affairs may give you a grant to go to a four-year college," she says, still in the dull, bleak voice.

The misery in her face almost wipes the joy out of me. I cradle my head in my arms, trying to take it all in, to believe it. But instead it is Rose's pain that rushes through me. I sigh. She doesn't know how to reach out, so I'll have to be the one. I lift my head.

"Rose, you wanted to help me yourself. I know that. I appreciate it."

They Called Me Bunny   193

Her breath comes out a gasp. It is the closest I've ever seen her to crying. "If Brad hadn't left when he did—"

"I know, Rose. That changed everything, didn't it?"

"He even took the car," she says.

I lay my hand on hers. "Rose, you've really tried. I'll always love you for that." I want to say more, ask a million questions, but she isn't ready. One thing though, I have to ask.

"There's an address for my tribe, isn't there? There in the letter?"

Rose gets up and walks quickly into the living room.

"We won't be needing that, will we? You can write down your address for me to give the adoption agency. I'll tell them to let those people know to send the check directly to you. That's what you'd like, isn't it?"

I can't believe my eyes as she tosses the letter and envelope into the flames. I hear myself scream. The next thing I know the flaming letter is in my hand. I blow violently to put the fire out. Then I feel a sharp, stinging pain and see my scorched fingers.

"Oh my god, Bunny." Rose reaches for my arm.

"Don't touch me! You burned up the evidence of me!"

"I'm sorry," she says. "I didn't know you'd feel this way."

"Well I do, dammit." Tears blind me and I stumble into her. "I've got to get out of here."

"Bunny, I'm a nurse. Let me treat that burn."

My hand throbs. I stare at the charred piece of paper I'm holding. "Why would you do this, Rose?"

"Don't go, please. Come with me to the bathroom." Her eyes plead with me and at last I follow her. We pass the room that is now hers alone and I glimpse an unmade bed with a pile of pillows, a magazine and an open box of vanilla wafers. Numbly, my mind registers that there is nothing in that room to be afraid of anymore. In the bathroom a teddy bear guest towel hangs on Brad's rack.

Rose holds my hand under cold running water. "Not too bad a burn. It's what we call second-degree. It would be better not to bandage it. Come and rest for a minute. I want to see if the skin gets puffy or weepy." I know she's worried about my hand, but all I can think about is the piece of paper.

She leads me back to the living room and we sit on the couch and stare into the dying fire.

"I'm a failure, aren't I? As a wife and as a mother."

I think of the unmade bed where Rose has been reading and eating cookies. Has she always wanted to do things like that? "You've tried so hard, Rose."

"It's always been you comforting me, hasn't it? What would I have done without you?" Her face is open, like a child's. "Brad and I were never happy, you know. That's why we wanted to adopt. Or I did, anyway. I hoped it would make us happy."

"Nothing could make Brad happy. There's something wrong with Brad, Rose."

"Do you think so? You don't think it's just me?"

"Of course it's not just you."

She grabs hold of my hand that is not burned and squeezes it. "Please forgive me, Bunny." Then suddenly she drops my hand and turns her head away. I think about her father hanging himself, how brutal that must have been for her, and in that moment I feel close to her.

"But please, Bunny, don't ask me again about that family you were born to."

The moment evaporates.

I write my address on the pad by the telephone and leave.

51

I return the next evening and find Rose at home. I have been in a daze, I've said nothing to Cork. The struggle to take in what I've learned absorbs me. I drop into a chair at the kitchen table, feel momentary blindness and wait for it to pass.

"Rose, there's one more thing."

Right away she looks guarded.

"I know it pains you to talk about it but it pains me a hell of a lot more not knowing. Is there anything," I pause, wanting her to know how much hangs on this for me, "anything at all you can tell me about my mother?"

I fasten my eyes on her, willing her to come through for me just this once. Her face crumples. "We knew she was some kind of Indian. I never wanted you to have to know that."

"You knew she was some kind of Indian," I repeat, trying to keep my voice from shaking, hoping to elicit more words.

"I wanted to keep it from you." She gazes at me with tired eyes. "But nothing seems to matter now, the way it used to."

"Why would you want to keep it from me?" I ask, proud and defiant in defense of my newly found identity. "I've gone through my whole life, Rose, with people asking if I'm Italian or what—" I break off, struck by something in her eyes.

"It just didn't turn out at all the way I dreamed," Rose murmurs. "Maybe we got you too late. You were already the way you were going to be."

"Rose?"

"What?" She seems surprised to see me across the table

from her, as if she's forgotten I'm here.

"What did you say about getting me too late?"

"Nothing."

"You meant something, Rose! What?"

"It doesn't matter. Nothing matters."

"If it doesn't matter, then tell me! Maybe it matters to me, Rose, these little devastating tidbits."

"Why do you hate me, Bunny?"

I let out an angry breath. "I don't hate you, Rose."

"When did you start calling me Rose? It was after Brad left, but when?" I notice she doesn't bother calling him my father anymore.

I hate myself for not feeling sorry for her the way she wants me to. Some impulse gets me up from my chair and around the table. I crouch down beside her and put an arm around her thin shoulders.

She gives a little shudder. "I wanted to keep all that pain from you, Bunny."

"What pain?" I murmur, as if we are both in a trance and I can get her to keep telling me things if I don't talk too loud and break the spell.

"Oh, there's more, much more," she says wearily. "It would only hurt you to know."

Goddammit, I want to scream. This is my life you're talking about, or wishing away, or whatever it is you're doing.

"Rose." I speak as calmly as I can. "You've always told me you went and picked me out from all the other little babies, remember? I was this cute little baby—"

"No, you weren't," she says.

"I wasn't a cute baby?"

She sits sullen and silent.

"Or do you mean you didn't pick me? I always knew that. I wouldn't have been the one you would have picked if you'd had a choice."

Rose's eyes turn suddenly bright and feverish. "You were three years old," she says. Then she jumps up and runs from the room. I hear her bedroom door slam. I never before heard

They Called Me Bunny

Rose slam a door. She has finally opened a door and now she wants to slam it shut.

Where was I those first three years of my life? What happened during those years?

I'm back the next morning. Cork got in late and is sleeping when I leave, but Rose will be up. I still haven't told Cork. I'm afraid she won't understand how important this is, won't react the way I need her to. And part of me wants to keep my Indianness locked away inside myself. I don't know why.

Rose comes to the door several minutes after I ring the bell. I have a key but it doesn't seem right to use the key as if I belong. It's clearer than ever that I never belonged here. Rose is wearing a new print dress and medium-heeled shoes with stockings. She must be planning to go out. I don't take my coat off. I just plunge into questions, standing there facing her in the hallway. Her eyes meet mine with apprehension.

"Please, Rose, is there anything you can tell me about my parents?"

She looks off toward the coat closet. "Your mother wasn't all Indian. She had French in her, too."

"What about my father? Did they tell you anything about him?"

"He was a white man, a German." Her drawn features ease a bit. She looks pleased to be able to confirm my white blood.

"Was I with them those three years?"

"You're driving me crazy, Bunny, with all these questions!" She takes her hat and coat from the closet, puts them on in haste and announces she's going grocery shopping. She picks up her purse from the hall table and I follow her out. We head toward our separate bus stops.

52

"Take a closer look," Cork says.

I do but I still can't tell what it is. She has just told me this is one of her most accessible paintings. I decide to go with what I understand.

"The colors are gorgeous. I think this is the best yet."

"Really?" Her brow wrinkles and she shakes her head. "No, I don't think so. But it's getting there. Bunny, you're not doing anything tomorrow night, right?"

I pause on my way to fill the teakettle. "No. Why?"

"Good! My mother wants you to come to dinner tomorrow. I told her we'll be there at six-thirty. Is that fine?"

I plunk the teakettle on the kitchen table. "Dinner at your parents' house? You said I'd come?"

"Don't look like that, Bunny. They won't eat you. They'll eat roast beef and peas and new potatoes and asparagus and—"

"Cork, don't. This isn't a big joke to me. Maybe it is to you."

"Come on, Bunny. Don't sweat it. Just be you. They'll love you."

Later I can't go to sleep, thinking what to wear, wondering if I'll be able to swallow. Maybe I'll ask for a small piece of roast beef.

The next evening I am ready at five-thirty. Cork is still in the bathroom. She's been in there a long time. When she comes out, she's wearing a pleated skirt with a blouse and her old green cashmere cardigan. She looks like she's been crying, but that couldn't be true, could it? I feel the urge to help, but I don't even know if anything is wrong.

She looks at me critically. I've never seen that look on her. "Bunny, why don't you wipe off some of your lipstick?"

Quickly I run to the bathroom and blot my lips with toilet paper. Probably I look cheap. I went to so much trouble and ended up looking cheap. She's right. I look better now.

"I bet that's the dress you wore to eighth grade graduation," Cork sighs.

"It's still like new."

"That's because you've never worn it since. Until tonight."

"I wore it one other time," I mumble.

"Oh Bunny." She puts an arm around my shoulders and squeezes me. "They're just people, you know."

"Rich people."

"Okay, rich people. So I'm a rich people too, right? Are you scared of me?"

I smile. "Only a little."

I wish I weren't having my period. It makes me walk funny. I'm bleeding heavily, like always when I get nervous and keyed up. It's a good thing I'm wearing two Kotex. We get off the bus and walk two and a half blocks, the houses getting more impressive as we go. Then Cork starts up the steps of a place the president of the United States might live in. It is even bigger than Lance's house.

"Wow," I comment.

Cork points to an upstairs window. "That's my room. I used to climb out into that tree."

"Yeah, I can see you doing that."

"I spent a lot of time in that tree." We are at the front door with me peering up at the tree, trying to figure out how she got from the window into its branches, when the door swings open to reveal a tall woman as vivacious and confident as Cork, who almost, but not quite, puts me at ease with her wide smile and shining brown eyes. There is something hard in her face. Will Cork's get that way? Even the brightness in her eyes is hard and fixed. I don't see that until we sit down in a room off the

huge entry room.

"Your father will be a little late," she says to Cork.

"Will he be here at all is the question," Cork responds.

"An emergency came up—"

"An emergency always comes up. That's why I don't want to be a doctor or marry one."

Mrs. Newberry's smile is strained. "If he's not here in half an hour we'll start without him."

"Like we're so accustomed to doing," Cork says. I am surprised at the level of tension between them.

"You've been out in the sun," Cork's mother says, looking at me closely. "Been on a trip to somewhere nice?"

"She's that beautiful color naturally," Cork replies for me.

"Well, you're lucky," Mrs. Newberry says smoothly. "Cordelia's father loves to get away to somewhere he can get tan. But I haven't been able to pry him away from work for months now."

"You went to the Bahamas last year," Cork says, looking distant and preoccupied. Not like her usual self at all. It dawns on me that she's been like this the past week or so.

Mrs. Newberry rises from her armchair to rearrange a bouquet of dahlias, then returns to her seat. Her dress, in soft hues of green and rose, swings gracefully as she walks. You never find colors like that on a rack. My navy blue dress with its long sleeves and white collar and cuffs feels stiff and out of place in this room where everything is understated elegance. At least I know it when I see it. I wonder if my inward grin shows, thinking that.

At the sound of the front door opening and closing, our three heads turn to the oval archway, where a tall man appears, gray-haired and distinguished, with strong handsome features. He removes his hat and lays it on the table with the beautiful dahlias.

"Sorry I'm late," he says, as Cork's mother rises, picks up his hat and takes it into the entry hall. I stand, awkwardly waiting to be introduced. What a romantic family. All of them at ease in their opulent surroundings. My heart quivers. I wish

I were someplace else, where I wouldn't feel like a tin fork in a sterling setting. But this home is part of who Cork is, it's where she comes from. For an instant I see the Cork I thought I knew as an illusion. The free-spirited artist. Will she sustain that identity or will breeding and background win out and turn her into a socialite, one with more flair than the others but belonging among them nonetheless? I want her in my world. She told me she wanted to escape this stifling atmosphere. But how seductive it is, the comfort, the easy charm, the sense of being someone who matters. I can see that. Deeply-cushioned furniture, expensive plush rugs . . . what fun it would be to walk on them barefoot. Probably no one does. Even Cork, who goes barefoot on our wood floors, has not kicked off her shoes. Good! I want it to be our apartment where Cork feels at home.

Mrs. Newberry is introducing me. I hear her voice, not the words, and step forward, extending my hand. He takes it briefly, looks at me searchingly with keen blue eyes and isn't pleased. I am not what he wants his daughter's roommate to be. That is why I was invited, to be looked over. No doubt Cork's mother came to the same conclusion, but she hides it better. I even sense a certain sympathy coming my direction from her, especially in this moment her husband appraises me and finds me so utterly wrong. There has to be compassion hidden away in one of them, they have after all produced Cork. Cordelia. Cordelia Newberry. Will I ever again see her in quite the same way? And what would they say if I told them I'm this color because of my Indian blood?

Mary Anderson Parks

Usually Cork is out of the classroom like a flash, but today I wait as she gathers up books, drops her pen, absentmindedly picks it up, stuffs it in her pocket and at last heads out of the building.

"What's the matter, Cork?"

"What?" she responds, a couple of beats late.

"You're a million miles away."

"I'm thinking about those statistics Professor Runyan threw at us."

"Oh yeah, I didn't get all that. Do you think it'll be on the test?"

"Bunny, that was really scary stuff. It's not the test I'm thinking of, it's the future."

"Runyan has that droning voice that makes me sleepy." I'd been thinking about Richard, that he's the one I'd like to confide in, but I can hardly tell her that. Rose hasn't been answering the phone when I call. I'm sure of it. I've tried in the early morning and evenings and late at night, but no one answers.

"Wait!" She sits on a nearby bench and opens her binder to the purple zoology section. Cork color-codes her notes by subject. She writes down the important stuff practically verbatim. It makes me lazy about taking notes, knowing I can borrow hers.

"I don't need to see your notes right now, Cork. Later is fine. You do think those statistics will be on the test, don't you?"

"Bunny, will you quit babbling about the stupid test? We're

They Called Me Bunny

here to learn stuff, did you ever think of that?"

"Okay, okay, I'm just not into animal life the way you are." I roll my eyes, hoping to make her smile.

"Listen," Cork says. "Listen to this." She reads from her notes: "Thomas Robert Malthus was an English economist and clergyman who lived from 1766 to 1834." She darts an intense glance at me. "That's a little over a hundred twenty years ago that he died, right?"

"Right." I nod obediently.

"In 1798, this guy Malthus predicted a doubling in world population every twenty-five years."

"So what?'

"So what? Do you just play stupid or are you really that dumb, Bunny?"

"You don't have to get insulting about it." Cork has been so edgy lately. She gets irritated at the least little thing. Something's bothering her, but I don't know what. Still, she doesn't have to take it out on me.

"Sorry, I didn't mean to say that. Maybe the mathematical significance of doubling is hard to understand."

"Just 'cause you're pretty good at math, Cork—"

"What Malthus theorized," she interrupts, reading from her notes, "is that population tends to increase faster, at a geometrical ratio, than the means of subsistence, which increases at an arithmetical ratio, and this will result in an inadequate supply of the goods supporting life, unless war, famine, or disease reduces the population or the increase of population is checked."

"Well, it hasn't happened yet."

"What hasn't?"

"We have enough food, we just don't distribute it properly. I did hear Runyan make that point."

"What you seem to have missed is how it's an exponential thing, the way population grows."

"How many people were there in 1798?"

Cork skims down the page. "I'm not sure he told us."

I feel again the urge to make her smile. "Is it like that old trick where you ask somebody to give you a penny today and two pennies tomorrow and keep doubling it every day? They think sure, why not. But by the hundredth day, they owe you . . . what, I wonder?"

Cork scribbles down numbers in a column, multiplying by two as she goes. She stops to count, then shakes her head. "I don't believe this. Am I making a mistake? I'm only up to the twenty-fifth day and already the amount is eighty-seven thousand, seven hundred seventy-two dollars and sixteen cents?"

"That can't be right." I plop down on the bench beside her to check her arithmetic. "Okay, on the tenth day it's five dollars and twelve cents. On the fifteenth day it's a hundred sixty-three and eighty-four cents. On the twentieth day it's, gee whiz, five thousand, two hundred forty-two dollars and eighty-eight cents."

"And five days later," Cork finishes, "it's almost eighty-eight thousand."

I let out a slow whistle. "The meaning of exponential is beginning to sink in."

"Runyan said we're going to run short of food if the population keeps increasing at the rate it's going. We could be in trouble as soon as seventy years from now."

"How many people will be here by then?" I ask, to humor her. Doing these calculations is putting her in a better mood.

Cork runs a red fingernail down her page of notes. "Okay, in 1950 there were around two billion people. Runyan says there could be as many as five billion in fifty years. We'll still be alive in fifty years, Bunny! Can you imagine a world with five billion people?"

"How often did you say the population doubles?"

"Malthus thought every twenty-five years, but Runyan predicts doubling every forty or fifty."

"It's just going to keep on doubling?"

Cork shrugs. "Twice as many people have twice as many babies. It's that simple."

"Cork, by the middle of the next century there could be ten

billion people, and then fifty years later—"

"Stop it, Bunny! I want to go home and get in bed. I don't feel very good."

I notice her eyes look tired. But her point has taken hold. I can't let go yet. "We're all in this together, Cork. All of us animals! I mean, think about it, the more humans there are, the more cows and pigs and chickens we'll need."

"There won't be enough room," Cork says, "for all of them and all of us. Runyan said a time will come when each human will have only one square meter of land. I sure wouldn't want to share mine with a cow." We both giggle.

"I guess people try not to think about this stuff."

"Yeah, the problem seems so big."

"But every person's decision matters. It all adds up."

"What are you talking about, Bunny?" The anger in Cork's eyes takes me by surprise.

"Well, I guess what it comes down to is birth control."

Cork glowers at me, and we set off toward home.

Something besides Malthus and his theories is bothering her. I keep silent, trying to match her long stride.

After a while she says, "You can borrow my notes." So I figure she's not mad anymore.

"How about stopping at the drugstore for a milkshake?"

"Yeah, milk would be good," Cork says.

It isn't until we're sitting in our favorite booth, sucking up chocolate milkshakes through paper straws, that she tells me.

"Bunny, I missed my period twice."

I see fear in her eyes.

54

I curl my legs under me and settle deeper into the basket chair. We love this chair. We pooled our money to get it. Cork was willing to pay the whole cost but I don't want things to be like that. I want to feel, not equal to Cork, I'll never be that, but at least like I'm not taking advantage, not that she'd ever think that but . . . I realize Richard hasn't said a word since we both sat down. He is on the daybed, staring at one of Cork's paintings, the one that is supposed to be a dog but no one knows that unless she feels like telling them. You can sort of see a tail, after she tells you.

Richard must be in one of his moods. My mind is full of thoughts I am unable or have been forbidden to speak. Cork was adamant about not letting Richard know. Maybe she'll have a miscarriage, is what she hopes. She said neither she nor Richard is ready to be a parent, it would ruin what they have between them. I asked her what she plans to do if she keeps on being pregnant. I guess adoption, she mumbled. I willed myself not to feel anything when she said that word. If I really try, I can achieve numbness.

Richard keeps silent so long it startles me when he speaks. His voice thrills me. Every time. It makes me want to be closer to him. I have to curl my hands around the edges of the chair's thick cushion to keep myself safely in place.

"She's amazing, isn't she? She has so much . . ." He pauses, his eyes raised to the ceiling. "Vibrancy, that's the word, don't you think? Have you ever seen anyone more vibrant? Her painting has the same energy! I get bowled over."

"Me too." I hope he doesn't hear the glumness in my tone.

"You do, don't you?" He fixes his dark eyes on me with an intensity that sucks the breath out of me. "We share that, don't we?"

I kick myself mentally for building fantasies on nothing. But he's right, we do think alike. I'll get over him, I'll have to. He'll be gone to Europe and . . . what about the baby?

"I'll have to be gone from her quite a few months," he says, "but every time I see a painting, I'll feel her there next to me. I'll feel how she'd be taking those long strides backward to get a better view, see all the angles. Remember that time we were in the DeYoung Museum and she crouched in a corner? And we wondered why?"

"Yeah. She wanted to see how it would look to a child."

"I'll be okay though, without her. I know someday she and I will go there together." Again his eyes fix on me, intense and searching. "Bunny, if I tell you something, it's just between you and me, right?"

A shiver goes through me. "Right."

"You wouldn't tell Cork?"

"No, I wouldn't tell Cork."

"Okay then." He holds my gaze. I struggle to keep upright as I feel myself melting away. I am grateful for the cushioned chair cradling me, holding me up. "It's that I've always wanted to go to Europe by myself," he says. "It's a dream I've had since I was ten years old. I want to do it alone. So I'm glad really that she can't come because of the school year not being over and her parents and all. To me this is way more important than school. And I've finally got the money together. I can stay a year maybe."

I guess Cork is right, this guy isn't ready to be a father. But shouldn't he be asked? My heart cries out the question. It doesn't reach the level of words, he can't hear it. And she never will ask him. Isn't it possible that if he knew she was going to have his child, it would change everything?

"You understand, don't you, Bunny? You're really easy to

talk to, you know?"

I smile. Apparently none of my torment shows on my face. I've gotten good at that over the years. It makes me feel nauseated. I pass my hand over my forehead. Cork has hidden her nausea from him. He commented once that he'd never seen a girl go to the bathroom as often as she does, but he said it with the same fondness he says anything that has to do with Cork.

"I do understand. It's different when you're alone. Any experience is more intense when you're alone."

"Yeah, that's it! I want that intensity. And I don't want to wait, Bunny. I've saved just barely enough money, but I've already waited too long. Europe's going to change, you know that?"

"How? How will it change?"

"It'll be overrun by Americans. And they're a new breed. It's already so different from when Hemingway and Fitzgerald were there. God, this dentist I went to last summer, I couldn't believe it! You should see this guy. He was chortling about how they had pictures of naked women hanging right up there in the museums for everybody to see. That's all he came away with, Bunny."

I giggle.

"Yeah, it's pretty funny in a way. But to me it's the greatest loss I can think of, not to have been there when . . . who's the guy who wrote *Winesburg, Ohio*?"

"Sherwood Anderson."

"Yeah, him. You read a lot, don't you? Sometimes I wish Cork was a reader. She never knows what I'm talking about. I mean, when I talk about stuff like this." He looks vaguely puzzled.

"I don't read all that much. I had to read *Winesburg, Ohio* for a class."

"You do too, Bunny. I've seen you. How come girls pretend to be stupider than they are?"

"Now we're on the edge," I say, grinning. "We've gone from one girl, the queen of them all, down to the dirty depths. But it's cool, don't worry."

A sudden squall of rain beats hard against the window. How exciting to be closed up in this cozy room with Richard just a few feet away! Yet I am behaving myself. I'm not doing anything to attract him to me sexually. I just want him to keep talking to me. None of my questions can be asked. How many girls have you loved in your twenty years, Richard? How old will you be when you're finally ready to get married? Do you have any thought of marrying Cork? How could you? It would ruin the bohemian image both of you have of yourselves. I sigh.

"What's that about?" he asks softly.

"I was thinking about those people who went over to Paris in the twenties, like you said. What bohemians they were, and yet a couple of them were married and still they hung onto . . . what? What did they hang onto?"

He laughs. "Zelda was crazy. She sure hung onto that."

Suddenly Cork bursts in, with her usual rush of energy. I am startled by how guilty I feel.

"It's just something I have to get through, Bunny." Cork settles deeper into the basket chair, still limber enough to cock one foot on the other knee and paint each toenail bright red. Her stomach is bigger but her height helps hide it, and she's been dressing in looser clothes. Doesn't Richard notice her stomach is bigger when they have sex? I stop my mind from going to that place. He's been coming around more often because he's leaving soon to go to France. Not always when Cork is here, and I wonder about that. He knows her schedule.

"I hate it when you say that," I mumble.

"What?" She waves her foot around to dry the polish. She is wearing shorts and a loose top. The heat is up to seventy-eight. She's been doing that lately, even turning it up to eighty. I turn it down when she's not looking. I am hot and irritated.

"I hate it when you say that." The words come out so emphatically I surprise myself.

"Look Bunny, you're not the one who's pregnant. You didn't have to wake up every morning for three months ready to puke. You're not the one who's going to have to give birth, dammit. That's the only way out, you know?" She glares at me. "Do you think I *want* my body to get all distorted and stretched out of shape?"

"I hate that you don't want the baby."

"Will you shut the fuck up? I'm nineteen, for god's sake. How could I raise a child?"

"There was a way out."

"An abortion? There's nobody who would do it. I asked Susan."

"You did? You told Susan you're pregnant?"

"She said no reputable doctor would do it. It's too dangerous. They could lose their license."

"It's dangerous for the woman, too."

"Not if it's done right. That's what Susan said. She thinks it ought to be legal."

"Wow. Really? She said that?"

"Confidentially. Just to me. She wouldn't say it at med school. She's already the oddball, just by being a girl."

"Cork, don't you ever think about keeping the baby?"

She plops both bare feet down on the floor. "No."

"I do."

"Look, Bunny, get this straight. This is not your baby. And it's not some sappy romance story. This is the rest of my life we're talking about." I'm getting used to Cork's new toughness. I answer back with my own tough questions.

"What about Richard? It's his baby, too. Have you told him, asked him what he wants?"

"No, I haven't told Richard! He'd want me barefoot and pregnant, slopping around cooking meals for him in some hovel in Italy. Richard doesn't know what the hell he wants. Richard's going to Europe."

"When's the due date?" I've never dared ask before. Up until now she's pretended it wasn't happening and I've gone along. But the bulge in her abdomen is taking on its own reality.

"The first of July. My mom's mad as hell. She doesn't want her Fourth of July party ruined. Can you imagine her saying that?"

"Yes," I respond, smiling. "From what I know of your mom, that's exactly what I'd expect her to say."

Cork grins. "Yeah. I told her it's too bad it's not due in January. I could've dressed up as Santa for their Christmas party. I wouldn't need any padding."

"That killed her, I bet."

"Oh, I don't know. Sometimes I wonder if Mom's real. I mean, her hair color is fake, her eyebrows are fake. She pads her bra. She never comes out of her room without makeup. Where is she, under all that?"

"She doesn't want to be like Queen Lear."

"What's that supposed to mean?"

"Everybody talks about King Lear, but where is his wife? It's like old women don't count. Your mom wants to make sure she's noticed. That's why she does all that stuff."

"She had me when she was thirty."

"So why are you saying that?"

"I'm supposed to have a youth, I'm supposed to be an artist. I am not ready to be a mother. She wasn't even ready at thirty."

"Is she going through the change of life?"

"Why do you ask that?"

"Maybe that's what's wrong with her."

"No, she's always been like this."

"If it were my baby—"

Cork comes up out of her chair with remarkable agility and rushes at me. "Don't! Don't say it!"

Unexpectedly, her head is in my lap and she is sobbing. "Bunny, Bunny, how could I have been so stupid? I'll lose Richard, I'll lose everything."

All you're going to lose is your baby, is what I'm thinking but don't say. Nothing she could do would drive Richard away. He'll go to Europe and then he'll come back to her. But if it were my baby, I would keep it and love it and follow Richard wherever he wanted to go if he'd let me. I'd make a home for him. We'd be a family of three and I'd do all the work. He could be gone as much as he needed, and I'd be there waiting when he got home and we'd love each other like crazy and make more babies. Cork lifts her face. Snot runs out of her nose. She wipes it off with her bare arm and looks at me suspiciously. "What are you thinking?"

"Nothing," I say.

"Yes you are."

"I'm thinking what I'm always thinking. How could a mother

give away her baby? It's what I've been thinking all my life."

"A million reasons," Cork says. Her lips compress and her jaw tightens. "Look, I don't want to talk about this, okay? This is just something I've got to get through."

"Does your dad know?"

"What do you think?" Her eyes challenge me.

"You mean he doesn't, don't you?"

"He'd never give me my trip to Europe when I graduate, or anything else, if he knew."

"But how can you keep it a secret?"

"I have so far, haven't I?"

"You don't see him much, do you?"

"The story of my life."

"But Cork, how do you know what he'd say? Maybe he wants to be a grandfather."

"Are you out of your mind?"

"Yeah, I'm out of my mind. I just wish I could do this for you."

"That's a laugh."

"I'd look like a balloon, wouldn't I? You're so tall, you hardly show at all."

"Well, Dad hasn't noticed." Cork looks thoughtful.

"What?" I ask. "Why are you looking like that?"

"Richard hasn't noticed either," she says slowly. "I wear smocks now, a lot of the time, and he thinks it's because I'm painting more."

"Cork, can you really keep him from finding out?"

"I think so. If he leaves next month like he told me he's going to."

"My god," I breathe.

She looks at me sharply. "You haven't said anything, have you?"

"No, of course not."

"Well don't."

We are both silent, thinking our thoughts.

I feel Cork watching me. "How can you be sure you would keep it if it were yours?"

She has no way of knowing how often I think about that. Sometimes I wonder if I have sex just hoping to get pregnant so I can prove I'd never give up my baby. Joe Doolin and I get together during my safe period, but we've done it sometimes when it wasn't safe, too. I worry that I'm barren like Sarah in the Bible. That scares me more than anything.

"I just am," I say.

"But you can't know for sure, Bunny." Her face crumples. "It's easy to say when you're not the one who's pregnant."

I don't answer.

"Mom's getting Dad to take her on a trip to Greece. They'll leave five weeks before my baby's due. She wants it to be all over and done with when they get back. She's hoping it'll come early."

"What about the Fourth of July party?"

"She's given up on it. We agreed I'll stay away from Dad for the next few months. I'll call him up on the phone. So he won't think anything's wrong."

"Just like it never happened," I murmur.

"Yeah." Her eyes are immensely sad. Why haven't I seen the sadness until now? She hides it behind all the toughness and carrying on. She's so good at hiding it maybe Richard really will never know. My eyes well up with tears. I think he'd like knowing.

Then she turns her full gaze on me and when she speaks, I know I am hearing the truth. Perhaps for the first time. "I'm talented, Bunny." She says it with quiet assurance. "That's what will always come first for me. If I ever have children, it will be with someone like my dad, who can afford to hire people to help take care of them. But he'll have to be different from Dad. He'll have to know my art comes first."

This is the Cork whose spirit I fell in love with when I first saw it shining in her eyes. This is the Cork Richard sees.

I lie in bed for what seems the thousandth night and imagine Cork's baby growing in her womb. It is real to me, palpable. How could something so perfect in its tiny minute wholeness be destroyed? How could she bring herself to do that? And then, as I lie imagining, feeling the fetus now in my own body, an image comes of a world alive with fetuses, all waiting in wombs, waiting to come out, growing inexorably, inevitably toward their birth into a world teeming with people, animals, organisms. I see it all at once, not in sequence, but as a sudden present horror.

I get up and go sit on the toilet, and without willing it or wanting to, I see women and men and children crouching on toilet holes, swarms of us all over the planet, filling the earth with our excrement.

But Cork isn't going to destroy her baby. What have I been thinking? My hand grips my forehead, squeezing like a vise. Its identity! Cork is destroying its identity. The little baby knows who it is there in her womb. It knows it is Cork's, part of her, part of her bloodstream, sharing life with her, connected by water and blood and genes, veins and bones. It is hers as much as it is itself. Its self grows in her, born of her genes and his, nourished by her body, taking what it needs. If she casts the baby away from her after it emerges naked and howling, not wanting to be wrenched from her, isn't that a greater crime against it than to kill it now and spare it all that heartbreak?

Tears come so fast they blind me. I want to be blinded. I

don't want to see what I am seeing. I am filled with yearning for my mother. I get up from the toilet and wash myself with soap. I wash that part of me out of which I came from her, that part we share, and it feels pitiful to be connected with her only through these wild imaginings that strike me in the night. I want to be pure and clean for her. Lovable. So lovable she would never dream of casting me away. I crawl back in bed and draw my knees up, lying on my side with my hand pressed warmly between my thighs. That's what Cork's baby is doing, safe inside her, curled up just as I am. I wish it never had to come out and face the world, but it will. So think positively, Bunny. That baby can invent itself just as you do, day after day. But oh how I'd love to stay with it, be with it, comfort it, tell it who it is and how beautiful and vibrant its mother was.

How would I explain that she gave it away? How could I possibly explain that?

I feel like I could die from the pain I'm feeling. Then Mother's spirit flows into me. She is trying to comfort me. I cry aloud, our pain so mixed up together I might as well still be floating in her womb.

They Called Me Bunny   217

We have a sad little party the night before Richard leaves for Europe. Sad for me and Cork. I'm not sure how Richard is feeling. He brings a bottle of wine and the three of us share it. He gets all wound up and excited and talks a lot. He keeps giving Cork big hugs and telling her how great she is. When he finally leaves, Cork falls asleep on the daybed. She looks exhausted.

Cork drops two courses and gets her other teachers to give her the assignments for the rest of the semester and let her mail in her work. I don't know what she says to get them to do that. So she's around the apartment all the time except for when she goes to see her doctor or the adoption counselor. One day in early June, I go downtown to hunt for a new blouse but instead I drift through the baby department, torturing myself. Out on the street, a black cat crosses my path and I feel sick. Lately anything sets me off. It's like I'm the one who's pregnant. I slow my steps and grab my stomach. What is a cat doing on this busy street? Did I say that out loud? I get crazier every day, talking to myself, moaning. It is happening right now. I catch myself in mid-moan and straighten up. The worst of it is this fleeting sense I am all right and then the next second I'm swirling, falling, nauseated, no one to catch me, nothing to break the fall or end it but hitting bottom, and I don't know what bottom is because I've never been there, and that seems like a blessing, not to have known the worst. Maybe my mother knew the worst and wanted to save me from it, or is that only a dream I hang onto, like a balloon floating high above me?

On the bus I run into a girl I vaguely remember from high school. I run right smack into her because of not looking where I'm going.

"Sorry I'm such a klutz," I say with a grin. Who is she anyway, gazing into me with serious dark eyes when she turns to see who backsided her. There is pain in her. So much pain, everywhere. Most of the time I don't see it, until it rises up like bile. Where does her pain come from? I note the black, naturally curly hair. The pale skin. The Jewishness.

"It's okay." She says only that, but the kindness in her eyes makes me want to throw my arms around her. I want to ask, "*Is* it okay? Is it really okay? Will we live through the pain?" But she moves on into the bus and sits next to a colored lady with an orange hat and I wonder about that, too, why she chooses that seat when there is an empty one she could have had all to herself.

I take the empty seat, but can't stand being alone. I go to the front of the bus long before my stop and wait near the driver.

"I get off at Ocean," I tell him.

"We've finally got our rain," he says. "You try to stay dry out there!"

"Thanks. I will." I run the short distance to our building.

Alone in the apartment, I sit by the open window smelling the freshness of rain, listening to it splatter onto the pavement, and I can't bear the pain of not knowing. Who was she, my mother, why am I not with her? Was I with her for three years? I can't stop yearning for the family that gave me away. I feel in my bones that I am one with them. Rose refuses to tell me anything more. Doesn't she know not knowing could drive me crazy?

I go to the kitchen, pull out the bag of flour and start making brownies. Something for me and Cork to munch on when she comes home from her appointment with the adoption counselor.

I stir into the brownie batter my hope she'll change her heart and want to keep the baby. No wonder I can't study. My mind

They Called Me Bunny

is always there in her womb, pulling for the baby. That too could drive me crazy, because it isn't likely what I hope for will happen. It's just me, all alone, against the adoption agency and Cork. Richard left for Europe without knowing. I hold the spoon in the air, fudgy-brown batter dripping into the blue and white striped bowl, and a picture forms in my mind, clear in shape and color, the edges sharp. I see a manila folder, like the one the counselor is filling with records on Cork, with the answers Cork gives and her full name, Cordelia Newberry.

The answers to my questions are hidden away in that folder I see in my mind, hidden among stacks of other folders with other children's histories. Children like me, adults now, with part of our brains empty.

I scrape the batter into a greased Pyrex pan and stick it in the oven. I spoon up the sweet mixture left sticking to the bowl and eat it, then wash and dry the bowl and spoon and measuring cup, put everything back in its place and wipe the counter clean. Remarkable how the smell of baking can help a person think. While the brownies bake, I start calling the adoption agencies in the phone book. It surprises me to find six. Is adoption a big business?

Do agencies get paid by the adopting parents? If they do, it doesn't seem right a girl like Cork has to rely on them for counseling. They'd have no reason to encourage her to keep her baby.

I won't call Cork's agency until I've called the others. I don't want it to be the one.

I tell them who I am, who adopted me, and that I am eighteen. On the fourth call I get the right agency. A lady with a stern voice admits they have my records, but says she can't tell me anything else over the phone.

My heart pounds and I know what I will do next, but it doesn't seem like a good time to tell Cork.

I glance at the clock, wondering why she isn't back yet. It makes me furious when I think about what happened at her first appointment. The counselor, Mrs. Williams, asked her if she had priced what baby things cost. Together they made a four-page list of what the counselor said the baby would need. "Do you really think you could afford all that on your own?" Mrs. Williams asked her.

I hear the front door open and Cork comes in, looking subdued.

"What's up?"

"Mrs. Williams has a couple picked out to adopt the baby. She says they are very nice people from her church."

"What church is that?"

"She can't tell me any personal details."

"Great."

Cork takes off her trench coat and lays it over a kitchen chair. Her eyes look like she's been crying.

"I made brownies."

"I can't eat brownies. I'm on a diet." She gets out a skillet, heats oil and pours in a cup of popcorn, then covers it with a lid.

"You shouldn't be dieting," I blurt out.

"Bunny, I'm eating better than I ever have in my life."

"Popcorn doesn't do the baby any good, it's all air."

"It keeps me thin and that'll make the birth easier." A few kernels pop and Cork pushes the skillet back and forth. Soon the popping comes thick and fast. When it slows to a stop, she takes the blue and white bowl from the cupboard and fills it with popcorn.

"No butter or salt," she announces virtuously. She sits down at the table, sweeps a big handful of popcorn into her mouth and munches hungrily. "Mrs. Williams thinks I should be gaining more weight, but I don't want to talk about her, okay?"

"Fine with me." I watch her admiringly. "Gee, Cork, you're a month away from your due date and you look terrific. Is being pregnant this easy for everybody?"

"I don't think so. Not from what I've heard. Evidently I take after my mother. Her doctor, who's now my doctor, told me she had no problems at all."

Cork will be like her mother in other ways, too. Suddenly I see that. She has good taste in clothes, she always likes the expensive stuff. Maybe for her, hanging around with me is slumming. Maybe even Richard is only a phase, someone she'll remember from time to time when she's safely married to someone of her own class. After all, she's giving up his baby, isn't she? Without even telling him. A knife turns inside me.

"Cork, have you ever really thought about what being adopted has been like for me?"

"I guess I haven't. Not all that much. I mean I do when you talk about it."

"When I talk about it." I repeat her words, not wanting to let her off the hook now that I've found courage to ask.

"You're usually so happy and bubbly. We all have our down moments. I sure have stuff that bothers me."

"I haven't told you everything, Cork."

"Well, neither have I. And I know lots of adopted kids who are really grateful they got such wonderful parents."

"You do?"

She takes hold of the bridge of her nose the way she does when she's trying to remember something.

"There was this girl in third grade, I remember she had more dolls and cuter clothes than anybody. She was spoiled rotten."

"And she told you how grateful she was she had such wonderful adoptive parents?"

"No, she didn't exactly say that. You could just tell how lucky she was." She strokes her nose, thinking. "Then there was a boy in high school I found out was adopted, and he was homecoming king."

I stuff popcorn into my mouth, then push the bowl away. "So that's how you see your baby turning out?"

"What do you mean?" She grabs a huge handful of popcorn.

"Like that lucky girl in third grade who had so much stuff. Or turning out to be homecoming queen or king or jack or ace of spades or whatever?"

"Gee, Bunny, you don't have to get all worked up. I'm the one having the baby, you know."

"How do you know how you'll feel after it's here, Cork?"

"What?"

"You heard me."

"Look, Bunny, can you see me as a parent? All by myself, thrown out by my family? What kind of life would that be for a child? A kid roaming around museums in Europe with me, can you see that?"

I stare right back at her, holding her eyes. "I'd love to have you for my mother. If I were the baby inside you, I'd have my share of your artist genes and I'd love trailing around with you and you showing me what to look for and—"

"There's nothing to talk about!" she yells. She is up and out of the room, slamming her bedroom door behind her.

"I tried, baby." I let the tears come, sitting by myself at the kitchen table. In my mind is the motherless kitten I brought home, that Rose and Brad wouldn't let me keep. I never found out what they did with it.

They Called Me Bunny   223

58

I step on a wad of chewing gum, then rub my foot back and forth but can't unstick the gum. By the time I take my seat among the waiting fathers, I have picked my favorite. When he pulled the gum off the sole of my slipper, I felt like Cinderella, with pink bunny slippers I hadn't known I had on. Calling a cab and getting Cork here to the hospital took all I had. It's a relief to find I'm not wearing my bathrobe. Other than my feet, I'm appropriately dressed in a pleated green plaid skirt and white blouse.

I feel different from any way I've ever felt. One of the fathers is saying something, but a throbbing in my left wrist and behind my right ear makes it hard to hear, so I grin at the ashtrays, at the walls, at the fathers' properly shod feet. Odd that none of them flew out with slippers on. That is my one coherent thought. Then the throbbing drives me out for air, out of the windowless waiting room and down the corridor.

"Some things you know from the day you were born." A nurse standing next to a bouquet of red roses says those words to another nurse, adjusts her white hat and dashes off. I run after this woman who says wise words, and that is how I learn where the nursery is. She turns on me, fierce and protective of those babies behind the glass.

"You can't come in here, you know."

How odd it would be if this were Rose's hospital. But Rose works somewhere else, and knows nothing of what Cork and I have been going through.

"I'm kind of lost."

"Well you can't come in here," she says.

"Is there a cafeteria somewhere?"

"Go back to the desk, take the elevator to the next floor and turn right." She watches me take a step backward, away from her domain. I turn and amble along in my slippers, wondering if she noticed them and figured out I am one of the waiting fathers. Don't we have a right to visit the nursery? I walk slowly, trying to remember what it is I have known since the day I was born.

Cork was in the prep room four hours. I stood out in the hall most of that time, until a nurse told me they were ready to take her into labor and made me go back to the waiting room. Time is moving, or not moving, in a way it never has before. I stare at the clock on the wall until the elevator doors open and then close behind a large, sturdy lady wearing a navy blue suit and matching hat, a fox fur draped over her shoulders.

"Oh good, you're here," the nurse sitting behind the roses says with a smile. "We have the paperwork ready."

She is well known here, the determined-looking lady in navy blue. I feel caught in this life of the nurse's station, in these corridors and rooms, these boat paintings on the wall, the smell of disinfectant. I hate the place, I hate what Cork is doing here. Not the birth, not the birth. It's not the birth I hate. I love the birth. The sailboat starts to sway, I fight a sudden weakness . . . the floor comes up at me.

On what seems another day, I open my eyes to see a thin-faced nurse bending over me. My head feels heavy when I turn it. I am lying on a white bed in a white room.

"This isn't right," I tell her. I want to bound up and off and away. I know there's someplace I need to be. But the skinny nurse holds me down with no trouble at all.

"You lie here," she tells me, firm and commanding. "I've just given you a shot to help you rest."

"I don't want to rest. I'm not a patient."

She lays a cool hand on my forehead. "Just stay quiet."

A bell rings.

"I'll be back in a shake to check on you," she says, hurrying out of the room. I try to get up but my head feels woozy. So I wait for it to clear, but instead my eyes close and I drift into unconsciousness. When I come to, I lie very still until I remember where I am. Then I sit up, get off the bed and stumble around looking for my slippers. I find them in a closet. At the door, I peek out. No nurses. I dart off in the opposite direction from the nurses' station, toward the waiting room.

Only two fathers remain. They give me nervous nods. And then I see her, the lady in navy blue, using a phone on a table in an alcove. Still feeling groggy, I sink into one of the couches. My brain moves in slow motion. It takes a moment to register her words: "This is Mrs. Williams calling in from the hospital. I've warned the nurses how important it is that she not see the baby. Even for a minute."

She means Cork. This is Cork's Mrs. Williams. Wearing a poor little dead fox around her neck. I strain to hear her next words. "We want to avoid a bond forming."

I remember what I have known since the day I was born. The feeling floods through me, warm and wrenching. I know what I have to do. I have to put that baby in Cork's arms.

If only I hadn't made such a spectacle of myself, fainting in the hallway. They'll spot me in a second. Wildly, I think of *I Love Lucy* and her friend Ethel—they'd get themselves nurses' uniforms—somehow they'd do that. All I can do is follow Mrs. Williams and keep my eyes on the fox's tiny sharp face and claws. She and her dead fox will lead me to the baby. I follow her back to the nurses' station, where of course I am recognized.

"I wondered where you'd gotten to!"

"I'm doing just great. Don't worry!" I sing out, hoping they won't get any ideas about putting me to sleep again. Mrs. Williams' navy blue bulk stays near, but she is filling out dreadful documents, like the ones that took me away from my mother. I want to scream and tear them up. I want to stop the world from falling apart for Cork's baby. She is here, I can feel that she is. She is here and she is a girl. And she will never know who she is if I don't do something fast. One of the fathers flashes by. I dash after him, take his arm and ask, "Has your baby come?"

"Yes!" He grins at the whole universe. "Come see!"

He grabs my hand and leads me to the magic place, the place where the babies are. He pulls me up close to the window. We peer in at the sleeping babies in their white cribs and I can tell which one is Cork's. She has Cork's dark hair, or maybe it is Richard's. The other babies are bald or capped with a ring of blond fuzz, like the one the proud father points to. I put my hands against the wall of glass.

I can feel in the strength of the glass, in the bones of my hands, that they've taken Cork's baby away from her forever. They drugged her and me both! I didn't get to put the baby in her arms. She never got to hold that dear child. Maybe she never even saw her.

59

I wander away from the nursery dazed, down a hallway I haven't been in. The doors of the rooms are open. I see mothers sitting up holding their babies and others lying down resting. I look into each room until I find Cork. She is asleep in the bed nearest the door. In the bed by the window, a young mother about her age sits propped against pillows, humming softly to the baby in her arms. I go stand close to Cork, relieved she is alive and breathing. I guess I've been worried for her as much as for the baby.

Suddenly a heavyset nurse strides into the room. "You can't stay here," she tells me. "If you want, you can wait at the end of the hall until she wakes up."

"Do you think she'll wake up soon?"

"Not likely! Not after the pills I gave her."

I go to a small area with armchairs and a pile of magazines on a table. No one else is there. I collapse into one of the chairs, then wake with a start, wondering how much time has gone by, and run to Cork's room to see if she's awake. She isn't, so I just keep running back and forth, napping a little in between.

A new shift of nurses comes on duty. I don't know if it's the same day or if it's night or what. A nurse with permed orange-red hair notices me checking on Cork and tells me in a kind voice that it's okay if I want to sit in a chair next to her bed. She pulls a white curtain around the bed and me. I guess I doze off because next thing I know my eyes open and there's Cork looking at me.

Mary Anderson Parks

"I asked to see my baby," she says. Her weak voice doesn't sound like Cork. "A nurse told me it was against the rules and gave me pills that made me sleep."

A squawk comes from the baby on the other side of the curtain. I'm hoping Cork won't notice but her head jerks in that direction, then back to me.

"She lied, didn't she?"

"Yes." My head aches with wanting to help her and not knowing how.

"Do you want me to tell you what the birth was like?"

I lean closer, nodding my head.

"I was having these awful pains, like what I had when I woke you up in the night. Only they were stronger and they were coming almost every minute. The doctor and nurse kept telling me 'Push, push!' and it hurt really bad. Finally I gave this one great big push and I felt the baby come out and I heard the doctor say, 'It's a girl,' and then I felt her weight on me, he laid her on my stomach, and Bunny, this is so terrible. By the time I could raise myself up to look, the nurse had taken her and wrapped her in a blanket, and she threw the edge of it over the baby's face so I wouldn't be able to see. But I saw her, Bunny. I did. I'll never forget her little face. I saw it in the instant before the blanket covered it. They had the wrong color blanket. Blue, not pink." She frowns, as if the blueness troubles her. "I'll know her anywhere, Bunny. I'll always know her face." She looks hard into my eyes. "Do you believe me?"

"Yes."

"I'm an artist, Bunny. Once I see a face, I never forget it. And I know the ways faces change over time."

She looks alive and lovely talking about her baby's face. But afterward, all feeling seems to drain out of her. She stares into space until her eyes close.

When the day comes to take Cork home from the hospital, I splurge on another cab. All the while I'm thinking how wrong everything is. She should have the baby in her arms. Richard should be sitting here close to her. Instead her arms are empty and I am the one holding her cold hand, not even sure she feels my hand around hers. She stares out the window, her head turned away from me.

After an endless ride through neighborhoods I don't remember ever seeing before, we reach our apartment building. I pay the driver and try to help Cork up the steps, but she won't let me. She uses the railing for support. The minute we get in the apartment, she heads straight for bed. Drops her skirt to the floor, climbs into bed, turns over on her stomach and wraps her arms around her pillow.

I meant to stay away from Cork. After going through those horrible days at the hospital and finally getting her home, without a baby, I didn't want to have to look at her. I don't know if it's Cork I'm ashamed of or me. I guess it's both of us. I hate what she's doing, I hate that I can't stop it and I hate that it's so damn final. I hate the idiotic rules that mean the fate of Cork and her baby can be decided while she's drugged. Here she is making the biggest decision of her life and they don't even ask her if she wants to think about it. You get more chance to change your mind when you buy a car for god sakes.

She regrets it already. I see the torment in her eyes. Most of the time she sleeps and I don't have to look at her eyes. I can hardly bear being here with her, but it would be cruel not to stay.

She only gets up when she uses the toilet. I make cups of tea that she takes sips from after they are cold. She tries a bite of the different foods I bring, then closes her eyes. I was wringing washcloths in cold water and laying them over her forehead until she told me warm would be better. "I feel empty inside," she said. "Cold."

I stare at her huddled under the blankets, her womb empty, her baby gone, and press my lips together to keep from screaming. I can't bear to think of the baby being handled by strangers. She won't know who she is. She won't know she is the daughter of Richard and Cordelia, two of the most beautiful, talented—

They Called Me Bunny

"Bunny."

"What?"

"You're still here."

"Yep, I'm still here."

"Good."

Am I imagining that she looks a bit more alert?

"What will we do, Bunny?"

"I don't know, Cork. We'll just try to go on with our lives, I guess."

"Can I talk to those people?"

"What? Cork, what do you mean?"

"I mean this was a mistake. I didn't know I'd feel like this, Bunny. How could I know how I would feel when I saw my baby? I can't even cry. I'm so empty without her I don't have tears."

I reach out and take hold of her cold hand.

"I want my baby, Bunny. I want my baby."

Something stirs in me. I try to think, but I can't remember how many days it's been, or even what day it is. It seems like we've been here forever, the two of us in this room full of emptiness, Richard far away in Europe.

Maybe it's only three days since she got out of the hospital. They kept her five days—no, they let her out early, they let her out after four, I think, and I'm certain we've only been back in the apartment since Friday. It must be Monday. It was yesterday Cork's mother called and Cork wouldn't talk to her.

"Cork, it's only been a week, not even that. Do you feel up to calling that counselor? She's the one, I think, you'd have to talk to. Do you feel up to it?"

She nods. Her eyes have a spark in them, the first spark of her old self I've seen.

"She could talk to them," I prattle on. "How attached could they have gotten? They've only had your baby a few days! Cork, they'll have to give her back! I know they will. When they find out you made a mistake. When they know the baby's own mother wants her!"

She smiles and nods. I grab her up in my arms and cry into

her neck, my tears mixing with her hair that still smells sweet because the nurse washed it before she came home.

Suddenly, with our bodies pressed together, I feel wetness on my chest. I draw back in awe. "Cork, your milk hasn't dried up yet."

"Isn't that wonderful?" She looks like a Madonna with her dark hair spread out on her pillow, a wan, hopeful smile on her lips.

I can't wait to see the baby in her arms. I'll be like an aunt or a sister. I try to curb my excitement, get back to the present, do what has to be done to get that baby to its mother.

"Do you have her number, Cork?"

"In my address book. Under the W's. Williams."

I bring it to her. "Can you get up and go to the phone? Do you feel strong enough?"

"I feel as strong as Diana," Cork says, swinging her feet to the floor. "Diana the goddess of the hunt, that's who I feel like."

I wrap her in a hug, pressing my face against hers.

"My milk's coming out again!" she squeals.

"I know! It's soaking my blouse!"

Cork goes to the phone and stands swaying on her feet, dialing the number, then waiting. It seems forever until someone answers. I sit in the basket chair thinking how lovely she looks and how happy the baby will be, held close against her mother, drinking milk from her breast, and then Cork is talking to someone, asking for Mrs. Williams, but Mrs. Williams isn't in.

"Isn't there any way to reach her today?" Cork's voice is trembling. "It's urgent."

She slumps down on a chair at the table.

"What?" I ask. "Where is she?"

"She's out of the office."

"They can't get hold of her?"

"She's 'out in the field,' whatever that means, and probably won't call me back until tomorrow."

"But when you told her it's urgent—"

"She just repeated, 'you'll probably hear from her first thing tomorrow.'"

My mind struggles to recover buried fragments from what I overheard in that murmured phone conversation in the waiting room. What did the all-powerful Mrs. Williams say about time limits? Something about how when the mother signs on a Friday there might not be time to file the papers until after the weekend. Will it be too late tomorrow? Are they doing this on *purpose*?

"Cork, I'm going down there!"

"Oh, come on, Bunny."

"No. I am. Right now."

"What're you going to do?"

"I'll go look in her office, see if she's there. I think they're evading you. You told them your name. They can't have that many mothers who just gave birth. They're afraid you're changing your mind, Cork!"

"I am."

"I know, but . . . Cork, did Mrs. Williams say anything to you about a time limit?"

"A time limit?"

"Yeah, like there's a period during which you're allowed to change your mind and then it's over and you can't?"

"Bunny, it's only been—what did you say, a week?"

"That's right, Cork. A week. But do you remember them telling you about any time limit?"

She rubs the palm of her right hand back and forth across her forehead. "I don't know. She read stuff to me off some form and said we'd talked about it all before. It was the day I left the hospital. I don't think the drugs had completely worn off. I just signed the papers."

"I'm going there, Cork. There *is* a time limit. I'm sure there is. I heard Mrs. Williams talking about it."

"But won't they be lenient? I mean, after all, the baby's mine. She's better off with her own mother, surely they know that."

I shake my head. "No, they're the last ones who'd know that."

She straightens up, moves her shoulders forward and back.

"I'm coming with you."

I was counting on that. We take quick turns in the bathroom, throw on some clothes, and in minutes we're out on the corner waiting for the bus.

Cork looks at me and laughs.

"What?"

"Do I look as bad as you, Bunny? We're going to make a hell of an impression."

I glance down at my mismatched colors. "We had to be quick. They should understand. They're the ones who make the stupid rules."

When we get there, after transferring from the bus to a streetcar to another bus, we find our hurrying was for nothing. The sign on the door says the agency is closed from noon to one-thirty. We walk two blocks to a Manning's cafeteria. Cork is nauseated by the food smells. She says Manning's always affects her that way, but I'm so hungry I could eat one of everything. I buy chocolate milk, a sugar doughnut, a tuna sandwich, potato chips, Jell-o, and a piece of custard pie. Cork ends up eating most of it. We're back on the steps of the agency when it opens.

"Are you the one who called?" the receptionist asks me.

"She is," I say, glancing at Cork.

The receptionist is about our age, dressed in a coral suit, white blouse and pearl earrings, with not a strand of blonde hair out of place. Her lipstick exactly matches her suit. What frights we must look, Cork and I. We should have used the time to dress carefully and look respectable. What if Cork doesn't get her baby back because we don't look right? Our clothes are all rumpled and Cork's slip is showing and I have on a jacket with two buttons missing.

"I'm afraid you've made a trip for no reason," the girl says. "Mrs. Williams is out for the day. An emergency came up."

"Let me leave a note in her office."

"That isn't necessary—"

"Which office is hers?"

"The first on the right, but—"

"I've already written the note." I march past her and quickly try the doorknob, but it is locked.

I wrote the note while we were at Manning's, and Cork signed it. It is as simple and clear as I could make it. "I, Cordelia Newberry, have changed my mind. I want my baby back." With today's date. I slip the note under Mrs. Williams' door.

"Does she ever check back in here at the end of the day?" Cork asks.

"Sometimes she does."

"We'll wait then," Cork says. "In case she does."

We seat ourselves in armchairs in the waiting area. Cork leafs through a *Life* magazine, casts it aside and sits staring at the beige wall. After what seems a very long time, she takes a deep breath, gets up and approaches the receptionist.

"Look, the message I really need for you to give Mrs Williams is that I've—"

"I'm sorry," the girl interrupts. "The only messages I'm qualified to give are your name and phone number. I'm not a trained social worker. I'm just the receptionist." She looks scared. "Please sit down if you want to go on waiting."

Cork slumps into a chair but soon she's up again, back at the desk. "Is the director in? I want to talk to the director."

"They're all at a meeting." The girl turns away and goes back to her typing. At five o'clock she covers her typewriter and pulls on her gloves. She has already cleared her desk. She holds the door open for us to go out. "I'll ask Mrs. Williams to call you in the morning."

"She's new," Cork says numbly, on the ride home. "That's why she didn't know me."

In the morning, after Cork leaves three messages, Mrs. Williams calls at ten minutes past eleven. She explains that because of the papers Cork signed it is too late to get her baby back. Mrs. Williams is unwilling to talk to the adoptive parents. It would disturb them unnecessarily to tell them the birth mother changed her mind, since the birth mother no longer has any legal rights. As of this morning. That's when Mrs. Williams filed the papers. The way I figure it, she filed the papers right before she got around to calling Cork.

When I grab the phone, Mrs. Williams tells me no, she didn't find any note. She thinks the janitor must have swept it up. "I have to run now," she says. "I'm late for my next appointment."

Cork changes after that. She isn't Cork anymore. She isn't the spunky beautiful tomboy her father nicknamed Corker. The music of "My gal's a Corker, she's a New Yorker" used to go through my head when I looked at her, but now she seems plain. The fight gone out of her. Whatever gave her that sparkle that made you feel more alive just being around her, disappeared with the baby.

I wonder if she thinks about the baby as much as I do. It's hard to know what she's thinking. Her thoughts don't come burbling out anymore. She stares at art books, hardly even turning the pages. I spend most of my time watching her. I can't focus on anything else. When crumbs start crunching under our feet, I sweep up, and when piles of dirty dishes topple over, I wash a few. It takes me one whole morning to sort through the clutter of mail and school papers on our kitchen counter. I end up throwing most of it away.

Often I make tea with honey and offer a cup to Cork. She isn't eating much but I cook anyway, hoping she will. I make big pots of soup, throwing in vegetables and canned stuff, tossing in any meat we have around. Occasionally I get up energy to go to the corner grocery and the bakery. And somehow I manage to make it to my job.

Saturday the thirteenth of August, one month to the day after the baby's birth, I cook up a huge pot of soup and am getting out the bread when our buzzer sounds.

"If that's my mom, tell her to come back another day," Cork

Mary Anderson Parks

says, her eyes big and staring. She's been sitting at the table while I make the soup, not even pretending to look at the book that lies open in front of her.

"I can't do that, Cork. It'd be mean."

"Then tell her I'm not here. I went out."

"Dammit, Cork, we don't even know who it is."

I lean forward and speak into the box on the wall: "Who is it?"

"It's me."

"Oh my god," Cork says. She runs into the bathroom and slams the door.

"Richard?"

"Let me in, Bunny."

I press the button that buzzes him in. Standing barefoot at the door, I remember my dark roots have grown out at least two inches, I haven't washed my hair for over a week, and I'm in an old terry cloth bathrobe that's worn down to the nub. Quickly I pull the sash tighter.

Richard bounds up the steps and gives me a hug that leaves me shaken. He fills the kitchen with his tall male self, his clean smell of the outdoors.

"Where's Cork?" His expression is eager, expectant.

"She's in the bathroom."

"Well, that's typical! Putting on her makeup?" He laughs and sprawls out in one of our three kitchen chairs. I notice for the first time how perfectly the number fits our situation. He looks wonderful, with his skin deeply tanned and his black hair so long it curls into his shirt collar.

"It smells great in here!" Richard breathes in the aroma from the pot on the stove. He acts like he hasn't been away, like the months of his absence have been erased. So I try to do the same.

"Soup's on. You got here right in time."

I ladle up a steaming bowl and set it in front of him. Then I get him a spoon and napkin and set a plate of bread and the butter dish at his elbow. He dives right in, spreading butter on the bread, blowing on a spoonful of soup.

I don't feel hungry anymore. It satisfies me to watch Richard eat. I pour myself a cup of coffee and sit across from him.

Gosh, it feels like we're married. I wish he'd stay in this kitchen and I could keep on serving him and Cork would never come out of the bathroom. Eventually he'd tell me about his adventures and why he's come back so much sooner than he thought he would.

"When's she coming out?" he asks, between mouthfuls. "Doesn't she know I'm here?"

"Yes. She does know."

I get up and pour him a cup of coffee, then sit down and push the cream pitcher to his side of the table.

"Richard."

"What?"

"You've been gone five months."

"So?" He pours cream into his coffee and stirs.

"Things change in five months."

"What do you mean, Bunny?"

"It's been a month since you last wrote and now you pop in on us like this! God, Richard! What did you expect? We'd just be waiting, I mean Cork would just be . . ." I'm stammering because by now I've figured out that maybe she's not planning to come out and I'm trying to think what to do next.

"You know, maybe you should just start all over." I rest my forehead in the palm of my hand.

"What do you mean, start over?"

My god, I look at you and I long to be yours, to be the one you yearn to see, yearn to tell things to. But I'm not. And yet you probably would talk to me instead of her if I urged you, and that confuses the hell out of me. But I can't think about how much I love to hear you talk, how much I love the sound of your voice. I've got to think about Cork, huddled up on the toilet seat or whatever she's doing, unwilling to come out and face the father of the baby she's given away. What the hell do I know about what's going on in either of your damn minds?

"What's the matter, Bunny?"

I take a breath. "Do you want more soup?"

"Sure. But what's the matter?" His eyes are full of concern. I get up and cross the space between us, leaning in close to pick up his empty bowl. How can he not know how he affects me? The nearness of his body makes me tremble. My hand shakes as I take the bowl. Why have I offered him more soup? If I want him to leave, why am I keeping him here?

"What's up with Cork?" he asks.

I bring another full bowl and he starts in on it.

"The man's starved!" I say.

He speaks as he stuffs bread into his mouth. "What did you mean, I should start over?"

"Call her, I guess. Give her some time."

"Five months isn't enough?"

"Was it enough for you, Richard?" I can't help asking. His eyes meet mine, then drift away.

"Yeah. It was enough." He slumps back in his chair, chewing on bread. "Europe got weird."

"It got weird?"

"It got weird being there so long and not really having anything to do. I found out you can only visit so many museums."

"Yeah, I guess I see what you mean."

"At first it was great. I took the train to all these different countries and stayed at youth hostels and met a lot of interesting people. But I kept to myself a lot, too. I wanted the intensity you get from being alone. Remember I told you that once?"

"Yeah, I remember."

"When I walked up the steps of the Pantheon, I felt like every artist or writer who's ever been alone in Paris . . . or at least I imagined I did."

"So was it really great being in Paris?"

"Yeah. But I missed her, you know. More than I knew I would. You, too. And by the end of five months I just wondered what I was doing in Europe. I mean, I wasn't writing or painting or anything. I'd go to cafes where everybody spoke French and I didn't feel like I belonged. It got lonely."

I can't resist the sadness in his eyes. I get up and stand behind him, put my hands on his shoulders. He leans back

They Called Me Bunny   241

into me, his head against my breasts. "I know the feeling of not belonging," I say.

And that's when Cork comes in.

She stops and stares, a question blazing in her eyes.

"Gosh, it's good to see you look that way." The words burst out of me. I go to her, wanting to hug her, tell her how wonderful it is to see her come alive, even if it takes anger at me to make it happen.

She pushes me away. She takes a step toward Richard, who stands up and goes to her with arms outstretched.

She has on a chocolate brown sweater that matches her eyes. She must have slipped out of the bathroom into her room. She is wearing her crystal necklace. It is her artist's instinct to bring attention where she wants it, distracting Richard from her too round middle. The gray skirt she has on is the only one she can button.

Ignoring me, she throws a challenge to Richard. "I assume you want to be alone with me. Shall we go out for coffee?"

He grabs his jacket and she goes to the hall closet and gets her coat. "See ya later," Richard mumbles as they go out. Cork says nothing.

I am left wondering what she will tell him and what she won't and what he will tell her. Later I can ask him more about Europe, what he did during those long months. Or can I? Suddenly I fling his coffee mug into the sink. Coffee splatters everywhere but the mug doesn't break. Only my heart. I am so filled with self-pity I could choke on it, thinking of his dear face and all the words I would love to be hearing right now from his mouth, only it is Cork who gets to be near him. She isn't even letting me stay in the background. But maybe I'm not good at staying in the background. It must have looked pretty bad to her when she came in.

Will she tell him about the baby? I would respect her then. All I've felt these past weeks is pity. And horror that it's happening again to another baby. Another girl who won't know who she is. It needn't have happened! It kills me to think of that. Cork would still be her usual buoyant self if the baby were here with us. I'm sure of it. And I would help! The baby would be so well cared for, so loved. Cork might find it hard at times, be inconvenienced, but we'd be wrapped up in meeting the baby's needs. Cork wouldn't be this shell of herself, this walking zombie.

She sure didn't look like a zombie when she sailed out of here with Richard. I hug myself, shivering as I go to the calendar on the wall to count the days. The baby was born the thirteenth of July. Thirty-two days ago. How could so much time have passed? Part of me has been thinking of the baby as dead, but the calendar reminds me she is alive, somewhere else, somewhere we can't see her, in the back room of an orphanage . . . no, that was my fantasy of myself waiting to be rescued. What do babies do at four and a half weeks? They had to feed her from a bottle. Did she take to that? So young? It's not how it should be.

The calendar mesmerizes me. Don't I have classes I'm supposed to be going to? Wasn't I enrolled in summer school?

I feel kind of dizzy on the way to my room. I sprawl out on the tumbled covers and relive the look on Richard's face when Cork laid her claim on him. Something primitive took him over. His eyes burned right across the room into her.

They'll want to be alone when they come back.

Reluctantly I get up, throwing my robe on the huge pile of dirty clothes. I slip into the last of my clean underwear, then a skirt and sweater. Somehow my textbooks have gotten pushed under the bed. I get dust all over me pulling them out. Sighing, I survey the clutter, the soiled sheets. Cork's room looks the same. Will he notice how changed we are? I swipe at my dusty clothes. Is all this my fault? Maybe I should have told him. This isn't fair to the baby! Or any of us. He might have talked Cork out of it. Shit, if she isn't going to let him know he's a father, she has no right to him. He's too good for her!

Defiant, with more energy than I've felt in weeks, I go to the mirror and apply lipstick, bright red, and eye shadow, green, then give my hair a good brushing. I can face the world now. I can go back to classes and tell the teachers I had a family emergency. It's something to do. It's a way to stay out of this mess of an apartment where lives get messed up. From the back of my mind comes the thought of leaving.

But where would I go?

Why can't I stay mad at Cork? Or she at me, for that matter. We sit in our kitchen sipping from Coke bottles, too dazed by an unexpected heat wave to bother with glasses and ice. I want her to talk to me. I'm not sure she's forgiven me, and I'm lonely for her. Ever since Richard's been back, she has been disappearing into her painting, hiding there. Today, heat forced her to take a break. I know it's good she's painting again, but I want her to talk to me.

"I can't get my mind to come to rest," I blurt out. "I'm looking for something!"

"We all are." She says it wearily.

"So where is it?"

"Don't ask me. I lost the clues."

"Cork, don't."

"I've lost everything, Bunny. Except painting. That's what I have left."

And Richard. Why doesn't she mention Richard? "Your painting is better, Cork. Better even than before. It's deeper, with layers, that you bury images in."

"Turn your face to the side, Bunny."

"Like this?"

"A little more. That's good."

"What do you see?"

"Your hair is so short!"

"It was breaking off and splitting from all the peroxide. I had to cut it. You just haven't been noticing things."

"You're not bleaching your hair and your perm's gone. You look completely different."

"I feel different." But I don't tell her about being Indian. "I can't wait for it to grow out so it'll all be dark."

"What is it you're looking for, Bunny?"

"Myself. Always. Forever."

"You're right here. Sticking to your seat, like me."

"I have to create myself every single day, Cork. It gets tiring."

"I don't see why you have to do that."

"'Because I have to make it all up."

"How do you mean?"

"Sometimes I don't feel real. I have to go look in the mirror to make sure I'm here."

"That's creepy." She sits up straighter. "Tell you what, Bunny. When the weather cools down, I'll paint you. So you'll know for sure you're here."

"I have something I want to tell you, Cork." She waits. I love the way Cork waits. Only her breath moves. Her chest goes slowly in and out. Her eyes stay quiet. Then when you talk to her, they light up. Or they used to. Is that why I want to tell her something astonishing, hoping those lights will go on? I hesitate, because it's scary, what I'm going to say.

"I remembered something, something that happened at the orphanage."

"How could you? You weren't more than a year old."

Good, I've gotten her attention.

"I just do," I say, not yet wanting to tell her more. "This little boy and I were playing in a sandbox. He wasn't my brother. He was towheaded, with blue eyes. He told me we shouldn't dig too deep or our shovels would hit the baby's head."

Cork's eyes open wide. "What baby?"

"He said his mommy and daddy buried a baby in the sandbox."

"Are you making this up, Bunny?"

"I'm trying to open doors, Cork. My mind is full of closed doors. They block me and I hate that. I want to run free but I come up against doors."

"That's funny. That happens to me with my art."

"What do you mean?"

"I'll be painting out of some place in myself that's free, where colors and shapes come easily, and then, like you said, a door closes."

"What do you do?"

"Put away my paints and wait till another day." She looks at me closely. "There's more, isn't there, you want to tell me?"

"Yeah, there is. Rose told me something recently, something she never told me before. I wasn't a baby when they got me. I was three years old."

"*Three*? But where were you for those three years?"

"She won't say. It's driving me crazy."

Cork frowns. "What you said about the baby, it could be real, if you were at the orphanage when you were three. Maybe that little boy came from a terrible family that killed a baby." She clasps her forehead. "I've got a headache coming."

It's my own stupid fault. Telling her that horrible memory about the baby. But dammit, she ought to worry. Who knows where her own poor baby is right now?

"I'm sorry," Cork says, heading for her bedroom.

What was I thinking? I should have left her alone. I really do see new depth in her painting. I wasn't making that up. I'm not making up any of what I said. And I know where the depth comes from.

Later, Richard drops by. We go out on the front steps to drink iced lemonade. For him I have energy to make lemonade. I love it when something happens so he's alone with me, even if the something is Cork having to go to bed with a headache I caused. What an awful person I am. I change into shorter shorts and a halter top, using the heat as an excuse. Richard thinks nothing of it. He never sees through me. Or Cork either. He especially doesn't see through Cork.

I sit on the top step, stick my legs out and wiggle my bare toes. "I wish I lived in the tropics."

"You'd hate it. You've never lived anywhere but here, have

you?" He settles himself on the step I'm on, facing me.

"Not that I can remember."

"San Francisco's the place to be. If you have to be in this country."

"Where else would you want to be?" I pretend I'm Cork, holding my body quiet except for breathing.

He considers, his eyes brooding. Only Richard could look cool and dark and brooding on a day like this.

"Russia," he says, "the old Russia."

"That suits you."

"Why do you say that?"

"It's where Dostoevski is from."

"So? What do you know about him?"

"Just that I love the way he thinks."

"Have you read any of his books?"

"Actually I have."

Richard hugs his knees, rocking slightly. "I've always liked Dostoevski. I took one of his books to Europe. What did you read by him that you liked so much?"

"I don't know. I like *The Idiot* a lot, and *The Brothers Karamatzov*, and *Crime and Punishment*—"

"You've read all those?"

"And *Notes from the Underground* and . . . *The Possessed*, is that the name of it?"

"God, Bunny. I don't believe this. Sometimes you act like a complete nitwit and here you've read just about everything the man wrote." I love the way his face breaks into a smile, but then doubt comes into his eyes. "Are you making this up?"

"Why in hell does everybody ask me that?"

"Sorry."

"It's okay. Actually I would have made it up if it weren't true."

He looks confused, probably because I don't tell him the reason I would have made it up is to see him smile.

"Tell me more about why you like his writing." He lengthens himself into a more comfortable position, as if expecting a long answer.

"I like the way his characters talk. They have so much to say and it's all interesting."

"Yeah, yeah. What else?"

"I like how passionate they are."

"That's it! They're passionate about what they believe. They're always searching, tormented. I feel like that, you know? And there's nobody who wants to talk that way. Or at least I haven't found them."

"Is that why you went to Europe?"

"Yes. But it didn't work, did it?"

I laugh. "You couldn't speak enough French."

"Only I didn't know that till I got there."

"Richard, let's go to the ocean! We could walk in the sand, listen to the waves—"

"How would we get there?"

"By bus." Excited, I reach out and touch his knee.

He gives me a strange look. "Without Cork?"

I draw in a breath and let it out. He watches me breathe, like I watched Cork, and his look recalls me to something I don't want to violate. I am not after all a hysterical Russian heroine.

"No, not without Cork. We'll wait till another day. Till she feels like going."

Does he look just the least bit disappointed? This is way too dangerous. I don't like the way I'm feeling about myself or Cork or Richard. I want to run away. But where is it I'm going? The answers are in that file cabinet I see so clearly in my mind. It's no longer a matter of getting up courage. I can't stop myself. I have to know. Nothing will make sense until I know.

I stand up. "Richard, I just remembered some stuff I need to get done today."

"Yeah, well I really ought to be at the restaurant helping my uncle." He gets up and stretches. "Thanks for the lemonade, Bunny." He gives me a lopsided grin. "And the literary conversation."

The minute Richard goes, I take the glasses inside, run to the phone and dial the number from memory. I've been holding it in my head all these weeks. I get the lady with the stern voice, the one who said she couldn't give me information from my adoption file over the phone. Now she tells me I need to see a Mr. Pirtle, but he's all booked up with appointments and then he's going on vacation. Before I can ask anything else, she gives me a clipped goodbye and hangs up. I keep my hand on the phone, thinking. When Cork wanders in, saying she feels better after a nap, I tell her my plan.

I awake feeling I could do anything. Giddy with excitement, I slip into a pink and white dotted Swiss dress and tuck white gloves into a shiny white purse. It's too hot for gloves, but Rose's training still has a hold on me.

A bunny outfit. Maybe a bunny can charm the dragon. That's how I see the lady with the severe voice, a dragon crouched near the door, breathing fire, guarding the records that hold my secrets.

"We all have hard things we have to get through," Cork says encouragingly as I go out the door. "You'll do fine." She looks wistful and sad, but that's how she looks most of the time these days.

I catch a bus right away and arrive at the transfer point in time to watch the connecting bus disappear in the distance. I'm so brimming with energy there's no way I could wait for the next one. I set out walking in my high-heeled white pumps.

If the dragon tells me I need an appointment, I'll say I'm going to sit there until Mr. Pirtle has a free moment. I saw a movie once where Danny Kaye was a salesman and he was in this waiting room sitting on the edge of his chair and every time somebody came through he'd jump up hopefully and the receptionist would shake her head, "No, that's not the boss." At the end of the day the guy finally comes out of his office and Danny Kaye jumps up, only by then he's so tired he loses his balance and everything spills out of his briefcase and the boss trips and falls on his butt. I smile, picturing Dragonlady on her butt.

"Hey, cutie!" The voice comes from above. I look up and see three workmen on a scaffold, leering down at me. I wave, and that surprises them into silence. Then come the whistles. Why do men act this way? I walk on, starting to feel hungry. Maybe I'll eat the Dragonlady, gobble her up. That thought is still zinging in my head when I open the door and plunge into the waiting room. There she is. She looks just like her voice. I march right up to where she sits in her brown tailored suit with an algae-colored blouse and a mistrustful expression.

I offer my best smile. "Hi! I'm Bunny Lundquist."

"Good morning." She barely moves her lips.

"I'm here to wait until I can see Mr. Pirtle. This matters to me more than anything in the world." My smile begins to wobble. "I've just walked thirty blocks to get here and I'm thirsty and desperate for information. I want to see my adoption file." She opens her mouth, probably to say I need an appointment. "So I'll wait here until he has a free moment." I plop down in the nearest chair and fasten my eyes on her. Won't that shake her up? It does, faster even than I hoped. She gets up and brushes her rear end with her hand, as if she's been sitting in a pile of crumbs, then disappears into a hallway. In a few moments she's back.

"Mr. Pirtle will see you for five minutes," she says, her tone disapproving. "Follow me," she says. I get up on legs that feel ready to buckle underneath me.

A short, balding man scurries ahead of us, heading toward a door marked Men's Room. He looks like he's trying to escape.

"Mr. Pirtle!" the dragon calls.

He turns, pale and wide-eyed behind rimless glasses. "Let her have a seat. I'll be along in a moment."

She shows me into an office furnished in shades of brown. "Mr. Pirtle is one of our busiest adoption workers," she says, frowning as she points to a worn leather armchair. She waits for me to sit, then opens the door wider as she backs out. "Don't touch anything," her sharp glance seems to say. Left alone, all I can think about is that my five minutes are evaporating while

Mr. Pirtle pees.

Then he's back, easing his round body into a chair behind his large desk. What a solid-looking place his office is. I sit up straighter in my dotted Swiss dress, determined not to be intimidated.

"I'm here to see my adoption file," I say, my mouth suddenly dry.

"Yes, yes, that's what I've been told." He moves his scotch tape holder so it and his stapler are lined up straight. There is nothing else on his desk. He takes a set of keys from his middle desk drawer, then slides his swivel chair over to unlock a file cabinet labeled "Closed Files." He pulls out a manila folder which he places on the desk, carefully centering it in front of him. My breathing stops. It looks exactly as I thought it would. He peers at me, his light blue eyes magnified by his glasses, then glances down at the file.

"I'll see if there's any medical information that might be of help to you." He opens the folder and begins going through the pages one by one with maddening slowness, stopping now and then to read silently, and at one page raising his eyebrows as if in surprise. It is all I can do to keep from grabbing the file and running full speed out the door. No dragon could stop me if I had that file in my hands.

He presses his thin lips together. "Well, there's a lot of medical information in here about your adoptive parents, but there's nothing at all about the medical background of the birth parents." He sighs and adds, "There often isn't."

I feel the beginning of anger. Why didn't whoever made these records bother to ask my real parents about medical stuff and write it down? It's not Rose and Brad I came here to find out about.

Slowly he flips through a few more pages, then stops at one that has four columns running down it. "I suppose you'd like to know about hair color, religion, height and weight, things like that?"

Eagerly, I lean forward. "Is the page you're looking at about my birth parents?"

They Called Me Bunny 253

He jerks his head up, covering the page with his arm. "Yes, it is."

I scoot forward in my chair. "What I *most* want to know, more than anything, is my mother's name, and also how many children she had."

Mr. Pirtle's eyes widen in shock. "I certainly can't tell you names! The law doesn't permit that. I can give only non-identifying information."

I struggle to take in what he is saying. "But it's names that I want. I'm nineteen. Don't I have a right to know who I am? Do I have to be twenty-one, is that it?" I won't cry. I won't.

"No." He shakes his head firmly. "The law requires us to keep names secret forever. We must, you know, protect the birth mothers."

Anger boils out of me.

"The birth mothers? What the hell do you people care about birth mothers? Tell me, would you have helped her contact me if she'd come asking?"

He frowns. "Of course not! We have to protect the privacy of the adoptive family. And don't use that kind of language, young lady!"

"I'll use any damn fucking language I want to."

Mr. Pirtle's pale face turns pink. "I want you out of here right now. Right this minute!" He gets up from his chair and prods me out the door and down the hallway. Two frightened-looking pregnant girls sit on opposite sides of the waiting room. Their eyes widen as they watch Mr. Pirtle push me along.

I hear myself yell, "You don't give a damn about us once we're adopted!" I can't believe it is me yelling. What happened to good little Bunny? But I can't stop. "You never came and checked to see how I felt about the home you put me in. You never asked me even once. I would have gone back to my mother in a second if you'd given me the chance. I don't care what problems made her give me up. I would have helped her with them."

Dragonlady springs from behind her desk. "You're hysterical," she says. "You're not making any sense at all."

Mary Anderson Parks

"I'm making the most sense I've ever made in my life. This *is* my life we're talking about, do you know that? Do you understand that at all?"

One of the girls stands up, looking like she's ready to bolt out the door. The other one slumps into her seat, shrinking away from us.

"Don't do it," I tell them urgently. "Think about whether there's any way you can keep your baby. Maybe there's somebody in your family who would help."

"You must leave this minute," Mr. Pirtle shouts. "You're agitating our clients."

Suddenly it hits me that I haven't accomplished a thing. He might have told me the name of the tribe I'm from, and now he won't even talk to me. What should I do? What should I say?

"I want to see the director," I blurt out. "I may be filing a complaint."

Dragonlady and Mr. Pirtle exchange looks. He gives a little shrug of his shoulders. She takes a step over to the big appointment book spread open on her desk. After studying it, she raises her head. "I suppose Mrs. Thompson might see you tomorrow at ten. *If* you can behave yourself."

"It's a deal. I'll be here." My heart sings as I walk out. I know where my file is! I'll get another chance to find out what's in it!

Mrs. Thompson has wavy gray hair so stiff it might be a wig. She points with the phone receiver to an armchair across the desk from her. The desk and chairs and dark wood cabinets, even the paintings on the wall, are all so huge that I feel very small. My heels sink into thick carpeting.

Once settled in, I see that Mrs. Thompson has planned it so she will always be at a higher level than anyone visiting her. It's hard to keep my dignity, sunk deep into the cushioned armchair. Mrs. Thompson lowers her glasses with her free hand and looks at me over them. Her glance tells me she is not impressed by my bargain basement green and white striped dress and matching green heels. And I took such a long time figuring out what to wear. She is in a well-tailored gray tweed suit. I pull off my white gloves and lay them in my lap, wondering why she had Dragonlady usher me in while she's busy on the phone.

I can hear the high-pitched voice of the girl on the other end, because for a few moments Mrs. Thompson holds the receiver far from her ear.

"This is a matter to discuss with your counselor, not the director," she interrupts. "I'll have her give you a call." She hangs up and turns her full attention to me. "I've heard about you. Aren't you the little girl who's been insisting so loudly that adopted children have rights? And speaking up on behalf of birth mothers. Is that something you have any experience with?" She doesn't give me time to answer. "I should think not!" She smiles as if she has said something pleasant, picks up a glass dish of chocolates, walks around her desk and holds it out to me. "Try one," she commands, in a firm, bossy voice. Feeling I have no choice, I take a chocolate, then pop it quickly into my mouth so it won't melt in my now sweaty hand. I think of Snow White biting into the poisoned apple her stepmother gave her. The chewy candy with cream filling is so sugary it hurts my teeth and sets me coughing.

"I'm the one who allows access to records." Mrs. Thompson says. "But from what I hear from Mr. Pirtle and our receptionist, who by the way has been with us a great many years, you, my dear, are the one who is out of line."

She laces her sturdy fingers together and stretches her arms out in front of her on the desk. I notice the thin gold watch. Everything from her silk blouse to her alligator shoes looks expensive.

"We need to come to an understanding, Bunny. We have pregnant women coming here, relying on us to find loving adoptive homes for their babies. We don't want them upset by someone like you ranting around in the waiting room. That should be obvious."

"But I—"

"Don't even bother to answer," she says, rising as if to dismiss me. "Just don't let me hear any more of this nonsense."

Things aren't going at all the way I planned. Bracing my hands on the armrests, I raise myself from the chair. She towers over me. "And then, if you choose to make an appointment when Mr. Pirtle gets back from his vacation, and come here ready to be respectful, he can tell you the non-identifying information he's allowed to give."

I leave the building feeling hopeless. I wish I'd brought along sport clothes so I could go straight to the school gym and hit tennis balls and sweat poisoned chocolate out my pores.

I need to clear my mind and think what to do next. I have to see that file.

A summer squall of rain hits me as I get off the bus. I break into a run, going as fast as my high heels will take me. As I come up to our apartment building, I see Richard sitting on the front steps. My god, he's crying!

"Come out of the rain," I tell him. "You're getting all wet." He looks up at me, his eyes red.

"Come on, Richard." I take him by the hand and pull him along. We sit down together on the top step, protected from the rain by the overhang of the porch ceiling. "What happened?"

"Cork . . ." His voice breaks. Tears stream down his face. I don't put my arms around him. I thrust my hands under my thighs and sit on them. His head drops to his knees and I watch him shake with sobs. I have to wait. He'll tell me if I wait. I don't dare say what I know, what I think he now knows. I can smell dampness rising from his corduroy jacket. Everything about him is dear to me.

It seems a long time before he raises his head. He sniffs, then wipes his nose with his jacket sleeve. I pull a handkerchief from my purse and put it in his hand. He blows his nose into it and gives it back.

"You and Cork have been talking?"

"Bunny, you knew! How could you not tell me?"

I look down, not able to meet the pain in his eyes.

He says in a husky voice. "I guess you couldn't. You're her best friend."

I steal a glance at him. It is awful to watch him cry. He keeps sniffling, passing his arm over his eyes to wipe them, trying to get control of himself.

"Do you feel like talking?" I ask. He looks like he might die of misery right here on our porch if he doesn't let out some of what he's feeling.

"Why did she do this?" He stares into my eyes and all I can do is look back, wondering the same thing, hoping he can't see my thought. It would be disloyal to Cork to let him know what I think.

"She said she needed to be free to follow her dreams as an artist." His mouth opens in disbelief as he shakes his head. "She said we have the same dreams, the same artistic soul. She thinks she did this for me! Can you believe that? Doesn't even tell me I'm a father! Gives our child away!"

I keep silent. I don't know what words to say.

"What did she think? That she could get over something like this? That things could ever be okay between us again?"

I wonder what moved her to tell him. The agony of keeping it inside?

"I asked her why she's so different," he says, as if in answer. "I told her it's not the same being around her anymore. She doesn't have that vibrancy that drew me to her. I said if she doesn't love me she should tell me. She started screaming then." He buries his head in his hands. "That was how she told me we had a baby together. Screaming like a madwoman. 'Am I vibrant enough for you now? You would have never been a good father,' she told me, but by then she was crying. I started crying too, because I wondered if she could be right. 'You're not ready,' she told me. 'I would have been stuck at home with the baby and you'd be out traveling, living like a bohemian.' That doesn't make sense, Bunny. We could have taken the baby with us if we traveled. Artists have babies, don't they? Sometimes?"

He looks at me searchingly. "You would have never done that, would you, Bunny? Given up your baby to strangers."

No, I think. I would never have done that. I might have had an abortion if I were brave enough, but I wouldn't give birth to a child and give it away.

I say to him, "We all do what we have to, Richard."

Without warning, his arms are around me. He murmurs into my neck, his breath warm against my skin. "I think it's you I want, Bunny. I've made a terrible mistake. You're the one I can talk to, the one who could help me." I feel my body shudder with joy. For an indescribable moment I surrender. Then, somehow, I summon the power to push him away.

"Stop it, stop! Don't do this to me, don't do it. You don't know what you're saying! Cork thought—oh, I don't know what she thought. I think she really did think she was doing it for you. She didn't want to spoil your dreams. She didn't know till it was too late how hard it would be."

He hangs on every word, his gaze locked into mine.

I manage then to tell him the most important thing he needs to hear, the thing that will make him go back inside and begin to forgive her.

"She tried to get the baby back, Richard. As soon as the drugs wore off, she tried to get the baby back. But they wouldn't even listen to her. That's why she's how she is now."

I watch something come back into his eyes. "Really? Cork tried to get our baby back?" He grabs me again and hugs me and I feel myself melt. I wish it would never end, that I could be wrapped in this man's arms forever. "Thanks, Bunny." He pulls away. "Do you think she'd let me back in?"

"Of course. Just go in there to her." I make myself smile. "I have to go somewhere. I won't be back home for a few hours. Be kind to her." But I don't need to tell him that. He doesn't know how to be anything but kind. He'd make a wonderful father.

The rain has slowed to a light drizzle. I walk three blocks to a corner phone booth, shut the door and stand slumped against the wall. I know I can't bear being alone right now, but it takes a few minutes before I can get myself together enough to find the right change and dial Joe Doolin's number.

He sounds groggy. I must have woken him up.

"It's me. Bunny." I tell him what corner I'm on. "Can you come and get me? Could we just ride around, not do anything?"

"I can be there in ten minutes." He sounds glad to hear from me. The last time he called, I didn't feel like seeing him.

We always say we're just going to ride around. And then we end up parked somewhere, steaming up the windows of his Cadillac. I'm not sure that's what I need right now, but I sure need something. Would Joe leave me alone if I told him this time it's different and I really mean I just want to ride around?

I think about Cork and Richard together in our apartment and feel like maybe for once I've done the right thing.

Cork and Richard are back together again and I can't help hoping that when their daughter grows up she'll find them and they'll be a family. But that's way off in the future, maybe never. Meanwhile, I can't concentrate on school. My mind swings back and forth from worry over the baby to anger at my adoption agency for shunting me off. I feel like any minute I might spill over with all the emotion I keep stuffing down. Then one day at work I read in the paper that Arthur Miller has married Marilyn Monroe. My god! Nothing makes sense.

Somehow that's the last straw, and as soon as I get off my job I go to the dean of students and tell him my sister gave up a baby for adoption and I can't handle it. I wonder why I say it was my sister? I tell him I'm falling apart, I'm a basket case, I missed weeks of summer school and I'm not ready for exams. I want to drop out of school because I can't get my mind into focus. Fucking helped, but I don't tell him that. It's what Joe and I ended up doing. Twice. But then I told Joe it was the last time and that this time I meant it. The trouble is the good feelings I get when I'm with him don't stay long. In fact I feel worse after.

The dean is a tall, thin, mild-looking man. He glances away as if what I'm saying embarrasses him. I guess he's not used to having messy feelings spilling out in his office. He pulls a sheet of paper out of a drawer and says he's going to sign a waiver so I can drop out without a blemish on my record. His words intrigue me. I've been thinking so much about records. Cork's

Mary Anderson Parks

baby's records are stored away now, like mine. Will she really ever succeed in finding them? In finding Cork and Richard? The agency won't make it easy. It seems odd to me that her records are in one agency and mine in another. I wish I could be with her as she grows up, help her through some of the feelings she's going to have. But she could be anywhere. She's as gone from us as we from her.

It is peaceful in the dean's office, sitting in his visitor's chair, gazing out the window at row after row of homes on sloping hillsides. I feel as if I could figure out what I need to do next if I could sit here a little longer, but he quickly signs the paper, hands it to me and tells me to take it to the registration office.

So that's that. I'm a City College dropout without a blemish!

67

A few days later I ask if I can leave work early. At a quarter to four, I stand shivering at a windy bus stop, sucking on my last Lifesaver. Not even Cork knows what I'm planning to do. "I'll go crazy," I mutter, "if I don't try it." A bus appears and rolls up beside me, a friendly, rumbling presence.

"Hi." I smile at the driver as I climb aboard and take a seat behind him. When we get to my stop, I leap up as I see my connecting bus about to pull away.

"You want that bus, Miss?"

"I do, yes!"

He honks twice.

"He'll wait!" A smile lights up his dark face.

I call out my thanks and run to get on the other bus. The two drivers give each other a brief salute, and I feel like a charm is working to protect me.

When I get off the second bus, I put on sunglasses, even though it's almost evening, take the scarf from my coat pocket and tie it under my chin, then pull it forward so it covers my hair. Thus disguised, I enter the adoption agency. It's a relief to see that Dragonlady is turned away from the front door, busy on the telephone. The waiting room is empty. In a few seconds, I am down the hall and in the ladies room locking myself into a stall, the third one, farthest from the door. I sit on the toilet seat for the next half hour hoping no one comes in.

Finally I hear goodnights being said as people leave for the day. I breathe easier. It's going okay so far. Then someone walks into the Ladies Room. Quickly, I stick my legs out in front of me, then worry whether I should have left my feet on the floor. God, I hope they don't try to open this stall. Good! Whoever it is goes into the one next to mine. I dip my head down to peek under the partition and recognize Mrs. Thompson's alligator shoes. My knees tremble as I wait to hear her finish. She flushes the toilet and soon I hear her washing her hands. Silence follows. What is she doing? I feel a sneeze coming and hold my finger under my nose. I manage to stop it. Then I hear Mrs. Thompson's heels click across the tile floor and the closing of the door.

Soon the restroom lights go off and moments later the big front door bangs shut. After stuffing the sunglasses in my coat pocket, I creep out of the dark, windowless room and down the dim hallway to Mr. Pirtle's office. It's unlocked! The charm's still working. His office has two big windows, so there is no need to turn on a light. From his middle desk drawer I get the keys that I saw him use to open the cabinet with his closed files. My file is under L for Lundquist. My hands shake as I pull it out. Suddenly there is a noise from the hallway. I freeze and wait, holding my breath. Minutes go by, and I don't hear anything more. I tiptoe to the doorway and peek out, but no one is there. The sound must have come from the street, or maybe the old building creaks with age. So I run back to the file and open it. I am expecting to see a letter from my tribe about the money they've been holding in trust for me, but there is nothing. Could Mrs. Thompson be handling that? Maybe she thinks money is the director's job! I flip through page after page where only Rose and Brad's names appear, then I come to one that has my name written near the top of the page: Baby Girl Tara Lee Wilson. My heart takes a leap, jolting a deep-buried memory. I remember being called Tara Lee! I remember the wild free feeling of being that girl they called Tara Lee. I remember dancing in a circle with my family. My chest is almost bursting.

Then I find this letter, dated November 10, 1941:

*To Whom It May Concern: I work with a program
here on my reservation to help our young Indian*

They Called Me Bunny

mothers learn about nutrition. Some months ago Marie Wilson joined in our work and soon became a group leader. Marie is twenty-six and has had seven children. She asked me to write to you for help on her behalf. She feels she is too emotional about her situation to express herself clearly.

Marie had to drop out of school when she got pregnant at fifteen. The child was the product of a rape. Marie is mostly Indian but also part Irish and French. She married an older man, a German storeowner, to give her child a father. They then had six children together. The man's drinking got worse and he lost the store. Marie found a job, but worried because she knew her husband brought drunken men to the house while she was away. When she argued with him about the danger to the children, he beat her up real bad.

I sit down. My legs won't hold me. That memory I had of the drunk men is real, and of my sisters protecting me and the other little ones. And Mother wasn't there because she had to work. I read on through tears.

It was during her third hospital stay that a social worker asked Marie to sign papers to keep her children safe. Marie was on pain medication and she thought it was about having somebody take care of the children just for while she was in the hospital.

When she got home and found out her children had been taken away by the state, Marie almost went crazy.

When Marie's husband was alive, he kept her relatives out of the home. The only time she could see her family was at tribal gatherings, so Marie went to all of them. It was after her husband was killed, in a tavern gunfight, that Marie began working with our program. Helping other mothers is helping Marie begin to heal. Her mother and father tell me they see sparks of the

Mary Anderson Parks

Marie they knew as a child, spirited and lively. They had thought never to see that in her again.

Now that she's getting back on her feet and has support from her family, Marie wants to find out if there is any way she can get her children back. I don't know if you are the agency that took the children, but I am writing to every adoption agency in San Francisco. The state authorities here tell me it is "out of their hands" because the three youngest children were sent to San Francisco for adoption. Parental rights were terminated as to all the children and they could not tell me what happened as to the older ones.

When not drinking, Marie is our most effective teacher. Yes, I regret to say Marie started binge drinking after her children were taken. Marie carries a sadness that will never end until she finds her children. Her first hope is to have them back. If that is impossible, she would like to have pictures and be allowed to write to them. Their names, from oldest to youngest, are Arlene, Vinnie, Bernice, Ed, Ramona, Tara Lee and Scarlet. Marie told me she read Gone With the Wind *when it first came out, just before Tara Lee was born, and it affected her deeply. She is a tender-natured woman and a very loving mother.*

Please reply as to whether you know anything at all about her children. Marie's hopes are very high because of this letter I am writing. I am afraid what effect it may have on her if she does not receive good news soon about her children.

The words at the bottom of this stationery are in our Sioux language. The meaning is: We are the Children of our Mother Earth, Brothers and Sisters to Each Other. I write to you in the spirit of our connectedness.

Sincerely, Harlan Plainfeather.

Frantically I search through the rest of the file. In my haste I almost miss it. It is on my second time through that I find the adoption agency's reply, dated November 30, 1941. I was four and a half.

> *Dear Mr. Plainfeather: We are the agency that handled the adoption of Tara Lee Wilson. Her sister Ramona's case ended up being transferred to another agency because we were unable to find a home for Ramona. I have no information about the other children you named.*
>
> *It would be inappropriate for me to give you any more details. It most certainly would not be possible for Marie Wilson to have any contact with this child. The legal relationship between them has been terminated and the child has a new name and a new family.*
>
> *I trust this information will be helpful and will conclude the matter.*
>
> *Yours truly, Thelma Thompson.*

I turn back to Harlan Plainfeather's letter. The Montana address is there, on the tribal stationery letterhead.

Finally I know my destination.

It is the last leg of my trip and quiet on the Greyhound bus until an old Indian gets on with a cageful of chickens. The driver looks as if he doesn't know what rule he ought to invoke. I guess he can't think of one. The man makes his slow way to the back of the bus, the chickens squawking their heads off. His gray-black braids have strips of leather woven through them. Maybe we're on the reservation already.

I've been on the bus a long time. I've thought about Richard, about how he's Cork's man, not mine. Because he is the father of her baby. I guess in my mind it's almost like they're married. It would be wrong for me to stay near them, loving him the way I do. But maybe I'm starting to get over Richard. Riding along, seeing California go by and then Nevada and Idaho, and now Montana, I'm struck by what a big world it is out here. And my place in it is with people I'm related to by blood.

I told Cork everything before I left. She asked did I have enough money to make the trip and I said I did, because by then I'd finally gotten the check for the money my tribe held in trust for me. It was two hundred eighty-eight dollars and ninety-five cents. I guess if I'd been able to wait, I would have found out the name and address of my tribe from the check. But I couldn't. I didn't quite believe the check would ever really come.

We've passed bunches of cows and miles and miles of sheep and now I see crops growing. Golden strips alternate with green. I figure out the golden stuff is hay when I see bales of it stacked up. Sagebrush I recognize from cowboy movies. At times we've gone miles without seeing a person or a tree. Roads stretch out in the flat, unending distance, the few vehicles on them dwarfed by the wide expanse of land and sky. The sky is bigger here! Even the clouds. How exciting a storm must be.

Low hills rise in the far distance, and occasionally the ground swells up into large bumps, then flattens out again. We pass a group of unpainted houses with no windows. The wind must blow right through. The houses lean to one side. One has entirely fallen in on itself. Then for miles there are no more houses, only wondrous rock formations.

Sit still and be quiet, I tell myself, but it is hard. I can't wait to get there and at the same time I'm afraid. I remember how Clarice Rawlins rejected me, didn't see me as Indian. If my own family rejects me, I'll die. I'll lie down on the dirt in my linen dress and die.

I feel lonelier after the man and his chickens get off. We made eye contact when he passed by. His eyes twinkled with encouragement, as if he knew I needed that. We were the only brown people on the bus and now it's just me. Since I've let my hair go dark, do people see me for what I am, or is it just that I think they do? That old Indian with frayed cuffs, dirty jeans and beat-up hat felt kinship with me, I could tell, even though I'm dressed in my best. It didn't matter that he was several shades darker. We recognized each other.

Should I have tried to get a phone number, let my family know I'm coming? I was too scared. I'm hoping when they see me on their doorstep, miles from anywhere, they won't send me away. To them, though, this place isn't miles from anywhere. It's somewhere. Maybe it's the only place they've ever been. It must be, or they'd have come to find me. I have to believe that. Isn't the letter proof how much Mother cares?

The next stop is mine. I've been counting. I get my suitcase down from the rack and pull on my gloves, then take them off and stuff them in my purse. Nobody in Montana wears gloves. It's hot. Eighty-two degrees, I heard at the lunch stop. I pull out

Mary Anderson Parks

a white handkerchief to wipe my chin and nose and forehead.

The bus lurches to a halt and I'm on my feet, suitcase in hand, bumping my way to the front, my heart beating so fast I feel I could fly. Just drop my suitcase and fly out through the bus roof!

I thank the driver and step down. A thrill shoots through me when the sole of my high-heeled sandal touches the ground. I have a sense of belonging to the earth beneath my feet. As a baby girl I walked on this piece of earth. I stand rooted to the dry dirt as the bus swooshes off.

There aren't any people around. It's too hot to be outdoors. I've been deposited in front of a one-story building with a battered sign over the door that says "Stanley's Grocery." I let my suitcase drop to the ground.

Down the road I see two gas pumps and a small shack. There are no paved roads other than the one the bus came in and went out on. A pickup truck disappears down one of the two dirt roads that angle out from the gas station, clouds of dust billowing behind it. I take a deep breath and raise my hands to fluff up my hair before remembering I don't have a perm anymore. I've let it go straight. It's a relief not to have to be Bunny, but I don't know yet how to be the person my mother named Tara Lee. My mother's a goddamn *Gone With the Wind* freak. That makes me smile, makes me feel like a real person, having a mother who named me after stuff she read in a book. A woman of imagination, with more than a bit of the romantic in her. I bet she named my sister Ramona after the Ramona in that book I read in junior high.

Is it possible that in a few minutes I'll see my mother? Won't we both just fall down in a faint like Scarlet? I want to sit somewhere and wait, think, prepare myself. There is absolutely nowhere to sit. I wish I smoked. I could stand here next to my suitcase, light up and look like someone in a movie who's just gotten off a bus.

I wish Cork were here. But I have to do this alone. Then I'll never have to be alone again. Will my mother recognize me? Will she even be here? How could I have come here, knowing nothing of what's happened during all the years since that letter was written? I take another deep breath. I tell myself, if I was gutsy enough to steal the adoption records, I've got the guts to go look for my family.

The records are in my suitcase. In case they don't believe I'm me.

The old man sees me first. He turns and speaks to the withered Indian woman who sits on a wooden chair like his on the small, sagging porch. She had been looking off into the fields across the road. This is the house I've been directed to, the last one before the bend in the road. Like the houses I've walked past, this one is small, squat, run-down, surrounded by a strange array of abandoned objects, the largest of which are two badly dented cars with no tires and a rusted tractor with no seat, also a pickup truck with its paint worn off. It is one of the yards that has no beer cans mixed into the clutter. I take that as a good sign.

Both old people are now peering down the road at me. I feel self-conscious, picking my way along in high heels, kicking up dust. Sweat trickles down my back all the way into my underpants. I've been switching my plaid suitcase from one hand to the other when it gets too heavy. I wish I hadn't worn beige linen. I'm sticky and mussed and soiled, and I wanted to look the best I've ever looked in my life. I want to be somebody they can love. Somehow, though, it doesn't feel like it's clothes that matter here. Something in me feels that everything is going to be okay, including me. They'll know I meant to look nice, whether I do or not. This whole scene is about as far from what Rose could accept as I can imagine, and that's just fine with me.

They don't stand up or move out of their chairs. They keep watching. And now, as I step onto the hard dry dirt of their yard, I see that he is a white man, the second I've seen on the reservation. The first was the large, red-bearded man I asked directions from at the grocery store. I told him I was Marie Wilson's daughter, looking for my family, and could he tell me where to find them. I wondered if he saw the thrill of pride it gave me to say those words. All he said was, "It's Marie's mother, Winona Peltier, you'll be wanting to find." He came out from where he'd been sitting behind the counter, went to the door and pointed me in the right direction.

The man on the porch looks to be at least seventy. Work pants held up by suspenders hang loosely on his thin frame. He has long wisps of white hair, sun-burned skin, and faded blue eyes. So there's to be another blue-eyed man in my life! The tiny brown-skinned old woman wears a blue cotton dress and black tie shoes that come up to her ankles. A long gray braid hangs down her back. She has strong features, especially her eyes, which even at this distance pierce into me with a steady, questioning gaze.

I resist the urge to set down my suitcase, toss my purse into the air and catch it in mid-fall. That would startle them even more than I already have, bouncing along this little traveled road toward them. I took three buses to get here. I've been on the way for days, but to them it must seem like I've appeared from nowhere.

My step is buoyant and hopeful. I try to rein in the hope and can't. "I'm Tara Lee," my mind sings, over and over, a refrain that won't stop. When I reach the porch and set my dusty white high-heeled sandal on the bottom step, I say it aloud. To them. "I'm Tara Lee." And I hesitate.

Slowly the old woman rises from her chair like something weightless, pulled by unseen strings. Her black-brown eyes read my face, searching deep into me. The glow in her eyes is like that of a fire that won't go out, that kindles back into flame just when you think it might be gone. Her arms reach out for me.

This is my grandmother! Tears swell in my throat and eyes.

"Tara Lee," she says, and her voice holds wonder. "The

Mary Anderson Parks

next-to-the-baby you were."

I drop everything, run up the three steps and clasp hold of her little thin self, wanting never to let her go. She hugs me back, swaying, moaning. I feel years and years of grieving envelop me.

A dog struggles to its feet and nuzzles in between us. An old collie with coat worn thin and haunches standing out from its body.

"Go down old feller," the old man tells the dog. The dog ambles over to a corner of the porch, his body moving in sections. He lies down and casts a reproachful look in our direction before closing his eyes against the heat. A light breeze starts up.

"Ah, feels good. You brought it with you, Tara Lee." My grandmother leans her head back and smiles.

How easily I can accept this woman as my grandmother! I see myself in her. She is a few inches shorter, skinny and wrinkled, darker, but this is what I'll be like when I am her age. I see the love that comes to me from her eyes. I see that I am welcome. She puts her hand up to touch the tears on my eyelashes, then guides me by the arm to where the old man has pulled up a third chair, close between the two of them.

"We knew you'd come home, Tara Lee." Her voice has a quality I'm not used to hearing. Rich and deep, it comes from the center of her. "The three older girls came right away almost."

"No, Winona, it was a few years," the old man says, edging his chair an inch or two forward to see her better.

"Well yes, it was. It was a few years. They came as soon as they could."

"They ran away twice and those people found 'em, dragged 'em back."

"They knew who they were," my grandmother says with deep, soft fierceness. "They knew their names."

"It feels good to be here." I say aloud the words I've been thinking and my grandmother takes my hand. "Where are they, my older sisters? Are they still here?"

She laughs, her eyes crinkling deeply at the corners. Her face can change so suddenly. A moment ago her expression was grim, dangerous. If I'd been the one keeping her grandchildren from her, I'd have been afraid.

"Arlene and Vinnie? They're right down the road, Arlene and Vinnie are. You have nieces and nephews runnin' all over down there. They've got houses right next to each other. Fight all the time, those girls do."

"And make up the next few minutes, then get mad all over again. It's those folks in the city made 'em that way. They just feel mad a lot, and they don't know what at." The old man emphasizes his opinion with shakes of his head.

"I feel that way myself from time to time," my grandmother says.

"There were seven of us, weren't there?" The question pops out. I feel that here it's okay to ask questions, that I don't have to be careful what I say. It has always been hard for me to be careful. Here I can be me. I know that already, so soon! Giddy with the joy of it, I lean toward her, my hand still in hers, which is rough but at the same time soft. It feels wonderful to have my hand in hers. Maybe it's the same for her to have hold of me after all these years. Both she and the old man gaze at me with beaming approval.

"You know that, do you?" Her eyes gaze directly into mine. Strong dark eyes that don't look old at all.

"I saw a letter at the adoption agency. But I knew already from my dreams, or maybe I remembered. I always saw seven of us around Mother in my dreams."

She flinches when I say "Mother," and I make up my mind to wait to ask what I most want to know. I'll be more ready if I wait. Ready for whatever made my soft, tough grandmother flinch.

"I dreamed too," she says. "I tried to dream all the way over to you children, wherever they'd taken you. I tried to reach you that way."

"What about my third oldest sister? Is she here? You said three came home."

Mary Anderson Parks

She draws a deep breath that goes up through her chest and back all the way down again. Her eyes turn to the old man, avoiding mine. "We told you how Arlene and Vinnie ran away more than once, till they finally made it here. Teenagers they were."

"Just kids," the old man says, "and they'd been in eight different foster homes."

"Thirteen and fourteen, when they came back," Grandmother says to the road or the fields or whatever she's looking at out beyond us. No cars have gone past. If one did, it would spray us with dust here on the porch, we're that near to the road. I remember my third oldest sister's name from the letter, but Grandmother isn't going to say what happened to Bernice. Not yet. "I had a brother, didn't I? I remember him."

She gives me a sharp glance of wonderment, or doubt. For an instant I'm afraid she thinks I'm an impostor, pretending to belong to them. But they haven't asked me a single question. They know who I am, they trust me. I see and feel that they do.

"It's not only reading his name in the letter," I tell them. "I remember. Part of it is dreams, but also it's memories. Some memories didn't come till I got out on my own. Something started to open up in me. I had a friend I could talk to, and she didn't really understand but it helped to talk to her. I began to realize there's a world out here waiting for me to find my place in it."

They listen and nod. They don't interrupt.

"I remember I had a brother. I loved him a lot."

The old man motions toward the doorway. "Come on out! Don't be scared." The screen door opens and a tall, stooped elderly man with a black braid down his back emerges from the shadows of the house. He does look scared. Who is he, what is he afraid of? Why has he been lurking in the house?

"Come sit yourself down by your old granddaddy, Ed. Your little sister's here." I try not to show my shock. This isn't an old man. It is my brother. But he won't look at me. He doesn't look at any of us. He scoots against the side of the house, his back to the wall, eyes averted, until he reaches the corner where the dog lies. He slides down the wall and slouches close to the old collie, who licks his hand. I turn wordlessly from one to the other of my grandparents. For they both are my grandparents. I know that now.

"Ed had it the worst," Grandfather says, his eyes on the bare floorboards. "Some military man and his wife adopted him. We found him through a shelter in Billings. He turned up there when he was sixteen. Tryin' to come home, weren't you, Ed? He's older than you, Tara Lee. He remembered home. But that military man beat him till he broke his bones and wiped the sense out of him."

"Can I go over to him? Would that scare him?"

"Course it won't," Grandmother says. "A gentle thing like you. You'll know to move slow."

I rise and take small steps toward Ed, careful to avoid the gaps between the floorboards. He tucks his chin down close to his chest. On an impulse, I lower myself slowly until I am sitting next to him, my feet stuck out in front of me, my back against the warm boards of the house. I take his hand gently. He doesn't resist. Something flickers in his eyes when I keep hold of his hand and press it. I remember holding my brother's hand when he was only a little bigger than I. Maybe this is as good as it gets, Bunny, you and your wasted brother and a slobbering dog, lined up like peas in a pod.

"She's like Vinnie," Grandmother says. "Goes on her instincts. That's what got her back home to us."

"They'll get along good," my grandfather says. "Her and Vinnie will."

"What happened to Bernice?" I ask.

I think Grandmother knows I have to ask these questions, knows I can't help myself. She sighs and comes to me, taking hold of my hands.

"Bernice was separated from her sisters. She started running away as soon as she was old enough to figure out how, but they just kept catching her and putting her in one home after another. I don't know what happened to her in that last place

Mary Anderson Parks

they put her, she wouldn't talk about it, but by the time we got her back nothing could save her. She dealt with trouble the way your mother did. Tried to disappear into a bottle. Both of 'em sweet as sugar when they weren't drownin' in that bottle."

My eyes implore her to say more, but she is lost in memory. I see the deaths of my mother and Bernice in her face. Her hands tighten on mine, so I don't feel alone.

Finally she speaks. "Ramona and your little sister Scarlet must both have got adopted. It's like they're dead to us." She looks saddest of all saying that.

A pickup goes by, slowing down as it passes. Is it out of consideration the driver slows the truck, so we won't be sprayed with dirt? He and the woman wave as they go past, not taking their eyes off us. Then they do a U-turn and pass by again, just as slowly. Grandmother, in one of her lightning-quick changes, shakes with laughter.

"You're a darned pretty sight, all right, in that dress and shoes," she says. "They'll all be passin' by before we know it, an' callin' each other up on the telephone."

"Winona, can you get a pair of moccasins made for Tara Lee by next month?"

"And why next month?"

"So she can circle dance with the rest of us. That'll give 'em another chance to see her an' welcome her home."

"You've got a whole lot of aunts an' uncles an' cousins been waitin' years, hopin' you'd find your way home." My grandmother's eyes are wistful. "You may not remember, Tara Lee, but you started dancing in the circle when you were just one year old."

"They think they can break our circle, but that's where they think wrong," Grandfather says, sudden anger flashing in his eyes.

"It's his stubborn streak, that streak of Crow in him," Grandmother says, surprising me. "They're as stubborn as they come, them Crows." A look of amusement passes between them.

"Ed will be out there, won't you, Ed? Ed can dance all night if he takes a mind to." When Grandfather grins at Ed, a miracle happens. Ed's face lights up with a smile that transforms him into the brother I remember.

Two weeks later, I write a letter for Ed to take out to the mailman next time he comes by. The mailman's schedule is completely unpredictable, but Ed has some kind of sixth sense and is always waiting on the step when the mailman drives up, honking, and the Ford comes to a shuddering stop. Grandpa says Ed puts his ear to the ground like Indians did in the olden days and hears the old rattletrap coming. He says it to see Ed smile.

So far the only mail was a short letter yesterday from Rose. She was answering the seven-page letter I wrote to ask how she's doing and to let her know I arrived safely and what I've learned about my family. She said what a strange address it is, and it must be strange for me to be in such a place, and to give her a call when I get back. She's working a lot of overtime and she's made friends with one of the other nurses. They go to dinner and a picture show twice a week. They have a lot to talk about because of their work. Sounds like Rose is having the best time she's ever had in her life. I'm glad I'm not the only one. Though even on that, Rose and I wouldn't see eye to eye.

Grandma is packing a box of beautiful things for me to send to Rose, a star quilt and other handmade items she kept carefully stored in a closet. She said it's the Indian way, to give away the finest you have. Grandma says it may be that Rose misses me now as much as they did every day I was gone, so I should write to her often. I'll try.

They Called Me Bunny   281

I write this letter to Cork:

Dear Cork. You would love to paint this place. The yards look like a bomb hit them. Stuff scattered everywhere, remnants lying about. It's a disaster. But sitting at the table drinking coffee, watching the kids play, it feels so good. I'm related to these people, Cork. They're my family. I wonder if you can know what this means to me. And there's so much to do, Cork. That's another reason I'm staying. I hadn't meant to stay. You know I brought just that one dumb suitcase. I don't have anything at all for winter, and from the stories they tell winter is something serious. This place is nothing like San Francisco. I hope you'll come see for yourself. Meanwhile! Can you please box up the rest of my clothes and send them? Mucho mucho thanks!

I'm at my grandparents' house, where my brother Ed lives, but when my ankle heals I'm moving down the road to my sister Vinnie's. Yes, I found sisters! And my brother! There were seven of us, Cork. Hardly fairy princesses! Or maybe we're in really good disguises! Anyway, we love each other. When not squabbling. Then, too. And my brother's an angel.

Vinnie's goofy like me, if you can imagine two of us. She broke her leg in the same place I did, isn't that weird? She had to run away from a foster home with her leg in a cast! She couldn't have done it without our oldest sister, Arlene. Vinnie has four kids and she's five months pregnant. She can really use my help. Her husband went to the city to find work, but she hasn't heard from him in a month. Everybody's worried about him.

It turns out I'm good with kids. I never knew that. I'd never been around any. Arlene's older kids, seven and eight, have been staying with me here at my grandparents, to help take care of me. We all sleep on the same mattress and tell each other stories at night until we fall asleep.

What happened to my ankle is I fell through a rotten porch step. The doctor says it's fractured. He's got it wrapped up with a splint and he comes by every day to rewrap it. I like the doctor a lot. He's from a different Sioux tribe. Everybody here is really proud of him. He's one of only two Indian doctors in the whole state of Montana. They have trouble getting doctors out here on the reservation. Maybe your sister Susan will want to be a reservation doctor. She could teach birth control!

Vinnie teases me about the doctor coming by every day when the clinic is so under-staffed. Grandma says he's sweet on me. He's going to get me a job in the clinic when my ankle heals. Part-time, so I can help Vinnie with the kids and bring in a little money at the same time. He knows how to help me apply for Indian grants to go to college. I could be more useful to my tribe if I have a teaching degree. I think it would be fun. I'd make up games for the kids to play, to help them learn. The doctor was stationed in Japan after the war, and he told me the kids there sing their multiplication tables!

Cork, I look at the big Montana sky and imagine you painting it. You could sit out under it in the clutter of my sister's yard, adding your own mess of pots and jars and brushes. No one would care if you spilled paint on things here. It's art that matters. They'd know that. They know what's important. Maybe because so much has been taken away. Do you know what I mean? It's hard to explain. I just know you'd want to paint the rusted wringer washing machine lying on its side next to the skeleton of a car. You'd want to paint the kids playing around it, especially my seven-year-old niece Annie, who reminds me of myself at that age. She's missing three front teeth and usually wearing at least five Band-Aids! Some things are innate.

They Called Me Bunny

Oh Cork. It's another world here. It's so different from anything I've ever known, yet it's home to me already. Somewhere deep inside I remember it. Please tell Richard I think of him. I hope things will work out for you both.

Here my hand stops and thought takes over, but none of the things I am thinking can be said. It's best to end here. How shall I sign off? I write the word "Love" and rest my hand on the paper until impulse kicks in and I scribble, "from Tara Lee who they called Bunny."

I don't tell her I think about her baby every day. That would be poking a stick in an open wound.

I hope you heal, Cork. I hope we all do.

Photo: George K. Parks

Mary Anderson Parks worked as an attorney for the Puyallup Tribe, the Seattle Indian Center, and United Indians of All Tribes Foundation, specializing in foster care and adoption, over a period of twenty-three years. She then moved with her husband from Seattle to Berkeley, California, to be closer to family, which includes three wonderful grandchildren.

She is the author of *The Circle Leads Home*, a novel, and several articles and stories.